# LOVE ME GENTLY

## A DEER CREEK NOVEL

### BOOK ONE

#### STACEY LYNN

**Love Me Gently**

**A Deer Creek Novel**

**Book One**

**Stacey Lynn**

Content Editing: My Brother's Editor

Proofreading: Virginia Tesi Carey

Cover Design: Shanoff Designs

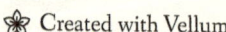 Created with Vellum

# DEDICATION

*To the survivor -*
*To the hurting-*
*To the one who thinks they've made too many mistakes-*
*It's never too late to find healing.*
*You're worth fighting for.*

## AUTHOR'S NOTE AND TRIGGER WARNINGS

Implications and descriptions of both physical and sexual violence and abuse are mentioned in this story. An effort has been made to be as compassionate as possible in describing these moments, but if these are sensitive topics to you, please take care.

If you, or anyone you know is, or has been, a victim of domestic violence and/or sexual abuse, there is help.

**Sexual Assault Hotline:** 800-656-4673 or reach out to www.rainn.org for resources and help.

**Domestic Violence Hotline:** 800-799-7233 or reach out to www.thehotline.org for resources and help.

# ONE

## TRINA

**Now**

I *SUCKED* AT BEING PERFECT. No one had to tell me that.

The bruise and cut on my face confirmed it.

I hissed in a breath as I gently applied retinol serum to my face. Normally on nights like this, I was a master at avoiding looking at my face in the mirror but tonight had been worse than it'd been in months. The evidence of the bruise blossoming on my left cheekbone far too evident already.

At least it'd been a backhanded slap and not a punch. But the jagged edges of his ring left a nasty cut that took a while to stop bleeding. The swelling and discoloration would have to heal if I had any hope of being allowed outside tomorrow. I'd need heavy concealer to hide it, and I was running low, so a trip to Sephora for more was questionable.

"What a mess."

It wasn't just my face. It was everything. My body. My spirit. My life. My choices.

I could no longer count the messes I'd made in the last twelve years, but I'd never forget the one that was the catalyst for the ruin I'd made of everything since then.

"Come to bed, Katrina."

I quickly hid my flinch at Jonathan's voice from the bedroom and swallowed down the bile rising in my throat.

"One more minute," I called back. I peeked my head out of our bathroom door.

He was already in the bed, covers folded back. He'd been handsome once. Almost the most handsome man I'd ever seen in my life.

To the outside world, he still was, but now all I saw was his ugly evilness.

I plastered a kind smile on my face that did little to soften the irritation tightening the Norse-God features on his. "I need to use the restroom and then I'll be there."

"Hurry. You know how I feel about waiting."

I dipped my chin in acknowledgment, closed the bathroom door, and quickly finished up and prepared myself. I'd learned a long time ago to keep a bottle of lubricant hidden and applied it.

My husband had already taken his pound of flesh, but in a few moments when he took my body, at least it wouldn't hurt so much.

The pain deep inside, though, would never heal. I had twelve years of life behind me to prove it.

# TWO

## TRINA

**Then**

THE HOTEL GLITTERED WITH CHANDELIERS.
Streamers and balloons hung on every available surface, and
my wide eyes, filled with excitement, took it all in.

Next to me, Cole Paxton stood tall and broad-shoul-
dered with his hand at my lower back. I'd almost melted like
the wicked witch after being doused with water when I saw
him earlier, when he came to pick me up with a corsage that
matched the color of my dress and shakily slid it onto my
wrist.

Since then, we'd gone to dinner with my best friends,
Heather and Ashley, and their two dates, Cole's best
friends. The six of us were always together, walking a fine
line between rebelling, being typical high school teenagers,
and following the rules. Considering who my father was,
with a large target on my back expecting I was perfectly
behaved at all times, I was the one usually on the side of
following the rules.

Not tonight, though. I leaned into Cole's hand at my back and briefly thought of the rule we were about to break.

For the daughter of Deer Creek's, small town Baptist minister, what I was planning to do later was a big one.

"This is awesome!" Heather shouted. She had Ashley's hand in hers on one side of her and Paul's in her other. The rowdiest leader of our group, like usual, she was in the front, dragging us all behind her.

My stomach rolled with nerves while my veins bubbled with excitement.

This was it.

Senior prom.

The night us girls had dreamed of for four long years. Me, longer, ever since I saw my oldest sister dressed in her sequined gown six years ago. Kari had looked like a princess, and while junior year prom had been fun... this was *so* much better.

"Drink first or dancing?" I asked, grinning up at Cole.

My boyfriend since we were thirteen, he was the only boy I'd ever kissed. The only boy I could ever think of doing *anything* with. Yes, tonight was going to be so much fun.

"You're in charge, doll. Lead the way."

I took his hand and led him straight onto the dance floor, laughing at his nickname for me. Created in middle school when the winter chill had frozen my cheeks pink and chapped my lips, he'd shoved his shoulder against mine and bopped me on the nose. "You look like a little doll."

I'd hated it then.

Much like everything else about Cole, I'd grown to love it.

We danced. We slow danced and held hands and kissed when the chaperones weren't looking. We took breaks for drinks, and then Ashley and Heather and I spent the rest of the night on the dance floor while the guys sat off to the side.

Near the end of the night, I dragged Cole onto the dance floor. He'd been chewing his lip, the only tell he ever had that he was nervous, and it was a rare sight. But I knew what he was waiting for.

He was leaving this up to me.

Ashley and Heather's parents thought they were staying the night at my house, mine thought I was at Heather's. All of us had gotten hotel rooms upstairs.

Cole slipped his hand against my lower back and held me as close as he was allowed to, and I couldn't wait any longer.

I had to lift onto the tips of my toes, even in the heels I wore, and whispered in his ear, "I'm ready."

His throat dipped as he swallowed, and I lowered back to my feet.

"You sure?"

His dark eyes turned stormy and his fingers pressed into my lower back. "I told you I'd wait."

He'd wait for me forever. I already knew that. Cole was that good of a guy and while my sister was following my parents', and the church's rules, I had different dreams.

None of them included leaving Cole in a few weeks and both of us being virgins.

I was off to the city.

He was going to college and then becoming a police officer.

I wanted to walk runways in Milan and Paris.

Our dreams were taking us to different places, and we'd soon be over, but my first time needed to be special.

No one would make it more perfect than Cole.

"I'm sure," I finally said. "I'm ready."

# THREE

## TRINA

**Now**

"THIS WAS MY FAULT." Valerie, the only friend I was allowed to spend any true social time with, had her lips pressed together. Proverbial steam billowed from her ears as her minty green eyes narrowed on my cheek. "I'm sorry."

"It's not your fault, and you know it. It was Jonathan being Jonathan."

I'd long since given up making excuses for him. A few years ago, when Valerie had shown up after one of our worst nights and I was icing my cheek on the couch, dried blood on my lips, and ribs so bruised I could barely walk, I hadn't bothered trying to come up with an excuse. She plied me with wine until the dam inside me broke, and I spilled all the horrid secrets I'd held on to for so long.

She would have seen right through it anyway. To this day, I was certain she knew the kind of man Jonathan was from the moment we met, and it was the only reason why she stayed friends with me. Valerie Sutton was desperate to save me, even while she was helpless to do so.

We both were.

"We were late. All because I wanted that vase."

All true. I'd been allowed to shop yesterday. I was supposed to be home at four in order to have time to prepare myself for Jonathan, make us dinner, and have his bourbon ready for him when he arrived home. Instead, we'd wandered into an art gallery and had gotten lost among the vases and ceramics, all gorgeous, all from a local artist. I'd been an hour late getting home.

While I'd been changed and ready for him and had his drink ready, he'd been *displeased* he had to wait for his meal.

He took the wait out on my face.

But it didn't matter what the reason or excuse was, he would have found me lacking in some way. Always did when the mood struck him to strike me. Eight years together, closing in on nine, and I could never figure out what the trigger was, or how to stop it. I just knew I couldn't leave.

I'd never been dumb enough to try.

There was nowhere for me to go where his reach wouldn't find me and drag me back.

Besides, where would I go? I no longer had a family, not one who'd want to see me after the way I treated them. Valerie was the only person I knew and since her husband and mine were co-managers of the Georgia Gators football team, they could only do so much.

Kip had tried to talk to Jonathan once. I ended up in the hospital and then an extended Spa Stay in Greece until I fully healed.

Lesson learned for everyone. Our business was ours and I was to keep my mouth shut.

"The vase is gorgeous," I told Valerie. She was sweet as pie, southern born and raised in Augusta, Georgia and while we all now lived in Atlanta, I'd met her when I was still in New York.

We claimed our accents cemented us as friends. Regardless of the reason, I was thankful for her.

"Come on. I'm only allowed a couple of hours, and I need a new concealer at Sephora."

"We could stay in and have it delivered." Her eyes dropped again to my scrape.

Usually if there was any evidence of his treatment of me, I'd be locked up. I wasn't lucky he was allowing me out. I'd earned it.

Both before and after his shower this morning. Neither had given me time to prepare myself, so while I was thankful I could get out of my jail, the pain I felt with every step I took made Jonathan, and any further punishments, a very vivid reminder.

"No. Please. I need this." I blinked rapidly, forcing away my tears. It was a miracle I had any left, any ability to feel *anything* anymore. "I can't be here today. I need to get out and breathe."

"The fresh Atlanta air?"

Her brows arched. Her sass was clear. She could always make me smile.

"Exactly." I chuckled and grabbed my purse. "Let's go before he thinks you were here too long."

"Right." She scanned the rooms, but she wouldn't see the cameras.

I couldn't see them either, but I knew Jonathan received

alerts every time I opened and closed the front door. Every time someone was in the house.

At first it'd made me feel protected.

At first, a lot of things had felt good.

Those days were long gone.

"Shopping and lunch," Valerie said, and looped her arm through mine. "And we'll pray that someone, someday soon, comes along and chops off Jonathan's favorite body part, shoves it down his throat, and he chokes to death on it."

I gagged. "Gross, Val."

"I wasn't born and raised a sweet Southern Baptist," she teased. "I'm allowed to be."

Fat lot of good that upbringing did me now.

*Till death do we part...*

I'd never thought the vow would be a bad thing... but that was before... back when I was naïve to the true horrors of the world.

---

"YOU LOOK BEAUTIFUL."

I stood tall and lithe on heels, in my silk nightgown and robe Jonathan insisted I wear when he was home. At one time in my life, I'd been called a doll.

Now I was forced to dress and behave like one.

"Thank you. How was your day?"

"Better than yesterday. You were home early."

"I wanted to make sure everything was perfect for you." I plastered on a smile and handed Jonathan his drink. The table was set, the salad and sides ready. The roast was cooling on the stove.

Jonathan sipped his bourbon, thumb playing with his

wedding band that had left me cut last night. I was certain I saw an excited gleam in his eye as he caught sight of the mark.

Normally my bruises made him more disappointed in me. He *hated* having to discipline me that way.

Sometimes, like tonight, he enjoyed them. He'd press them, hurt me further, and kiss them like they were his trophies.

The trophy he currently watched with eagle-precision eyes was tarnished and broken and nothing but dirt and bile on the inside. Jonathan and the rest of creation only saw my outer shell.

"Aren't you going to give me my kiss?" he asked.

"Of course. I've missed you." I closed the space between us, heels clicking on gleaming wood floors, and pressed my lips to him. He tasted of darkness and alcohol, and as his hand rested at my hip, I forced myself to relax into him. "I've been looking forward to kissing you all day. You know how much I love you."

"Beautiful," he murmured against my tongue. "You've always been so beautiful and exquisite when you're like this. You'll try harder, won't you?"

His lips slammed to mine and his tongue dove into my mouth, I took the kiss like I took everything else. Pliantly. Regretfully.

"I'll try," I whispered when he pulled back. "Of course I'll try to do better. I only want to please you."

I smiled up at him and hoped he believed it.

"Very well." His fingers dug into my hips before he pushed me back. "Let's eat then and see what the night brings."

I already knew what the night would bring, but thankfully, this time I was prepared.

And when the darkness pulled me under later, I barely felt the pain.

Only the sheer regret of what had led me down this path in the first place.

# FOUR

## TRINA

**Then**

OUR LEGS SWUNG BACK and forth from the back of Cole's beat-up Chevy pickup truck. He was sitting next to me, but he might as well have been in Alaska for all the anger pulsing off of him in heavy, thick, pulsing waves.

Not that I could blame him.

I had just handed my boyfriend of five years all of his dreams and then told him I was ripping them away. In my defense, it wasn't the right time, and I'd tried telling him we had different dreams.

"Please don't do this." His voice sounded like it'd been rubbed against sandpaper as his plea fell. "Don't, Trina. Please. We can make this work."

"We can make it work for you, you mean." My legs swung back and forth, dangling from his tailgate, and I resettled my hands beneath my backside. If I pulled them out, I'd do the unimaginable, like reach for Cole or run them along my stomach and give him hope.

I wasn't trying to hurt him. I didn't mean to sound so harsh. It was the only way I could keep from sobbing, from falling into his arms and letting him protect me, protect *us*. This wasn't what I wanted. Not when I had dreams of my own and we were days away from high school graduation.

My older sister, Kari, was at the university in Boone, a half an hour away. She was getting her degree in education and wanted nothing more than to return to Deer Creek, teach at the very high school we attended, and then get married and have babies.

Her life was normal and sweet and calm and drama-free.

I didn't want what she wanted, or what Cole wanted for us. Not *now*. Not before I had the chance to try to chase my dreams.

Getting pregnant wasn't part of my plan. I'd heard the sayings. *It only takes one time...*

We'd been careful on prom night. Both times. I still blushed when I thought of how the night went, well into the early morning, and then the frantic rush to get home before any of our parents busted us for lying. The night hadn't been *good*, but like I predicted, Cole had made it perfect. For me. For us.

I'd hold the beautiful memory close to me and treasure it forever.

What I didn't want was the consequence that we tried to prevent and hadn't.

I couldn't, however, go through with the procedure...not without at least telling Cole. Maybe that made me an even more selfish brat than it would have been had I simply broken up with him. But I knew Cole. He was relentless and patient in his love for me. Leaving without destroying us would give him hope.

"I want to give you everything. You know that." Cole jumped off the truck and paced back and forth. "I can take care of you. When I get out of the academy, I'll be able to get us a place. It'll be a good life, you know it."

It would be. It would be good and calm and simple...and I didn't want any of it. Sometimes, at night, I viewed our end. Four years of dating in high school, one in middle school, friends since years before, Cole was etched into the fabric of all of my best memories. He was the only guy I could imagine being with, but our end was always on the horizon, moving like a slow train wreck you couldn't help but watch.

The end was now.

The train was barreling down on us, and we were unable to escape the wreckage. I knew it to the depths of my bones, and while I wanted to take everything he offered, it wasn't me.

It never would be, and I couldn't bring myself to surrender to Cole's dreams for us, dreams we've argued over ever since he decided to go to the police academy.

I would end up despising him.

It was easier to imagine leaving town in a couple weeks, having him despise me instead.

"But what about my dreams?"

His hands slid to his hips, pressed tightly against the belt loops of his jeans. His face twisted into the same condescending look he gave me every time I told him I wanted to go to New York and model. That I had dreams of making it *big* and seeing my face on billboards and on magazine covers in every grocery store in every size town across the country.

He called them big city dreams. Even from where he

stood feet from me, I practically felt him patting me on the head like I was a sweet little thing.

He didn't understand. I wanted more than Deer Creek, population 2,433. A small mountain town that was dying more than it was growing and relied on winter tourists to stay afloat, we would never grow into anything more exciting.

"Trina," he said, and his voice carried that sigh I was so used to hearing. We'd had this discussion for over a year now.

"No, Cole." I jumped off the truck and marched to him. "Why don't you go to the academy in New York? You can be a cop anywhere. You don't have to stay here. Why can't we both have what we want? Come with me."

I reached for him, took his hand in mine. I could do this, we could do everything, but I couldn't be the one giving up everything.

"That's not me," he said. He squeezed my hand and let go. He skimmed my arm with his hand and stopped at the side of my neck. He held me firmly. Maybe he thought if he held on tight enough I wouldn't go through with this. Pain shouted from his eyes and silent expression. "You love me, Trina."

"I do." Tears swelled in my eyes as I nodded. "I do love you, Cole. So much, so very much."

He swallowed slowly. Every muscle in his throat rippled with the slow, forced movement. He pulled his hurting gaze off mine and looked over my shoulder. His voice shook as he said, "But not enough."

"No." I shook my head, my tears streaming down my cheeks so hotly they burned my skin. "I suppose not enough."

He was right. If I loved him, I'd keep our baby. If I loved

him, I'd start a family with him. I'd do everything I was supposed to do, and it wouldn't feel like such a chore.

It would be an honor, and Lord knew, I wanted to love Cole Paxton as much as I knew he loved me.

Except he didn't love me enough to support me in my dreams, either. If I gave in now, I'd end up sacrificing a part of my soul that beat for more.

"I don't want you to do this." He put enough space between us so he could settle his hand on my stomach. "I hate you for even considering doing this, and I love you, too. How can that be?"

"I don't know."

"I don't want to hate you." His voice was thick with gravel and nails.

We said nothing then, as the breeze of the field swirled around us, tossing my blond hair into my eyes. I shoved it away, peeling it off my cheeks that were slick from tears.

We were behind the high school, and all the other students had long since left, but I'd talked Cole into staying instead of heading to the Dairy Queen where all our other classmates hung out after school.

With graduation next week, we were all trying to spend as much time together as we possibly could before drifting off into our futures.

I figured after this conversation, no one would want me around anyway. Perhaps not even Ashley or Heather.

"I'm sorry." It was all I could think of to say.

He shook his head, and the muscles bunched in his arms. He would make an excellent police officer some day. He was bold and brave, strong and humble. He was handsome and fair. He was noble. A good man. The best man.

"You're sorry. For what?" He spun around and faced me, glaring daggers at me that sent a chill straight to my heart. "What are you sorry for? Breaking my heart? Ruining this relationship? Killing our child before even giving it a chance? What exactly are you sorry for?"

"All of it," I croaked, stepping back. Every word he spoke lashed across my chest like a leather whip.

"Of course you are. But not sorry enough to change any of it."

I stayed silent. Too afraid to speak, too afraid to move toward him or tell him what he already knew.

We stared at each other, like opponents facing off against each other, when we'd always faced everything together, side by side. Now we were in a standoff, one I wouldn't back down from even if a small part of me wanted to, and he was equally stubborn.

"Right," he spit out and pulled his keys out of his pocket. "I should get you home then."

"I'll walk."

I lived less than two miles away. I'd never walked home from school. Cole had been picking me up and driving me to school since he got his license. The pain of my statement jolted him back, as if this hurt him more than me telling him I was getting an abortion.

"You'll walk." He blinked and then scanned the field behind me. When his gaze came back to mine, it was filled with heavy resignation. "So this is it?"

I didn't want it to be. Not at all. It had to be, though. "I think it has to be."

"Fine." Cole gritted his teeth together. His eyes were wet, and as much as I wanted to look away, to flee from the pain I was causing him, I took it and absorbed it. "Take care then, Trina. Have fun in the big city."

He said the last two words like they were a curse. I suppose to him, they were.

At some point in my life, I would have been happy staying in Deer Creek. When I was younger, it was all I wanted, much like everyone else I knew. But then our eighth-grade band class took a school trip to New York City. We saw Broadway shows and strolled through the Met and spent hours upon hours in Central Park. By the time I came home, I had fallen in love with something that still ran deeper in my veins than I ever felt Cole. It was a living, breathing, desperate *need* in my blood that pulsed for the excitement and adventure.

I had never hidden my dreams from the man in front of me. His features etched with a pain I would never forget and a fury I equally deserved.

"Goodbye, Cole."

I stepped out of his way as he moved to his tailgate. He slammed it shut, and the truck rocked back and forth from the force. Then he reached in and grabbed my backpack. He handed it to me, arm extended like he couldn't bear to be within touching distance of me.

I took it from his hands and slipped it onto my shoulders.

He looked at me, opened his mouth, and closed it. And then he was in front of me, his hands on my cheeks and his breath skating across my lips right before he shoved his mouth against mine.

He kissed me harshly, painfully.... passionately, and I reached out, covering his wrists with my hands so tightly I wanted us to meld together.

Right as I surrendered to the kiss, he yanked back, throwing my hands away from him.

"I will always love you." He swiped the back of his hand across his face, wiping our kiss away. "I hate you. Right now, today, I hate you for this and for everything you're doing, but despite everything, I will always love you."

Without giving me a chance to say a word, he jumped into his truck.

I stood in the field and watched him throw the truck into reverse. I stayed still as he peeled out of the parking lot, the stench of rubber burning my nose as he turned down the street.

And once he was gone, his truck gone, and I knew he couldn't see me, I crumbled to the ground and I sobbed.

Because I knew, even as I knew I had to do it, that I was throwing away the best thing that would ever happen to me in my entire life.

# FIVE

## COLE

**Now**

I DROPPED my phone to the desk and buried my face in my hands. Life, man. It certainly had a way of kicking you while you were down. Some days I couldn't believe where I was, other days, I didn't dare look back.

"You all right?"

My partner, Eddy Ferentz, dropped into his chair, the creaking sound making his moves obvious.

I let out a groan and pushed back into my chair. "June's mad at me. Again."

June had been mad at me for the last two years. I kept hoping she'd adjust.

She kept wanting her dad and mom back together. Couldn't blame my four-year-old daughter, but life didn't give you what you wanted all the time. June was just learning it earlier than most.

And she was *not* happy about it.

"What was it today?"

I huffed. My little Junie bug's tantrums were well known in the police department where I worked and had proudly served for the last eight years. "She wants ice cream and thinks it's *stupid* I can't take her out for some tonight."

"They just went back to Marie's yesterday."

"And I'm sure Marie will take her out. She didn't even ask for it when I had her."

My custody arrangement was simple, much like my marriage had been, much like the divorce had also been. I didn't blame Marie for leaving. The blame rested solely on my shoulders. I'd never fully loved her and we both knew it. She was the one smart enough to admit it out loud first. I had a week on, a week off, and if I was called in for a case while I had the girls, either Marie helped out or my family did.

My girls didn't lack for family in their lives, but Junie wanted her dad. In her home. With her mommy.

"It's not cool of Marie to keep calling and telling you these things."

It wasn't. When I had Ella or June for my week and they got sad, I handled it. Marie had always been softer than me, more of a pushover. She couldn't help herself from trying to please everyone, and nothing broke her more than alligator tears on one of our girl's round cheeks.

"June's a daddy's girl," I told him and then blew out a breath and shook my head. "It'll be fine. She'll be fine. She'll adjust."

Parents divorced. Kids adjusted. Junie needed more time. She was my mini-me in all the ways. When I'd have football on, Ella and Marie would paint their nails and read books or go shopping. Junie would fling her tiny body at mine while we played indoor football with me on my knees. The game usually ended with her on my back, me running around the house, while she single-handedly declared herself the winner.

She had no idea I was the true winner. I had two beautiful girls I couldn't live without. I won hands down. Every time.

But I wasn't about to pop Junie's balloon and tell her that.

"Paxton."

I turned toward our chief, Tim Lannister. He was leaning half out of his office.

"Yeah, Chief?"

"Need you. Come here."

I shoved to my feet as Eddy oohed, "Oooh someone's in trouble."

I chucked a pencil at him and hit him square between the eyes. "Do something useful with yourself while I'm gone."

"I hear Heather Samson is single again. I could go do—"

"Don't." I shivered. I didn't want to know anything about anyone *doing* anything with Heather. "Do your job, idiot."

"Aye-aye, captain."

I snorted. "Not yet." Not even close. I was perfectly content being a sergeant and getting to stay out on the streets with the men and women I supervised. Someday, when I was ready to give that up, I'd be aiming for that job, though.

---

"YES, CHIEF?"

Tim sat in his chair, leaning back in it, while waving me into his office. "Come in. Come in. Have a seat."

I scanned his cluttered office, stacks of papers piled high, including the two chairs on the opposite side of his desk. The man was an honorable and excellent chief of police, had lived in Deer Creek his entire life, and was staring down the retirement age. He had shining white hair, what little was left, a robust stomach from both age and a fondness for

American beer and had the respect of every man on the force.

He also couldn't organize his office if his life depended on it. "Where? On the floor?"

"Smart aleck," he muttered. "Move that stack."

He waved his arm toward the chair closest to me. I grabbed the files, set them haphazardly on top of the chair and in their own pile next to me, and said a quick prayer that the whole thing didn't topple before sliding into the chair.

"So, what's up?"

"There's a conference next month I want you to attend. Think you can work that into your schedule?"

Benefits of being in a small town and having a good boss, was the understanding of having to share custody time with my children. "What's the conference? And when is it?"

"It's the National Detective's Conference in Atlanta. Think it'd be good for you to be the one to represent us this year."

He handed me a flyer for it, and I took a quick glance. "This is for lieutenants and higher ranks."

"And both Bo and Jack nominated you to be the attendee." Bo Parker was our captain and had been for the last three years. Jack was a lieutenant and like our chief, was closing in on retirement age.

"Is that because they hate me?"

Atlanta was my least favorite city on the planet and anyone who knew me for longer than ten years knew exactly why. I'd vowed to never step foot in the state of Georgia if I didn't need to, and so far, I'd succeeded. Outside of a few bathroom stops on family vacations on the way to Florida, anyway.

"No. Jack said he thinks it'd be good for you to get the experience in the training, and Bo said if he attends another conference this year, he's going back to being a street cop. So, you're next."

Atlanta. If it were anywhere else, I'd jump at this opportunity. It was ridiculously stupid to boycott an entire city, but my impulse was to say no.

"It's three days," Chief continued, like I wasn't having a crisis of morality mixed with stupidity. "Can you clear your calendar?"

I scanned the pamphlet again. He'd probably already reserved my spot since the deadline was near. Probably had my hotel room booked too. I didn't *actually* have a choice in this unless Marie would refuse to help with the kids, and that wouldn't happen.

Besides, some of the sessions would be helpful. We were a small town, but we tried to stay up to date with the newest technologies. A sprawl from larger, neighboring towns and a boom at a nearby university hit Deer Creek about six years ago and since then our population doubled. So did our crime. Most of it was petty crime. But domestic violence was on the rise, as well as drugs. Learning more de-escalation techniques was always helpful. As well as community building.

"I'll go." I folded the pamphlet. "Anything else you need from me?"

"Update on the call we got about the Humphrey boy?"

A call came in from a teacher at the middle school for possible child abuse. "I've put Nix on it. She's meeting with Thomas at the school first."

"Good call," Chief said and nodded.

I didn't quite need the approval. I'd been in this town my whole life, in the police department as soon as I graduated the academy, entering after my second year of college and decided doing the four-year thing wasn't for me. At twenty, I went to the academy and several months later I was back here in Deer Creek, driving a patrol car and writing traffic violations. I'd worked hard since then, though, and I knew the chief respected me. But Sarah Nix was the best officer for cases like this, mostly because she was one of the few female detectives we had and the school resource officer, Bill Thomas, tended to overwhelm the middle school kids with his booming personality.

The kids loved him, and he was great with them, but he was employed through the county sheriff's office, not the local police.

"Thanks."

"Good. Now if you don't have questions for me, you're excused."

"None at this time, sir." I shoved to my feet, crumpling the pamphlet in my hand, and headed back to my desk.

Eddy was tossing a stress ball in the air, feet kicked up on the desk when I reached mine. "You fired?"

"Worse." I tossed the pamphlet in his direction. "I have to go to Atlanta."

His brows popped high on his forehead, and he kicked his feet to the floor. "There's a half a million people in that city."

"Yup."

When Trina Mills decided to get rid of our baby, break my heart, and skip out of town with a smile on her face twelve years ago, saying I struggled was putting it mildly. It was half the reason I dropped out of college. I couldn't focus. Could never stop thinking of her. She made it worse by occasionally sending me letters, hoping things were going well for me. She rarely apologized, at least not after the first couple of times.

I should have burned them all, but I didn't.

It didn't matter where she'd been or what magazine cover she eventually starred on, I couldn't get rid of her.

And now I was going to Atlanta... where her husband was the General Manager of the Georgia Gators, their professional football team, and former CEO of one of the largest, and most well-known technology companies.

"There's not a chance you'll see her."

"Probably true, too."

It didn't matter that I wouldn't see her.

She'd still be everywhere.

"You still don't want to go."

"Not a chance."

"Yeah. I get that." Eddy moved to Deer Creek eight years ago, a couple years after I started on the force. We were partnered together because he had more experience, but I knew the town and people. Chief figured the locals would trust him faster if he was seen with me, and I could learn from him.

It hadn't taken him much time at all to learn the historical gossip of my high school crash-and-burn relationship with Trina. Over time, I'd filled him in on the rest, which meant he was one of three people in my life I'd ever told.

"That really sucks for you."

"Thank you," I deadpanned. "So very compassionate."

"What can I say?" He smirked. "I'm a compassionate man."

"Right."

"Now about Heather Samson..."

I flung a pen at him.

Atlanta...here I come.

# SIX

## TRINA

**Then**

TEARS SPECKLED the letter I finished writing, folded, and tucked into an envelope.

I talked to my parents every week, and up until last week, no one had mentioned Cole. Every one of my friends hated me after we broke up. They told me I'd destroyed him, but no one knew I'd destroyed myself right along with him. At graduation, I wanted to cry and reach for him and apologize. The blank stare in his eyes when our eyes met as he passed me in the aisle of our high school gym was the only thing that stopped me. By the time I left for New York, I didn't have anyone left in my life other than my family, and even if it was my own fault, it still hurt. I boarded my plane in July with a small amount of savings in the bank, enough for a few months of rent in a shared apartment I'd found online, and with my parents' reluctant blessing and help. I tried not looking back, but some moments were harder than others.

When my mom accidentally mentioned Cole's name last week, I soaked up every small bit of information I could learn from her. I missed him most of all. He'd been my best friend for so many years it hurt to not be able to pick up the phone and call him when I received my first callback on an audition, or when I'd gotten a small, teeny tiny part as a back-up dancer in a community theater play. It paid nothing, but I was waiting tables to make ends meet. The apartment I shared with Stella was barely affordable even with both of us working almost full-time at an Italian restaurant, and my room was smaller than my parents' bedroom closet back home.

Some days I woke up with fear choking me, telling me I'd made a horrible mistake.

Other days, the pulse of the city beneath my feet filled me with immeasurable hope and anticipation. I clung to those days like a lifeline.

I had to make it. I had to achieve my dreams because I knew if I didn't, breaking up with Cole and everything else I'd done would all be for nothing.

When would it go away? That aching, searing pain that pierced my chest when I thought of him, when I thought of what I'd done. It wasn't only losing Cole that hurt like someone punched a hole in my chest, it was the grief from the choice I'd made. Telling myself it was for the best didn't make things better, and I told myself that a thousand times a day.

I'd ruined something more special than Cole. I'd ruined more than one or two lives, and as the months passed, the guilt grew thicker, even though I tried to fight against it. Mostly, I stayed busy, doing everything I could to keep my mind off the past and keep pressing forward.

Except for these letters I couldn't stop writing.

I tugged the letter back out and reread it. The uncertainty I already felt grew into a tumultuous storm in my stomach. This was stupid. Cole was the last person who would want to hear from me. Reaching out to him only hurt us both. Before I could crumple it into a ball and toss it into the garbage, I scribbled his address on the envelope and sealed it shut.

A pounding thump hit my door, and I quickly hid the envelope in my desk drawer.

"What is it?" I shouted.

"Dinnertime, sunshine, let's roll," Stella said from the other side of the door.

We always grabbed a quick meal before we went to work. Stella had helped me land the job when I showed up at our doorstep, all innocent and exhausted—both mentally and physically from the trip.

At twenty-one, she might have only been a few years older than me, but she seemed decades wiser. She worked all day and did online schooling at night, insisting she'd end up better than anyone else in her family had ever done, even though she never told me what that meant. I would have been lost without Stella. She took me under her wing, taught me how to use the subway until I was confident I could get anywhere I needed on my own. She gave me tour after tour of the city my first few weeks when I was there and had even printed off a map, highlighting areas no single young woman should walk through alone.

Our apartment, as run-down as it was with paint peeling off walls and a heater we had to bang periodically to make it kick on now that the weather was turning absolutely frigid, was on the edge of a decently nice area of New York, and a really scary area, so we rarely went out at night alone.

Safety in numbers, Stella always said.

"I'm coming. Just give me a minute." I pulled my hair up into a ponytail and glanced down at the letter.

*Mail it. Don't mail it. Mail it. Don't mail it.*

I grabbed it, dug through my purse and slid a stamp onto it, and shoved everything back into my purse.

"Everything okay?" Stella asked as we walked toward a nearby diner that sold filling, but inexpensive food. I lived on their patty melt sandwiches these days. "You've been more mopey than usual."

"I'm not mopey." I grinned and shoved my hip against hers, laughing as she stumbled over a crack in the sidewalk. "I'm missing home, I guess. It's almost Christmas."

"You're not going home? I thought your parents were going to help you get a ticket."

"They were." I was lying through my teeth. I had no desire to return home. Not yet, not for Christmas when everyone would be home from college. "It didn't work out."

"Aw, that's too bad." She slung her arm over my shoulder. "I'll make this a Christmas you'll never forget. I promise."

"Thanks, Stella. You're the best."

"Nah, I'm not the best, but I am pretty awesome, and I'll be sure to plan all sorts of awesomeness for you."

Her grin was enchanting. Thinner than me by at least ten pounds and about the same height, Stella had slick, inky black hair that came to sharp points right at her shoulders. Her eyes were wide and blue, and she always carried a bounce in her step like she knew every day was going to be the best day of her life.

I pushed away thoughts of Cole and home and everything I wanted to forget, and I vowed to trust Stella.

This Christmas, this New Year's—it'd be the best of my life.

It was time to move forward, so with only minimal hesitation, I slipped Cole's letter into a mailbox we passed on the street and pretended it would slip him into my past as well.

There was no looking back.

It was time to chase my dreams until I caught them.

---

"HAPPY NEW YEAR!"

The cacophony of shouts rang in my ears. I was surrounded by an enormous group of Stella's friends, in an apartment in Brooklyn. A friend of hers, Zane, was hosting the New Year's party bash for all of his NYU friends who were hanging around the area for the holidays. I was, by far, the youngest person in attendance, although if anyone noticed, no one seemed to care. At least they didn't care enough to tell me I shouldn't be drinking beer from the keg.

It was my first New York party and while I wanted to be enjoying every moment of it, while I'd tried to enjoy every moment of the incredible Christmas Stella had wanted to give me, my heart was only half into it.

I might have made things seem better in my letter to Cole than they truly were. How could I not? I'd left him and Deer Creek to make it big.

I wasn't certain my last job of being a stand-in in a soap commercial that showed fifty other stand-ins in a group shot was making it big.

God, how I wanted it to happen. I wanted an agent and my name to be known in households all over the world. I wanted my face on billboards and in magazine spreads. I wanted to walk the catwalk wearing designs from Gucci and Hermès. I wanted to travel to Milan and France for their shows.

I wanted it all, and even though I could be grateful for some of the small successes I had, hell, even landing the non-paid stand-in role a couple of weeks ago, it wasn't enough.

It made me fear I wasn't enough.

And wouldn't that be the worst of the worst of all things?

Falling flat on my face and having to move back to Deer Creek, my tail tucked between my legs, facing Cole again with nothing but failure stamped on my forehead.

Everything I'd done...for nothing.

Tears burned my eyes as I thought about that possibility, and I tossed back the rest of my beer. I'd been drinking for hours but only finished two cups. The warm beer tasted like spit as I forced it down and headed outside for fresh air. Perhaps a frigid blast of icy wind would adjust my attitude.

The building we were at had a small front stoop that was so common in New York walk-ups. It wasn't smart to be outside alone, nor was it smart of me to holding a cup of beer while I was two months shy of turning nineteen, but the shouts and the cheers and celebration from inside the first floor apartment blared through the opened windows.

"Not into the holiday spirit?" a voice asked.

I was so startled, I jumped from my spot on the cement step and turned.

I was so into my thoughts I hadn't heard the heavy metal door open or close or hear Zane step outside.

"You scared me," I said. "And no, not this year, I suppose I'm not. What are you doing here?"

He held up a cigarette and flicked open his lighter. "Hate the smell of smoke inside my house."

I hated the smell of smoke anywhere, but whatever he was lighting wasn't a normal cigarette, the kind the guys in my high school used to steal from their parents so they could look cool around the fields and bonfires and beer kegs. It had a different smell than regular tobacco, sweeter.

"What is that?" I asked, stepping away from the plume of smoke as he exhaled.

"Clove cigarettes." He held it out to me. "Want to try?"

"No thank you."

"Right." He smirked and settled the cigarette back against his lips, speaking while he inhaled. "Stella told me you're from a small town, living in the big city to make dreams come true, am I right?"

Everything he said was factual, but there was an edge to his words, to the tone in his voice that didn't thrill me. It sounded laced with mockery, the merest hint of it though so I wasn't certain.

"Yes."

"And how's it going so far?"

He exhaled again and little smoke rings puffed out of his mouth. They grew larger and larger in the air above us before drifting away into nothing.

"It's going."

It was. I was. I had plans and ideas and ways to move things along, I just needed an in. For someone to not only see my talent or my physical appearance but to see my drive.

"Stella wanted me to talk to you about your modeling. I can help you, if you want it."

His lips thinned, and he dropped his cigarette to his

side, flicking the ash to the cement. I took a step back, almost plastering my back along the railing. He hadn't moved toward me in the least, and yet his dark eyes, the glint in them and the tone of his voice all set me on edge.

Perhaps I was doing what Stella had scolded me for before—judging people who were different from me because I hadn't been around so many kinds of different people in my life.

"How?"

He shrugged and pulled out a business card from his tight jeans that were faded and old and ripped. His flannel shirt he'd been wearing earlier was now tied around his waist, and his V-neck white T-shirt showed the curves of his chest. He wasn't built like Cole, but he wasn't a slouch, either. "I have a friend who works with an agent. Works with new models, helps get them their portfolios started, small parts until he can get agents to notice them. He does this work on the side, without any up-front costs. He takes a percentage of the jobs you get through him."

"Seriously?" I snagged the card out of Zane's hand and stared at it.

It was white card stock. Simple lettering. Something that could have been printed at any print shop and didn't have the professional sheen I'd seen on most modeling agencies' logos. But Zane had said this guy, Robert Madrid, was doing this work on the side.

"It sounds too good to be true." My thumb ran over the letters of Robert's name again, then the phone number.

Zane shrugged, took a puff of his cigarette, and dropped it to the cement as he exhaled. "Women seem to like him, haven't heard complaints about him getting them work. My advice, Deer Creek?"

I cringed at the way he said and knew my hometown name. "What?" The card stock in my hand crumpled from my tight grip.

"Take any help you can get, it might not always look pretty, but no one breaks through in the business without sacrificing their morals every once in a while."

I flinched at his advice. It sounded... questionable. I was going to ask him what he meant when he pulled open the door and before he could step inside, Stella jumped out.

"There you are!" She rushed me and grabbed my arms. "I've been looking everywhere for you! Come on. We have to party! This year is going to be fantastic!"

For the first time in my life, I was beginning to hope it would be. With Robert Madrid's card burning a hole in my hand, I tucked it into the pocket of my jeans and followed Stella back inside, Zane closing the door behind us and following.

We partied for the next two hours, where I eventually had to wrap my arms around Stella's waist since she was too drunk to walk by herself. I hailed us a cab and took us back to our apartment where I tucked her into bed and provided a bowl in case she woke up sick during the night.

Then I curled up in my own bed, back against the wall, legs crossed, and studied the business card again.

I needed a breakthrough, something to help pay the bills more than waiting tables.

I desperately needed to prove to everyone back home that moving to New York wasn't a mistake but my destiny.

And I really, really needed help.

Had I been older, I would have heeded the warning bells. I would have run far away from not only Zane but Robert Madrid. I would have listened to the whispering, small voice in my mind telling me not to pick up the phone and call.

But I was young. I was naive.

I was too hopeful with stars in my eyes blinding me to the truth.

Looking back, that one poor decision cemented the rest of my downfall.

# SEVEN

## COLE

**Now**

I HAD a view of the damn stadium. Of all the hotels, of all the event and conference centers, I got stuck waking up in the morning and going to bed for the last three nights with the Gators logo shoved in my face.

Thankfully, I was leaving tonight.

I shoved the curtains closed, the sadistic part of me compelled to open them every morning. Like I'd see her. Like in a city of a half million, people I'd somehow spy her on the street. I had no clue where she actually lived and had quit trying to follow up on her life hoping she'd come back to me after she got married.

Mostly.

I *had* stopped myself at seeking out Jonathan's address. Knowing what I knew of him it was probably buried under a half-dozen LLCs to keep his residence hidden.

Not a bad idea considering the kind of man he was. The wealth he had.

I could still remember the day I ran into Trina's parents at church, her mom crying, her dad angry. I'd tried to avoid them, but that didn't stop me from overhearing their conversation. They'd just gone to New York, begged by Trina to go meet the new man in her life. At that time, she'd been on the cover of a teenage health and beauty magazine. She was the face of a drugstore skin care company.

The first time I'd seen her face since she left Deer Creek was while I was in the checkout line at a gas station with a Mountain Dew and a fistful of beef sticks. I'd been equal parts appalled, ecstatic, and mournful. All three hit hard and fast, and I spent the weekend in my apartment, blocking out the world around me.

So tight was the hold she still had on me years later when her parents mentioned that man during summer break and were devastated that they weren't going to be invited to her wedding, I spiraled for weeks.

*Wedding.* At twenty-two years old, she was getting married.

I should have been able to let her go then, but it wasn't until another year went by and I met Marie.

Now, I was in Trina's city. Marie had given up and walked away from me and our family, and I couldn't blame her. Twelve years since Trina walked away from me and as I stepped out of the hotel to head to a coffee shop before going to the conference center, I was scanning the streets like I'd actually get a glimpse of her.

What good would that do? Nothing.

Yet I couldn't shake the feeling that she was close. So much closer than she'd felt in years.

The fall sun hit me hard and fast in the eyes, and I squinted. It was early October, and days like this made me glad I lived in the mountains. Hopefully, we'd be getting snow by Thanksgiving. Down here in Atlanta, they'd be sweating hanging outdoor Christmas lights. Around me, people bustled in their rush to get to work. Men in suits and dress pants and polo shirts hurried to wherever they went with their faces tucked into phones, unaware of anything around them. Women in similar style dress rushed right along with them, heels either clicking the pavement or peeking out of their work bag, while they had AirPods shoved into their ears, phones in their hands. Scowls were tossed every which way as they focused on themselves.

This was only one of the few things I hated about cities. Everyone thinking the world revolved around them, day in and day out, expecting people to step out of their way and no short amount of rudeness given if that didn't occur.

Manners were nonexistent. Thinking of your neighbor as your brother was gone. These days, people thought only of themselves. Their own worries and plans...

I couldn't wait to get back to Deer Creek.

Only nine more hours and then I was on the road.

I pulled open the door to the coffee shop, unoriginally named *The Coffee Shop*, and took my place in line. Ten minutes later, I had my double shot Americano in hand, pushed open the door and stepped out.

Immediately, a flash of light pink slammed into my shoulder, making me jump back. My cup, on the other hand, flew in the other direction and landed on the woman's shoulder that had barreled into me.

"Hey," she called out and spun.

And the world stopped. Right there, in the middle of the bustling sidewalk, in the doorway of The Coffee Shop, my entire world stopped as the woman in pink opened her mouth to say something and then froze.

Gaped at me like she was looking at a ghost.

And I suppose she was — if I was the ghost of the past. Pretty sure I was doing the same, but since I'd been thinking of her, I recovered first.

"Trina," I breathed, and had the wherewithal to step out of the doorway I was blocking. "I..."

"You spilled coffee on me," she said.

"Trina," I called her name again. Had to. Had to know this woman was who she appeared to be and wasn't a figment of my imagination.

She blinked and unfroze. "What are you doing here?"

I stepped further from the doorway, and hoped she'd come with me. She scanned the sidewalk, eyes focusing on something in the distance before she took a step, then another, toward me.

"Cole," she finally said.

My name exhaled from her lips like a song.

I cracked a smile. "Hi, Trina."

Her lips curved, fell. "I...I can't believe you're here."

"Detective conference."

"Oh. You're a detective. That's good." Her bottom lip found its way between her teeth and the world around me silenced.

"Yeah..." It was just her and me, her gorgeous, thick and blond hair and wide, round blue eyes, lighter than I remembered. Somehow duller, too. And was that... "What happened to your cheek?"

She jerked back like I'd slapped her and whatever light remained in her eyes dimmed. "I should go. It was nice to see you."

She stepped away. On instinct, I reached for her. She flinched, yanking her arm away from me as she turned white as a sheet.

My voice was softer when I called her name again.

I swore there were tears swimming in her eyes when she shook her head. "Don't, Cole. I need to go."

"Hey! There you are!" A woman's voice rang out, and Trina froze, head whipping in the direction.

I followed her gaze and found a woman in cream-colored, wide-legged pants and a pale blue shirt with a wrap tied at her hip sauntering toward us, smiling widely at her friend. Her eyes widened as she caught me standing nearby.

"I was waiting for you at *Delu*. But it seems you got held up." The woman's eyes jumped from Trina's to mine and lingered. "And you are?"

"Cole. An old friend."

"Cole." She said my name with intention, drawing it out, like she'd heard it before. I knew the moment recognition hit. Her eyes slid to Trina's. "Oh."

"We ran into each other on the street."

Like she had to defend herself. Irritation spiked in my veins. The hidden bruise. Her flinch. The caution in which she held herself now, even though this woman had been excited to see her...

Something was wrong. Definitely.

"And your name?" I asked the woman.

She blinked, maybe surprised I'd asked. Maybe surprised I didn't know who she was considering Trina's current social status. "Valerie. Nice to meet you, Cole. What brings you to the city?"

So she did know who I was. "Police officer's conference." I really needed to get going but my stomach rolled at the thought. "Can I see you again?" I asked Trina. "Before I leave town?"

"No," she said and stepped further away. "I don't think there's any point in that."

"We should go, Katrina," Valerie said. Regret flashed in her eyes when she looked at me.

I couldn't figure the two out. She was either a genuine friend to Trina or something much darker.

"You're right." Trina steeled her spine and rolled her shoulders. The coffee stained her pink shirt, but it was forgotten. At least to her. "It was nice to see you again." Her tone had gone cold.

Vapid.

I detested it.

"Wait." I pulled out a business card. "If you change your mind, or need anything, Trina—"

"Katrina. It's Katrina now."

"You'll never be that to me." Besides the fact she'd always hated her name and hadn't even used it when she modeled, this *Katrina* in front of me was definitely *not* Trina. "Take the card. Call me. If you need anything. Help. Or want to talk."

She kept her arms crossed. "I'm fine."

I ignored her. "I'll drop everything and be here. Swear it. You need me, I'm here." I focused on her bruised cheek again. It was hidden well, and a couple days old, but no makeup could make it vanish completely. It only told me she had practice doing it.

Which meant she'd had one before, and there were few ways a woman repeatedly got bruises on her cheeks.

Valerie reached out and plucked it from my fingers before she tucked it into a side pocket in Trina's purse.

"Goodbye, Cole." Trina spun on nude heels and looked back. "Valerie. We can't be late."

"Right." She pushed out her lips, looked at Trina, then back to me. "It was nice meeting you."

And as the woman hurried to catch up with Trina, slipping her arm through Trina's, she looked back once... genuine worry on her face.

Something was wrong. Something big and dark. I didn't need to be a police officer to put the pieces together.

It wasn't until she was gone that I realized I didn't have the chance to say goodbye.

Which was probably good, because I wasn't sure I had the strength to say it to her again. Instead, before they vanished down the sidewalk, I cupped my hands around my mouth and called out, "See you again, soon, Trina!"

She didn't respond, but the friend lifted her hand in the air in acknowledgment.

It was something. At least I knew she heard me.

My phone buzzed on my hip and suddenly, the noise of the city returned, yanking me out of the last few minutes. I grabbed it without paying attention to the name or number. "This is Paxton."

"Hi, Daddy! Mommy said I could call you before school!"

I glanced at my watch. Nine. Her bus would be coming any minute. "And I always love to hear from you, Junie bug. You ready for the bus?"

"Yep! When will I see you?"

"Tonight, pumpkin. I'll be back home tonight, but it'll be late, so Grandma's going to get you from Mommy's, and I'll come and tuck you in when I get back okay?"

"Or you could come tuck me in at Mommy's."

I could...but I wouldn't. "But then Grandma will miss seeing you, too. So let's go with Grandma nicely today and tell your sister I love her, too?"

"Do you love me?"

"With everything I have and everything I am, sweetie pie."

"DID THE CONFERENCE NOT GO WELL?"

My mom, Bridget Paxton, could know everything about me with a look. Today, it didn't take her mother's intuition to sense anything considering I held a glass of bourbon in my hand. I rarely drank, and yet ever since my run-in with Trina I'd been craving one. Fortunately, I'd held out until I finished the conference, got on the road, and got home and tucked June and Ella into bed.

Both were sleeping, but their murmured *love you's* and soft, sweet hugs had managed to dampen my fury to a simmering anger.

"The conference was fine." I sighed and scrubbed a hand down my face before gathering the strength to meet her concerned gaze. "Ran into Trina on the street."

"You did? How? What? How is she?" My mom clasped her hands together in prayer. Ever since her parents weren't invited to her wedding and essentially cut off, they'd been desperate for her to return home. Something wasn't right. We all knew it.

Trina might have gone to New York to chase her dreams and managed to catch them against all odds...but she'd changed. Now I suspected why, and it was worse than what her parents thought.

They thought Trina got swept away with wealth and celebrity-status and decided her small, southern town pastor dad and stay-at-home mom were too simple for her. That they weren't good enough.

I doubted their professions or their simple life had anything to do with Trina's distance, but had everything to do with the man who caused her bruised cheek.

"Chance encounter on the street." I chuckled at the

memory. Crazy how it was twelve hours ago. Seemed like a lifetime already. "She slammed into me leaving a coffee shop and I spilled my coffee all over her."

"That doesn't tell me how she is."

"Yeah, well, she didn't really give me anything. Barely said hello to me and couldn't wait to get away."

My mom's lips flatlined and her eyes narrowed. "That's not Trina."

I debated for a minute. My parents were still close with hers. Hard not to be when we all still went to the same church, gathered at the same potlucks, and went to the same local stores they always had. The population of Deer Creek might have doubled, but those who were here before the growth were as tight-knit as ever.

"Nothing about her was," I admitted. "And you gotta *promise* not to say a word to Mr. and Mrs. Mills." I might have been close to turning thirty-one, but I'd used their first names maybe twice in my life. It never felt quite right, despite their constant reminders for me to do so.

"Cole, I don't know..."

"Then I can't tell you. It'd kill 'em, Ma. I swear it'd absolutely destroy them."

Her chin trembled and I waited as the fight raged through her before she sighed. "Okay. I promise. It'll stay between us. And maybe your father if I need to share."

"She's been beaten." My throat clogged as I said the words. They'd been trapped so deep inside of me all day it was almost a relief to get them out. Not so much when Mom winced with sympathy for her.

"You sure?"

"Covered bruise on her cheek and she had a practiced hand in doing it. I can tell, Ma. She wasn't...she's in pain. That much was obvious."

"The poor thing." My mom hugged herself and shook with sorrow.

The girl we'd all loved...so many still did, even if she'd turned her back on us all. I knew why she did it to me and had long since forgiven her for her decisions.

I stayed true to my word. I hated her for a day...maybe more, but after the hatred and anger faded, there was still only the love I had for her remaining. No matter how hard I tried, I could never quite kick that either.

And now the only woman I'd ever truly loved was in danger. In pain. Living with a man who thought he owned the world...or at least the South, and my hands were tied.

Mostly.

"What are you going to do?" my mom asked.

"I'm going to save her."

Somehow. Some way. I'd stand by my word. I'd always be there for her. Now I just needed to figure out how.

# EIGHT

## TRINA

**Then**

AFTER NEW YEAR'S EVE, I spent days seeking as much information as I could find on Robert Madrid. His name was mentioned in a handful of local modeling agency catalogs, and once I found the name and address of Whisk Agency, where he seemed to work, I took the subway and strolled around the neighborhood.

Zane's warning about girls having to test their morals every once in a while, still lingered, so before I ever made contact, I did what I could to make sure this man was legit.

The building's entryway was modern, all glass and white marble floors and white cushioned chairs held together by gleaming gold metal.

The agency itself was located on the twentieth floor of the building, but the building's lobby sent relief coursing through me and washed away my largest concerns.

Whisk Agency was legit. The model Anna Molin was

one of their clients. She appeared in makeup commercials for luxury makeup brands I hoped to one day be able to afford. She was on billboards and the sides of buses modeling underwear and swimsuits in the spring and summer months and covered in thick, cable sweaters and plaid button up shirts in the fall and winter.

She was a beautiful model from Brazil, and I wanted to be her. And then more famous.

It was with only a small remaining amount of trepidation that I picked up the phone on January sixth, giving Robert a few days to get back to work after the New Year, and made the call.

To my further appeasement, he was incredibly professional, and when I told him I received his name and number through Zane, he scheduled me into his office for an initial consultation and meeting on his first available appointment. Which happened to be almost two weeks away.

Thrilled, I spent the next two weeks mulling over more books and websites and videos on modeling and posing, how to adjust my frame to allow light to hit me better, how to smile or shift my eyes to appear either sultry or fierce.

Stella giggled every time I passed a mirror and struck a pose, but even she noticed a fresh quickness to my step.

My customers at Laredo's apparently noticed the difference as well, because my tips increased substantially. It left me with an extra small chunk I squirreled away into a tin can I kept under my bed, slowly growing my savings and a smaller coffee tin for "splurge" funds.

When my appointment came, set late on a Friday afternoon at Whisk Agency, I ensured I'd spent an appropriate amount of time curling my blond hair and working on my makeup to look a few years older. I was wearing my best dress and tights. Wearing an ultra-long white shirtdress, I left the collar opened and the top couple buttons undone. It wasn't enough to reveal cleavage, but enough to see skin tone and my collarbone. My heels were in my shoulder bag so I could put them on as soon as I reached the building. My heavy, gray snow boots clunked on the slushy sidewalks, remnants of snow earlier from in the week, but like life in Deer Creek, New Yorkers prepared for the weather and went on about life as usual. It was one of the only similarities between the two places I'd been able to find in the last six months.

My nerves were at an all-time high by the time I reached the building. If everything Zane had told me about, and everything I'd read about on Whisk, was true, this had the potential to be my big break. I desperately needed it. How amazing would it be to not only start off the new year with this opportunity, but also to be able to phone my parents and let them know?

I had to nail this appointment.

Taking a few minutes, I changed into my heels on the covered and dry sidewalk, before doing a quick makeup scan with my compact mirror. All done and looking as good as I was going to, there was nothing left than to go for it.

Summoning up all the confidence I had, which was approximately the size of a mustard seed, and faking everything else I needed, I curled my hands around the brass handle on the glass door and opened the door.

Instantly, I was hit with a blast of heat as I stepped into the lobby and headed straight for the lobby's receptionist desk.

"Hello," I said, already digging into my purse for my driver's license. Robert had told me I'd need to show ID to be allowed on the elevator. "Trina Mills. I'm here to see Mr. Madrid?"

I cringed at the way I phrased it more like a question than a statement. If the woman behind the desk, beautifully and stylishly coiffed but old enough to be my mother noticed, she said nothing.

"Sign here," she said, pushing a blotter toward me for visitors. "And take this badge with you. It must be visible at all times."

She glanced at my ID, nodded, and picked up the phone. "Mr. Madrid, your appointment is here. A Miss Mills? Excellent. She's on her way."

She set down the phone and gave me a quick glance, with a barely-there smile, pointing at the elevators. "Twentieth floor, second bank of elevators to your right. Sign out when you leave."

"Okay. Thank you."

I tucked my license into my purse and grabbed the badge, clipping it to my purse as I walked to where she gestured.

As soon as the elevator doors closed shut behind me, my stomach rolled. By the time the elevator slowed to a halt, I was one more floor away from expelling my nerves all over my feet.

"Goodness," I muttered, and pressed a hand to my stomach. "You can do this."

When the doors dinged and opened, I stepped off the elevator, ensuring my steps were firm and confident. Spying the receptionist desk first, I headed straight toward it even though there was no one sitting behind the cherry wood and marble counter-height top.

I forced myself not to fidget with my purse string or the

hem of my shirt, and instead, I surveyed the area. Richly colored woods, beautiful marble. Frosted glass walls with the same cherry-colored wood doors behind the reception desk. A hallway to the right. Couches that looked built more for design aesthetic than comfort to my left. Glass top tables at the edges of the two small couches and one in the middle created a sitting area that, while made with warm colors in tans and chocolate brown pillows, none of it said "get comfortable and stay a while." It was exactly what I expected from a modeling agency's entrance. Everything was rich-looking, expensive, and screamed impersonal at the same time whispering, "*Notice me.*"

No way was I moving close to it.

A door opened down a hallway to my right, and I turned in the direction of the noise, hoping it was Robert Madrid. In an instant, I set my posture to how I'd been practicing for this moment for the last few weeks.

Shoulders back, breasts out, chin up, arms relaxed at my sides. I placed one foot in front of the other to elongate my legs and at the last second, as a shadow appeared from around the corner, I flipped my blond hair off my shoulder.

"Miss Mills," the man said, as he appeared.

He was stunningly handsome. Dressed in a well-fitted double-breasted black pinstripe suit, his shirt was stark white and his tie, a deep blood red.

He was at least a decade older than me. Old enough to be experienced and *hot*, young enough to not be anywhere close to my father in age. The lack of gray in his styled, dirty-blond hair and no wrinkles helped with the age.

"Mr. Madrid, I assume," I said, holding out my hand as he walked toward me. I swung my hips in one long stride of a step and reached him. "Trina Mills. Pleasure to meet you."

"Trina. Please, call me Robert. This is all informal, anyway." He shook my offered hand but held himself back. His rich, blue eyes did a scan of my body, and I fought not to falter in my step or my nerves.

The last thing I needed was my hand trembling in his firm, but professional handshake.

"Lovely," he said. He grinned, showing off sparkling white teeth. His approval of my appearance loosened tension in my shoulders. "Zane was correct about you."

"Thank you," I replied, my voice polite.

I was here to get approval on my looks after all, so the fact he'd inspected me didn't bother me.

However, he held my hand a bit too long. I tugged, signaling for him to let go, but his smile widened and his grip didn't falter. "Shall I show you to the room and we can get started? I know Zane mentioned I often photograph after hours, so I'm only allowed a short amount of time."

"Sure." I shook my head and corrected myself. "Yes. Thank you, that would be lovely." *Polite Trina. Be polite and professional.*

Seeing as he still held my hand, he pulled me forward and then I was next to him. His hand released mine but instead of gesturing for me to follow him, he settled his hand at my lower back.

Warmth hit where he touched, followed by a slight chill.

Did all men touch models and women they photographed?

It wasn't as if he was crossing a line, but the move felt too *friendly*, maybe? Like we hadn't just met.

Regardless, I didn't move away, but my posture stayed tight and tall as he guided us down the hallway and to the right. He then led me through an open door, and as soon as we stepped inside, my heart leaped and fluttered.

A photography room. Bright white lights were already set up, standing on top of and in front of a white background. In the center of the area was a gray one-armed chaise lounge. Comfortable, but not too cushy.

I turned to Robert and smiled unable to hide my excitement. "Thank you, again, so much for agreeing to meet with me."

His eyes seemed to almost dance with the same excitement I had. "I believe the pleasure will prove itself to be all mine. Now, I prefer to have you comfortable before our first shoot, so why don't you get settled in the chair, and for a few minutes, we'll just talk, okay?"

"Thank you." I couldn't hide my sigh of relief. Spying a small table next to us, I set down my purse and walked to the chair. Once seated, I crossed my ankles and settled my hands in my lap.

Robert went to where there was a stool by the wall, grabbed it, and picked up a camera with his other hand and brought both back so he was sitting in front of me. He sat down on the stool and settled his camera in his lap, the cover over the lens, straps hanging down as if he was in no hurry whatsoever.

"So, tell me about where you grew up," Robert asked, taking me by surprise. "Zane tells me you're from the South?"

A smile formed on my cheeks, unable to be helped. It'd been forever since anyone had asked me about home. "Yes," I said easily, almost breathily. "I'm from a town called Deer Creek, in the mountains in North Carolina.

"What's it like?"

My gaze shifted, and although I hadn't expected the

personal tone of the questions, he'd wanted me relaxed. Perhaps he was trying to get me talking so I quit thinking so much.

With that realization settled, I told Robert everything about life in Deer Creek. He asked me more questions and I answered, and soon, as I was telling about how my high school backed up to a cornfield, something he found entertaining based on his quiet but sincere laugh. Before long, I realized he'd started taking pictures. Every time I smiled, or every time I was lost in thought about a question of his, the quiet click of the camera registered in my mind. Yet the conversation still naturally flowed, and I knew, every time he checked his camera screen at the back of his camera and grinned and nodded, I was doing well.

Yes. This was what I needed.

I thought we were done when Robert set the camera down on the stool and sauntered up to me. His finger trailed along my cheek but his eyes stayed on mine.

"You are beautiful," he said. "The photos I've taken are wonderful. Some of my best yet."

I was no longer nervous, or thinking his behavior earlier might have been inappropriate, even as his finger drifted to my jaw, the side of my neck, and over my shoulder.

"Thank you." I grinned.

"Part of modeling, though Trina, is being comfortable in your skin."

At his words, his finger on my neck drifted to the edge of my top, tugging lightly on it. My skin warmed from either his touch, or the lights, or perhaps the excitement. I didn't know, but something new was buzzing beneath my flesh.

"I understand."

His head tilted. "Do you? I would like a shot of you,

softer than what we've taken, more natural. Would you mind unbuttoning your blouse for me?"

He must have registered my surprise because his finger disappeared and instead his hand settled on my shoulder. "Not nude, Trina. We'll keep you covered. I'm looking for something a bit more mature, seductive, to show your range."

Of course. It made sense. Models were photographed in almost nothing all the time anyway.

"It's okay," I said. "What would you like me to do?"

His grin softened, along with his eyes, and I allowed Robert to do the work.

He unbuttoned my top, spreading it open, but he stayed true to his word. My bra stayed on and covered. He brushed my hair over my chest and then pushed off a shoulder of my shirt, but the entire time he adjusted me, whispering quietly and softly, he stayed professional, working on keeping me calm and relaxed.

*Billboards and magazine spreads.* I repeated my goal in my mind. I was reaching for my dream, obviously it might mean showing more skin than just from the throat up.

"Beautiful," Robert murmured, clicking away. He glanced at me occasionally and asked if I was okay, and with each nod, he seemed more pleased.

He was checking the back of the screen when I made a decision.

While he wasn't looking at me, I dropped the rest of my top, and lifted my hair off my breast, letting it fall behind my shoulder.

His eyes jumped up at my movement, and his gaze settled on mine. "You okay?"

"Yes." I readjusted my position in the chair and gazed back at him. "I'm okay with all of this."

"Lovely." With a quick nod, the camera was once again in front of his face. He took photo after photo of me, all from the waist up, some with my hair in front of my bra, some with it behind my shoulders. He moved close and tugged a bra strap off my shoulder and then stepped back and clicked away. And when he declared us done, there was only a professional gleam of approval shining on his face.

"You're beautiful," he said, once I was redressed. He held out my purse to me, and I slid it up my shoulder. "The camera loves you. I won't make promises I can't deliver on, but I can tell you I haven't been this excited about working with a model in a very long time."

"Thank you." My voice went breathy again, surprised at his honest candor.

"I'd like to see you again next Friday. More photos, perhaps...even more natural?"

His eyebrows rose in question, one I quickly understood. I'd already made my decision. I was willing to do anything to reach my dreams.

I nodded. "Of course, that will be excellent. Same time?"

"Yes. I'll see you back here, and if you have any questions in the meantime, please call me. Okay, Trina?"

"Okay Robert."

"Wonderful." He pressed his hand to my hip and leaned in. Brushing his lips over my cheek so quickly I almost wondered if I imagined it, he whispered, "You'll be a star, Trina beautiful. I'll make sure of it."

His hand squeezed my hip, and he dropped his hand. Then he stepped back.

The moment was beautiful. Excitement and hope were drumming through my veins in unprecedented measure.

So I let him guide me back to the elevator, lean in and

give me another kiss on the cheek, this time I returned one to his, and we said our goodbyes.

When I returned to my apartment with Stella, I was so over-the-top excited about my afternoon, we were almost late for our shift at the diner.

I was thrilled. Living on cloud nine.

Robert Madrid was going to make me a star.

I was certain of it.

# NINE

## COLE

**Now**

"DADDY!"

I squatted in time to catch June as she flung her body at me at full speed.

"Oof," I grunted and picked her up, adjusting her feet so her heels didn't dig into my hips. Her arms wrapped around my throat, and if she were any stronger, she'd be choking me. "How are my girls?"

"Feral." Marie laughed and slipped the strap of their overnight bags off her shoulder. "And they keep getting worse." She reached out and playfully pinched the back of June's knee, making her shriek.

"Mommy!"

"Thanks for bringing them back." It'd been my night to go get them from her home, but I had a late call-out. It was nights like this I was thankful for how easy we co-parented.

"It's not a problem. You know that."

She grinned down at Ella who was studiously removing

her shoes, lining them up against the wall. She'd said hello to me as soon as the door opened and then was practically barreled out of the way by her little sister. Which almost knocked me down the stairs considering the entryway in my split-level home was barely large enough for me alone.

Not that Ella ever seemed to mind. It never ceased to baffle me how Ella looked exactly like me, June like her mom, and their personalities matched us the exact opposite.

"How's school, sweetheart?" I reached down and settled my hand at Ella's head.

She grinned up at me from her crouch on the floor. "Recess is stupid."

"Oh." I eyed Marie.

"What have we said about that word?" she asked our daughter.

"*You* said it wasn't a nice word." I hid my chuckle with pressed together lips and flashed wide eyes to Marie. She matched my look with an eye roll. "But I think it's true because there's nothing nice about recess."

"What's wrong with recess?" In kindergarten it could be anything from being bullied to taking a dodgeball to the face.

"I can't sit and read," Ella muttered. "Mrs. Lipton says I *have* to go run and play."

"Oh...The horror..."

Marie chuckled and quickly covered it, June popped off my shoulder far enough to screech right into my ear. "I *love* to run and play!"

I flinched at the ear-piercing squeal and gave her a tight hug.

"What's wrong with running and playing?" I set June down on her feet and got close to meet Ella eye-to-eye. "Does something hurt?"

"No. My hair gets sticky and gross."

Behind me, Marie's muffled chuckle sounded much like a snort. I forced the grin that wanted to break free to press into a frown. Only Ella, my five-year-old daughter going on twenty-year-old fashionista, could be upset with this. "I'm sorry. That has to be hard. What if we started wearing your hair up more? Would that help?"

"Maybe." She shrugged. "Do we get dessert before bedtime?"

"Absolutely. Cookies on the counter from Mellie's Cakes. If that's good enough for you."

"Mellie's!? I love Mellie's!" June's small feet thundered up the stairs, and Ella followed.

For being the older sister, she somehow ended up following after June most of the time.

"Sorry," I said to Marie when they were gone. "Couldn't help myself tonight."

She shrugged. "Your problem getting them to sleep after a sugar high, not mine."

I should have known she wouldn't care. It was my week, and outside of phone calls, we respected the differences, however minor they might be, in how we parented. "Thanks again for bringing them back. I do appreciate that, you know."

"I know, Cole. You've always let me know you appreciate me."

A flash of sadness hit her eyes that made me cringe. I *had* appreciated her. I even liked her. A whole lot. But I knew what that statement didn't say... I didn't *love* her, and she still felt the pain of that.

Before I could apologize, she had a wide smile on her face. "Well, I should go. There's a signed permission slip in

June's bag for a trip with her preschool field trip to go to the grocery store later this week."

"The grocery store?"

"They do some sort of healthy eating unit, and the kids get to pick their own healthy snacks."

"I'm guessing Mellie's Cakes aren't allowed in that cart."

She laughed. "Probably not, no."

"What a dull field trip."

She slapped my shoulder still laughing. "Shut up. Just make sure it gets turned in, so she doesn't miss out."

"On all the fun of picking out a zucchini? I would never deprive her."

She was still laughing and opened the front door. "Have a good week, Cole. Call me if you need me."

"I will."

I always promised but I never did. Sometimes I wondered if that made her sad or upset. June demanded frequently to call me when they were with her, but when they were with me, the girls rarely asked for their mom. I'd like to believe it was because I was more fun, but the truth was, I nipped it in the bud from the very beginning. Maria dug that hole on her own by caving at the sight of June's crocodile tears.

"Be safe getting home," I called out when she was at the door to her Highlander. "Lock your doors. All the smart things."

"You know I will," she called back. "See you, Cole."

I waited in the doorway until she'd started the car and pulled it back out of the driveway. Once her taillights disappeared down the street, I finally went back inside.

I hadn't seen my girls for a week. We had catching up to do.

MELLIE'S CAKES were a bad idea. It was an hour after Ella and June's regular bedtime when I finally had them bathed, teeth brushed, dressed in pajamas and ready for bed. And that was after I took them outside and we ran laps around the house in the dark, and I challenged them both to a push-up and jumping jack competition. Ella won the jumping jacks. We all dissolved into a fit of laughter as they watched me struggle with a single push-up while they knocked out a dozen.

A warm bath and two books later, both my girls were snuggled under my arms on both sides of me in Ella's tiny twin bed.

"You girls ready for sleep?" I kissed the top of both their heads.

"Not really." June snuggled in tighter and let out a loud yawn.

Sure she wasn't, but she'd fight sleep until the last possible moment.

"I love you, Daddy," Ella whispered and squeezed me as tight as she could with her arm over my stomach.

"I love you too. Both of you. Bunches and bunches." I gave Ella one last kiss and nudged June with my hip. "Let's let Ella sleep, okay?"

"Fine," June grumbled, but her voice was thicker, her words slower.

She slipped off the bed, and I followed her, tucking Ella's covers tight around her and then waiting until June climbed into bed to do the same.

I double-checked their window was locked, closed the blinds, and on my way out of the door, I whispered back to both, "I love you girls, sleep tight."

"Don't let the bedbugs bite," June whispered back.

Only soft breaths came from Ella's side.

No surprise there.

Back down the hall in my four-bedroom split-level home, I headed straight to the kitchen and began cleaning up. There were three bedrooms upstairs, one larger one downstairs that held a guest bed and dresser for the occasional visitors and my workout equipment. The rest of the downstairs had a full bath and a large playroom-slash-theater room. The girls shared one of the larger bedrooms upstairs for now, but eventually I knew they'd want their own, so it was set up as my office.

As soon as I stepped foot in this house when Marie and I split I knew it was perfect for me and the girls. We could do all our daily living on one floor, which meant the girls were kept close to me at night, but they had their privacy to run and play downstairs. And when I didn't have them and wanted guys over to watch a game, the ninety-six-inch projector screen I had downstairs was perfect. Also, the girls were small enough that after I had it installed, they lost their *minds* when we started watching their favorite movies on it.

I was loading the dishwasher and wiping down the counters when my work cell phone rang with an unknown call. My brows pinched, considering I rarely had calls it from someone I didn't know, but I couldn't ignore it, either.

"Detective Cole Paxton," I said as I answered the phone.

"Wow, you are even more handsome on the phone," a woman replied.

My spine jolted straight, and my hand clenched the phone tighter. "Excuse me?"

"Valerie Sutton," she said. "We met last month when you were in Georgia. Briefly."

Like I could forget. I hadn't been able to stop thinking about Trina since that day. I'd tried to push her out of my mind and get back to real life as soon as I returned, but whenever I had a slow moment, I was researching Jonathan, trying to find *anything* I could on him. Every time I blinked, I saw the bruise on Trina's face.

The fact that he was as rich as he was, and I couldn't find *anything* was suspect in itself. Call me paranoid, but I'd seen a lot in my day, and the fact there wasn't *anything*, not even a hint of a scandal as he gathered his millions, made me question who he had in his pocket to scrub his history so pristine it shined like crystal.

"I remember. How can I help you?"

"It's not me who needs help, Mr. Paxton."

Blood rushed to my ears as her tone changed. "Cole. What's going on?"

"I heard you tell Katrina you'd be there to help if she needs it."

"I did."

"Did you mean it?"

"Absolutely. What happened?" My tone was getting sharper, but it had nothing on the anger starting to boil my veins.

"I can't say much, and I'll need to hang up soon, but she's at Atlanta Community Hospital. She needs to get free, and right now the only way we can think of is if you're the man she told me you were."

*The man she told me you were.* It confirmed Trina had talked about me. I *knew* Valerie recognized me last month.

"What do you need me to do?"

"Come get her before Jonathan has her sent out of state to another hospital. Or out of the country. But Cole?"

"What?" I was already mentally packing and planning calls.

Shit. The girls were here.

My mom would come. Marie would come back.

I'd figure it all out, but nothing was stopping me from doing this.

"Get here quick."

"As fast as I can, I'll be there."

"You better...considering it was your business card that landed her here."

The call ended and I didn't hesitate. Didn't even question it. It didn't take a genius to figure out what she meant.

Jonathan found the card and lost his *mind* on his wife.

I'd shoot him myself if I could. Happily. And without remorse.

Grabbing my personal cell, I called my mom.

"Cole? Honey? What is it?" It was late, and if she wasn't sleeping, she was almost there based on her groggy voice.

"It's Trina. She needs me."

A soft thump echoed. My guess was it was my mom's feet hitting the floor, and then my mom spoke. "Your dad and I will be there in ten."

# TEN

## TRINA

**Then**

IT WAS HAPPENING. My dreams were coming true. The sky was hazy with thick, gray spring clouds and cool wind still whipped through my winter coat. I dodged sludge puddles left and right as I hurried down the sidewalk, now a master at weaving in and out of pedestrians in New York.

The city thrummed in my veins. The noise at night my lullaby.

It'd been three months since I met Robert. His photos of me landed me two small roles at open casting calls, one for a body soap ad and the other for a juice drink. Earlier today, he'd called and said we had to meet. He had exciting news to share with me.

Which meant that the dreary, wet air had nothing on my bright mood or my overly large smile as I shoved my way through the glass doors at the Whisk Agency. I strode with purpose toward Corinne, the woman I met that first day who sat behind the main reception desk.

"Hi Corinne," I said, breathless with anticipation. I unwound my thin scarf at my neck. "Is Robert ready for me?"

She checked my ID I handed to her every time and barely spared me a glance. "You may head up, Miss Mills."

I tried to get her once to call me Trina. I'd been Miss Mills ever since.

I still called her Corinne, figuring at some point, I'd break through her distant manner.

"Thank you."

She waved a hand elegantly toward the elevators as her eyes slid to someone behind me. "How may I help you?"

I all but skipped toward the elevator banks, Corinne's dismissal unable to put a pall to my mood.

I'd been on pins and needles, bubbling with excitement ever since our quick phone call four hours ago.

*I have excellent news for you, Trina.*

*"Well, what is it?" My fingers tapped a rhythm on the kitchen counter, and I flashed wide, hopeful eyes to Stella.*

*"I'll tell you tonight after the shoot but come prepared and ready to celebrate."*

*I hung up the phone, grabbed Stella's shoulders, and squealed so hard she flinched.*

This was it.

My moment. Good things were coming, just as Robert predicted.

The elevator doors chimed, and I stepped in, repeatedly pressing the button to take me away to the twentieth floor and my dreams coming true. He'd never called me before unless it was to change an appointment time. Eight times I'd sat for him, and now I was comfortable doing anything he asked of me.

Even today, knowing we were "stretching my limits," as he'd suggested on the phone, didn't make me nervous.

Robert was my catalyst to everything I dreamed of unfolding. So far, he'd shown me he was going to make good on his promises.

I trusted him.

———

THE PLUSH, black velvet beneath me was almost as soft as silk draped over my thighs. Every time Robert suggested I move a leg and adjust my position, it slid, threatening to expose the very last hidden part of me.

Two hours ago, the team he hired whisked me into hair and makeup.

He'd never done that before. I'd never sat in a chair, behind screens, while Robert prepared a shoot for me and a team prepared me.

It'd been a dream come true until someone came in, handed me a white silk robe and with a bored tone, stated, "Wear nothing besides this."

I'd barely managed to grab the silky robe before it fluttered to the floor. My gaze had jumped to the stylists while a lump formed in my throat.

"What?"

"Nude today," the makeup artist said, piling all her brushes and compacts into three large cases. "That's what the agenda said."

I considered refusing, and then the reminder of Robert telling me he was stretching my limits came to my mind. He had tried to prepare me, I just wished he'd done a more thorough job.

When I walked out from the screens, draped in nothing

but a silk robe, and Robert motioned me toward the lounge chair, he'd been as succinct and professional as always. He started with photos of me in my robe, slowly having me undrape it from my shoulders as my comfort grew. How he knew, I had no idea, but he must have seen something in my eyes soften because every time I reached that point of ease, he took me further.

My breasts were displayed, my blond hair draped over a shoulder. I was lying mostly on my side, propped on my other hand.

"Okay, Trina," Robert said, "let's remove that last piece. Slide your top leg forward and bend it over your bottom one."

I envisioned the position. It'd keep me covered, mostly, yet no one but Cole had ever seen those parts of me.

And just the reminder of him, thinking of him, nude, in front of another man even if that man was a photographer sent a cool trickle down my spine.

If Cole had his way, I wouldn't be doing photo shoots and magazine ads. I'd be back at home in Deer Creek, attending community college and waiting for him on Friday nights to get done with his studies so we could take his truck to a field and make out. I wouldn't be exposing my body to photo shoots, I'd be covering it with thick and warm maternity clothes, large as a house. I blinked that reminder away before I could linger on it and focused on the *now*.

My Friday nights were spent chasing my dreams, and they were coming true.

"Trina?" Robert asked, lifting his head behind the camera. "Are you ready?"

I shifted into the position he described, and once my legs still hid my most intimate areas, I brushed the silky drape to the floor.

"Beautiful," Robert muttered and ducked behind his lens. "Arch your back... tilt your chin up...stunning...look this way..."

I followed his cues, focused on my dream, and pushed thoughts of Cole to the background.

I still spoke to my parents, but I was answering their calls less and less often. In January when my mom brought up Cole, I'd asked her to quit mentioning him. She'd sounded disappointed, as if she thought the only reason I'd ever return home was for him, but she was mistaken.

I missed my parents.

I didn't miss Deer Creek.

I loved walking in Central Park or perusing the Met. I went and saw plays and wandered the city. I'd been to the top of the Empire State Building and taken a ferry ride to the Statue of Liberty. I wandered through SoHo and found a cute restaurant in Little Italy. Stella and I, with some girls she met in her online class, went ice skating.

I was seeing everything I wanted to, experiencing it all firsthand instead of in a glossy travel guide.

Deer Creek had nothing on New York.

"You seem distant today."

Robert's voice startled me, and I flinched, jerking my head only to see him no longer behind the camera, but in a chair facing mine. He reached out and brushed hair off the side of my face. "Not that I mind. The camera loves you even when you look a little sad. More so, maybe."

"I'm not sad." I tried to smile. "Are we done?"

"With the photos."

"Oh. Okay then." I leaned forward and reached for the satin robe I'd had on my lap.

"Don't."

"What?"

"I enjoy seeing you like this."

Unease slid through me. The robe on the floor called to me, and yet I couldn't move. Robert was still sitting in the chair, knees spread, lounging back like he always did when we talked, but he'd never looked at me like this...or placed his hand on his belt, slid it further down.

He rubbed his hand down the zipper, and I gulped. The hard impression beneath the fabric of gray dress pants was impossible to miss and I yanked my gaze away.

*No.* He didn't mean to do this. He couldn't.

I shook my head. "Robert."

"You're beautiful, prettier than any girl I've ever photographed. Let me look at you without the lens in the way for a moment."

A strange heat warmed my ears and my face, and yet I still didn't move. Was this any different than being naked and photographed? It felt like it, and yet he hadn't moved toward me. Didn't touch me.

But it had to be wrong. Right? I was too paralyzed to cover myself, especially more so when he spoke.

"Would you like to hear the good news I wanted to share with you?"

"Yeah." I cleared my throat. "Yes. Please." I'd listen to anything if it took my attention off his hand. Off that bulge beneath his pants. Off the way he played with his belt buckle until it opened.

"I've heard from an agent interested in representing you."

"What?" I forgot about my nakedness for a moment and jumped to sitting. "Who? From where?"

Robert smiled at me. That same friendly smile he always gave me, and he laughed. "Steven Cormack."

"What?" Steven Cormack represented some of the

largest models in the world. At least his agency did. But he was always mentioned. I'd never dreamed of anything so incredible. I had to have heard him wrong. "Are you serious?"

"I am." His gaze dropped and settled on my breasts and went further down. Remembering I was naked, I crossed my legs and draped an arm over my breasts. The robe was too far to reach for, and I eyed it before he continued. "I spoke with him today. He'd like to meet you next week."

His gaze rose again and all of it had happened so quickly I wondered if I imagined it. He'd never looked at me with such interest before. Still, I grabbed the robe and wrapped it around me.

This time, he didn't stop me. "This is. Wow."

I couldn't wrap my head around it. All the unease vanished, and a new rush of excitement suffused my every breath. "I don't know what to say. Thank you."

"You don't have to say anything," Robert said. His hands moved. The metal clink of something jangled, and I tightened the grip on the robe. "But you can thank me."

I forced my eyes to stay looking at his face. The excitement chilled in my veins.

His tone was clear. His movements more so as his body shifted.

"I don't want to," I said, my chin wobbling and tears already blurring my vision. "This isn't...this isn't what I want..."

Visions, horrible visions splattered into my brain on what exactly he wanted from me. Sex? Was he going to rape me? God. How could I have been so stupid to think he was nice to me? All those touches. All the brushes of his hand over my breasts. The soft smiles.

"Robert—" I said, trying again, but what could I say?

I was naked in front of a man who was older than me, much larger and stronger.

I'd willingly placed myself in this situation.

I'd ignored the warning flares. The touches and looks and kisses.

The room turned to ice. Fear pummeled my body as he spoke.

"You want to meet Steven, don't you? All I'm asking for is a little gratitude in helping you get there. Is that so wrong?"

I tried to look away from him, but the movement of his arm grabbed my attention and before I could stop myself, my gaze settled on his lap.

On what his hand was doing to himself. Stroking.

Vomit pooled in my throat.

"I don't want to do this," I said, a tear sliding down my cheek. "This isn't right."

"There are dozens of other girls, just as beautiful, willing to do whatever they need to make their dreams come true, Trina."

I flinched. The way he said my name. His voice was tight and even then, a small groan slid through it.

How would I get out of this?

"This is how the game is played. This is how pretty little girls like you end up on billboards. But if you don't want to meet Steven, your one and only chance..."

His voice trailed off. His meaning was absolutely clear.

I wanted to meet Steven Cormack more than my next breath, but to do it this way?

I was trapped in a room with a man who had the power to do anything to me. And I'd gotten naked willingly.

I was still naked.

I also *really* wanted to be a star. If I didn't make it, every other choice I made would be for nothing.

What was it Zane warned me? Everyone sacrifices their morals every once in a while...?

"What do you want?" I brushed tears off my cheeks.

Robert grinned and slid forward in the chair. With a glint in his eyes that would give me nightmares for years to come, he described in detail what he wanted from me. What he'd do to me if I refused.

In the end, I could see no other solution. No way out. Giving it voluntarily would be better than to have it taken from me.

I dropped to my knees in front of him and gave him everything he asked for.

# ELEVEN

## COLE

**Now**

IT WAS after two in the morning when I reached Atlanta and pulled into the hospital parking lot. True to my mom's word, she and my dad were there in ten minutes—the benefit of living in a small town close to family. They'd always been willing to drop whatever they needed in order to help out. I left them with instructions on getting the girls to school, reminding my mom about the grocery store field trip form—to which she had the same response I had—and telling them to call Marie in the morning to let her know what was going on.

My next calls were to the chief and Eddy, both answering their phones and telling me to go. Chief told me to check in when I got back.

Thank goodness for good coworkers and an understanding boss.

I had no idea what I was walking into. I'd had almost six hours to allow my imagination to run away from me.

Considering I'd been a police officer for eight years, I'd seen enough that I had to force my mind from thinking the worst.

The worst hadn't happened. She was hospitalized, not in the morgue, and I reminded myself of that truth while I headed straight for the doors.

I'd added Valerie's number to my personal phone and shot her a text letting her know I was on my way, and before I reached the elevator banks, I sent her another one.

**Me: What floor and room?**

Her text bubble appeared like she'd been staring at her phone, waiting for me. Which meant she'd clocked the ETA I sent her once my GPS calculated the fastest route. Good. I was starting to like this woman.

*Valerie: 417. Give me a few minutes. Need to get rid of Jonathan.*

Like I was going to stand around and wait.

I headed up to the fourth floor, and when I saw the signs for the hall that would take me to Trina's room, my pulse slowed and all the rage I was feeling on the drive started to cool. I was here now and could see her. Since I didn't quite know what I was walking into, I turned toward the waiting room and took a seat in a secluded corner, grabbing a magazine and ducked my head in case anyone Trina might know walked by. My ball cap was pulled low, and my clothes were bland. All the things I'd needed to be unrecognizable. Might have been overkill, but as far as I was concerned, her husband had deep pockets. Who knew who he had on his side in the hospital. Depending on what came next, no one would be able to describe my features. Or who the man was who snuck into his wife's hospital room.

My phone buzzed and I opened the text.

*Valerie: I'm with her. Convinced Jonathan to get me some coffee in the cafeteria.*

**Me: In waiting room. Be right there.**

I stood and wandered close to the elevators.

I'd seen numerous photos of Jonathan Wolf. More in the last five weeks since my trip to Atlanta. Footsteps thumped on the floor, and I moved to the coffee and water station in the waiting room. It allowed me to peek at the elevator banks out of the corner of my eyes and there he was.

It was the middle of the night and the man was dressed like he was prepared to head to a boardroom. Dark, navy suit, so dark it was almost black, but the dark brown shoes on his feet gave it away. The man had a gold watch and perfectly styled hair.

He didn't pay me any attention as he pressed the elevator button harder than necessary, and as he waited, he pulled out his phone. The screen lit up and then he was texting someone. He was completely at ease. No hint of distress tightening his eyes or features. No pursed lips or stressed jaw. Nothing to indicate he was the least bit upset about his wife being in the hospital.

Text sent, he slipped his phone back into his pocket and shook out his wrist, and that was when I saw it—a smear of something dark, staining his wrist beneath his watch, the outer edge of his hand.

Blood. Had to be.

I swallowed thickly, fighting down the urge to get some of his blood on my fists, and turned back to the water machine. Cup filled, I took a sip and slowly turned.

The elevators dinged, and as the doors opened, Jonathan strolled into them like absolutely nothing was wrong in his world.

And perhaps that was true. Who would go against him? Who could fight him?

People in Atlanta might not be able to…

But I sure as hell could.

———

I REACHED the door and turned the knob. I'd had hours to prepare myself to see Trina. Hours to imagine the worst and hours to imagine the swelling and whatever else I'd find. Considering I had no idea how much time I'd have with her, I didn't hesitate.

As soon as the door opened, Valerie jumped to her feet, faced the door, and stood at Trina's side. She moved to stand as Trina's protector, and the way she stood barely gave me a glance at Trina.

But what I saw was enough. Her bottom half was covered beneath a blanket, one side much bulkier than it should have been. IVs were placed in the backs of both of her hands and an oxygen monitor was pinched to one finger. Both hands were visible and resting on her stomach.

"Hey," I said to Valerie, and tipped my chin up.

"You're here," she breathed out, and it sounded like relief. "He'll be back soon."

I already knew that. I also knew she hadn't moved.

"You going to let me see her?"

"It's bad," she whispered, and her chin trembled as she said it. She had mascara streaks beneath her eyes and a rumpled, deep red blouse. A thick collar hung down from her collarbones and I imagined it'd once been tied into a bow of some sort at her throat. "He hurt her. So bad."

I swallowed the knot twisting my throat and nodded. "Move, Valerie. Let me see her."

Her hand drifted off Trina's arm as she stepped back

and as I caught my first glimpse of Trina's face, the world spun and came to an abrupt stop.

Her face was *mangled*.

I closed my eyes, drew in a breath to keep me in that room and not racing down to the cafeteria and when I opened them again, Valerie's gaze was frozen on me. "Damage. Tell me all of it."

"Bruised ribs. Doctors don't *think* the cheekbone is fractured but won't know for sure until the swelling goes down. He did something to her leg, it's braced but I'm not completely sure if it's the knee or what, but..."

"That's enough," I said, and forced my tone to gentle. "I get it."

"He's a monster." He was worse than that, much worse.

I stepped toward Trina and reached out, brushing the backs of my fingers down her arm. "Has she been awake?"

"She's sedated. She hit her head and has some swelling."

"*She* didn't hit anything," I grunted.

"I know. I know, Mr. Paxton, but —"

"Cole—"

"Cole. I know that, but somehow, she hit her head on something." I couldn't stop staring at Trina's face. She wasn't recognizable. Her hair, which was stuck to her temples and had clearly been washed which didn't work because blood still remained, was the only thing about her I could identify.

"And how exactly am I supposed to help her?" She was in a hospital, hooked to monitors and clearly unable to walk. I'd do anything for her, but this seemed impossible.

"She has to get out of here. They won't...he said it was a home invasion. Sent cops to his home and everything so I don't know if *he* did it this time or someone else. But as soon as I got here, he asked me about you and showed me your business card. Demanded I tell him how she got that."

"What'd you say?"

"I said I had no idea what he was talking about, but the cops didn't find anything at his home. And he said he'd just come home from a meeting with Kip."

"Your husband is his alibi?" My brows arched and I couldn't hide my pointed tone.

If she was surprised I'd looked into them, she didn't show it. Perhaps because the world knew her as well. Daughter to a famous actor and actress, one of the few celebrity couples who'd been married for over thirty-five years, their romance and marriage were inspirational. Valerie, their only child, met and fell in love with a professional football player while in Los Angeles before being traded to Georgia. It was there he met Jonathan, but it was Kip's family that helped fund his buy-in when they became General Manager and Assistant GM. Kip's family, generations prior, started a small bank in Savannah, Georgia, that now had branches all over the Southeast.

"Kip *despises* Jonathan," Valerie leaned in and whispered. Like we were being recorded. Like someone would hear her outside. "He's wanted to leave for years, but I'm the only person Katrina's allowed to spend time with. He tried to talk to Jonathan once." She glanced at Trina, sniffed, and came back to me. "It didn't go well."

"He stayed so you could be there for Trina."

"It took *years* for her to admit what was going on. And that was four years ago."

I closed my eyes at the revelation. How long had this been going on? They'd been together now for a decade. Had she been abused that long? The thought made my stomach roll with disgust and unbearable pain for her.

"What happens now? What do you need from me?"

If I could, I'd throw Trina in my arms and carry her out. There was no way I could move her, though.

"Cops can't do anything until she wakes up. Get her side of the story. Katrina would need to press charges."

She chewed her bottom lip.

I could surmise what she wasn't saying. "You don't think she will."

"She never has before."

"Right." Of course she hadn't. She *couldn't*. I glanced at the clock on the wall. Minutes had gone by. I wanted to pull up a chair, protect Trina, and beat Jonathan so badly when he returned that he'd be in a bed just like Trina or worse, but this wasn't the time. "Again, what do you need from me?"

"You'll help her?"

"I'll do whatever I need to do."

"Okay. Good." She breathed out and nodded. "Kip has a plan, actually. I told him about you. He's not certain, to be honest, if he can trust you."

"Then tell your husband I've loved Trina since she was fourteen years old and not a damn thing has changed."

Tears burned her eyes. We both glanced down at Trina, but I couldn't look at her too long. She was too damaged. She'd *hate* that I was seeing her like this.

"Tomorrow," Valerie whispered. "I can get Jonathan to let me stay tonight. Kip has a meeting planned for him...or is planning on calling an emergency meeting in the morning. We can get her transport, but we need somewhere for her to go."

She handed me a card with an address. A time. Nothing else. "What's this?"

"Meet us there. You have a hotel room? I'd offer you a bed at our house, but if Jonathan finds out..."

"I'll sleep in my truck if I have to." I packed for days considering I had no idea what I was walking into, but I'd try to get a hotel for the night.

"Okay then. Tomorrow."

"Give me a minute with her."

"If Jonathan comes..."

"Then you'll have to handle that. One minute. Alone."

"Okay." She walked toward me and set her trembling hand on my shoulder. "Please. I *need* her safe from him, and I don't think she has the fight left in her to do it herself. Please tell me she'll be safe with you."

"She lets me take her home, and I can guarantee she'll be in the safest place in the world for her."

Valerie must have seen the truth flaring in my eyes because she nodded once, squeezed my shoulder, and let go. Once the door clicked shut behind her, I turned back to Trina and got close to her ear.

"You told me you didn't go by Trina anymore, but I don't care because that's who you are and who you've always been. I don't know who that monster has made you into, but we're going to get you safe. Get you someplace warm so you can heal. You have my word, Trina. I'll take care of you."

My hand had drifted to hers and her fingers flinched. I glanced down, squeezed her hand back and her fingers tightened around mine.

"You can hear me, I know you can, honey, but right now you gotta pretend I wasn't here. Valerie and I will get you safe. We'll get you back to all the people who love you and can help you, okay?"

Her head fell to the side, so she was facing me. Her eyes fluttered like she was trying to open them, but I didn't want her to wake and see me.

Hearing me could be bad enough if she mumbled something while Jonathan was there.

"I love you, Trina." I leaned down and gave the softest lip brush to her forehead. It was one of the few areas of her face that hadn't been destroyed. "Swear to God, I kept my word. I don't hate you, couldn't keep doing it, and I still love you. We'll get you through this."

Me. My parents. Hers when she was ready.

She was never going to be alone again with that monster.

I'd make sure of it.

The door opened and I twisted to see Valerie peeking her head in. "Just saw the elevators open. Get out."

"Tomorrow." I dropped Trina's hand and hurried to the door.

"Tomorrow," Valerie promised.

I turned left down the hall instead of right and ducked into an alcove where there were snack machines and hospital coffee machines. Other items lined the shelves, like a pantry for those who were visiting.

But I didn't stay hidden.

As soon as I heard a masculine rumble, I peeked my head around the corner. Jonathan's back was to me as he handed his coffee to Valerie. She flashed me wide eyes as Jonathan entered Trina's room.

"Go," she mouthed, eyes flicking from the door that was still open to me.

I went. I did it quickly, wishing things could be different.

I did it with a heaviness in my soul.

That man had beaten my Trina beyond recognition, and that was only the damage I could see.

What else had he done to her?

# TWELVE

## TRINA

**Then**

STELLA TUGGED my arm so hard she almost yanked it right out of its socket.

"Stella! Slow down!" I was laughing as I shouted to her, but she paid me no mind.

Dodging and weaving through the late summer crowds in Times Square was dizzying on a good day. With Stella pulling me along behind her, it was a wonder I was still on my feet.

I couldn't blame her, though. I was so thankful I had found a friend as good as she'd been to me. For the last year, ever since I stepped foot into our small, run-down apartment that kept falling apart on us, she was there, supporting me. Encouraging me.

Hugging me on the days when I truly didn't think I could sit through another photography session—with either Robert, or my new agent, Steven. I didn't have to tell her why I came home crying.

She never asked.

But the first time it happened, she swept me in her arms and let me cry for hours. Then she went and bought us a couple of bottles of wine, and kept my glass refilled. Since I first met with Steven in April, my life had been a roller coaster.

Photo shoots. Model calls. Jobs booked. Everything was moving at lightning speed.

I was *doing* it. I was making it, and I, more than anyone, knew how special this moment was.

And yet that pit in my stomach continued to grow, making me feel sicker as we approached our destination, until Stella came to an abrupt stop, and I slammed into her back.

"Look at you." She wrapped her arm around my lower back and hugged me tight to her side. With her free hand, she whipped open the magazine spread she had earmarked to my face.

My face in a full-page spread featuring a new, low-priced, line of makeup that was going to be in all drugstores across the nation. *I* was the one, at least my face, who would be associated with all of it.

This was it. The beginning. I'd be able to get Stella and me into a better apartment once my checks rolled in. I'd be able to go to Fashion Week. I'd be able to do *all* the things I dreamed of...

As long as I continued to keep Steven happy.

A shiver rolled through me at the thought and the rush of the crowd and music pumped from speakers pulled me back to the present. Now wasn't the time to mourn how I got to this place. It was a time to celebrate. Soon I'd be so well known, I wouldn't have to do the things Steven demanded of me.

Soon, I'd be popular enough I could find a new agent who would take me on because of my skills and my résumé. Doing what Steven made me do was temporary. Someday, I'd be free of it.

"Look!" Stella cried and held up the magazine.

My gaze followed and excitement flittered through my veins. I glanced up, beyond the magazine in Stella's hands and found it. A matching billboard to the magazine spread.

My face was on a billboard in Times Square.

I was on a billboard in Times-freaking-Square.

"Holy cow," I breathed, and my limbs trembled. "I can't believe it."

I leaned against Stella as tears burned my eyes. Of all the horrific things I'd had to do to get here, I was still here. Still standing. Still chasing dreams and then wrangling them.

"I'm so proud of you," she exclaimed and shoved the magazine into my hands. "Turn around. Let me get a picture of you being so beautiful and awesome. Soon everyone will know your name and I'll get to say I was the one who helped make you into the awesome person you are."

I barked out a laugh, shaking my head. "Of course you did, Stella."

"Well, outside your parents and all. Have you told them yet?"

I glanced down at the now crumpled magazine in my hands. It'd be on the shelves in their grocery store any day. If I told them, they'd buy every single copy and hand it out to their friends as they left church. They'd be thrilled for me, I knew it. They'd supported me with their words ever since the day I left, even though they desperately wanted me to come home.

They'd be proud of me. Happy for me.

But then they'd ask how all of this happened, and there was no way I could look my father in the eye and confess to him I had to sell my soul to earn it.

"Not yet." I frowned and glanced up, camera-ready side in place. "But I will. Soon."

Stella pushed her lips to the side. Her parents weren't great, and she'd been on her own since she was eighteen, too. My relationship with mine was vastly different. It was the one thing she could never quite understand. To her, I was turning my back on loving parents who were always there for me.

To me, I couldn't shake the guilt and regret I constantly carried. One look at my mother and I'd crumple.

I couldn't do that. I wasn't ready.

I doubted I would ever be ready to risk it.

"Okay." She shrugged and pulled her digital camera out of her oversized faux-mink bag. "Whatever, woman. Hold up the magazine and smile. Your first... and most definitely not the last billboard ad in the middle of Times-freaking-Square!" She bounced on her feet, and I couldn't help but follow her enthusiasm.

"Who would have thought?" I grinned as I said it and held open the magazine to the correct page.

With the billboard behind me and Stella snapping shots in front of me, for a moment, I could believe that everything was perfect.

⸻

MY HAIR WAS ATROCIOUS. My eye makeup smeared. I couldn't bring myself to look at myself in the mirror as I scrubbed the taste of him out of my mouth. It lasted forever, and he'd been rougher than usual. It didn't matter what I said or how I smiled, it seemed Steven always knew the days I *hated* him.

And I did. Truly. I hated everything about the man, despite my success since July's billboard ad and my first magazine spread. Jobs were coming faster, but it was my soul that was leaking like a sieve. It didn't matter how often I tried to plug the holes to keep my sanity, to maintain some sense of myself, I was losing it.

I was losing *me*.

I spit one more time, gagged as I scrubbed my tongue and then shoved my mouth near the faucet so I could rinse and spit. The entire time, I tried to forget.

Forget the contract Steven had me sign that meant if I canceled it and found a new agent, he'd take *all* the royalties I'd made. I'd owe him back pay. I'd lose my current deals, including the *Mynx* skincare that was getting me more attention.

I wasn't even sure it was attention I wanted anymore. Every time a set of eyes landed on me these days, I wanted to hide. Thankfully it was December and I could walk the streets of New York huddled in an oversized, puffy coat with a thick scarf wrapped around my throat, hiding the lower half of my face, the rest covered by a thick beanie with a popcorn ball on top.

I could hide in plain sight and I was only starting to regret the return of spring when I'd have to shed it all.

Not like I didn't *shed* everything every time I stepped foot into Steven's office, anyway.

Glancing in the mirror only long enough to see the devastation smeared all over me, I grabbed a paper towel and ran it under water. By the time I was done cleaning my face, my cheeks were red, my eyes were swollen, and I looked like death.

Which wasn't all that far off from how I was feeling these days.

I opened the bathroom and stepped foot into Steven's office.

He was resting his backside against the edge of his desk, arms crossed over his chest. The fact he'd only gotten redressed and resumed the place where he was standing when I entered wasn't lost on me. He intimidated me on purpose, and I fought against cowering in front of him as I retook my seat in the chair. It was a replay of how our appointment started. Fortunately for me, he'd never once demanded a second round.

"Are you over your snit?" As he asked, he adjusted his shirt sleeves. The cufflinks rattled, taking me back to earlier, when his hand had pulled my hair until I cried out.

I pushed down my skirt and kept my eyes on his face. Who knew what he'd do if I showed any emotion or balled my hands into fists like I wanted to. "I'm feeling better."

"You don't appear to be nearly as thankful anymore as you once were, you know? It's disappointing." He reached for paper on his desk. Not paper. A gold envelope with a shiny black embossment on one corner.

Considering I most definitely was not thankful anymore but trapped in a hell of my own making, I stayed silent.

"Nevertheless, you are still becoming one of my agency's most talented models."

I perked up at that, pulse increasing. Someday, I'd be able to call my own shots. Make my own rules. Forge my own way. Only two more years with Steven, and then I'd be free. "Thank you."

"No thanks required. You've been invited..." He held out the envelope in my direction. "To?"

He shook the envelope until I reached for it. I tugged. He held on tighter until I glanced up at him and met his gaze. "I would hope, with this, that you'll show more excitement for our meetings in the future."

My stomach rolled, and I swallowed the disgusting, still lingering taste of him, even as I fought a cringe. This could be *anything*, but I knew exactly what he wasn't saying.

"Of course, Steven."

"Good." He grinned and let go of the envelope.

I wasted no time opening it and pulling out the contents. The first one on top was all I needed to see.

Paris Fashion Week.

February.

Nine weeks from now.

"Are you kidding me?" I shrieked and grinned up at him. For a moment, I'd forgotten who he was. The power he had and all he made me do. "I'm *going*?!"

He nodded once, that disarmingly friendly smile he wore the first time I met him. He licked his lips, and my excitement dwindled. "As long as you continue to please me, yes. Your travel plans and everything else is included in that envelope."

*As long as...*

Of course there was a hitch, a leash tugging me back.

"Of course." I stood and made the small step toward him, leaning up and kissing his cheek. "Thank you, Steven. I won't disappoint you."

He slid his hand down my back until his hand landed on my backside. He squeezed, harder than necessary, enough to make me flinch. "See that you don't."

# THIRTEEN

## COLE

**Now**

I WAS EARLY to the location Valerie handed me. I hadn't slept. I didn't even bother going to a hotel room. Once I climbed in my Tundra, I was unable to leave. Trina was so close to me after so many years, and it didn't matter to me how beaten she was.

Strike that. That mattered a whole lot, and it was the worrying about the pain she was in, the recovery she would have ahead of her, and how in the hell Valerie and her husband were going to get her free that kept me rooted to hospital's parking lot.

How did they plan on getting her out of that hospital without Jonathan knowing? And what were we supposed to do with her once I had her?

I'd do anything they asked, as long as it meant Trina came home with me, but her safety in all areas came first.

It was on that thought I picked up the phone. Despite the middle of the night hour, I called Deer Creek's primary physician. Sheila McElroy had been a physician in town for as long as I could remember. With long, gray hair always wrapped in a low ponytail or bun, she was nearing retirement age and probably needed her sleep. However, there were many times we needed her in the middle of the night on cases, so she it wasn't unusual for someone on the force to draw the short straw and wake her.

Considering this was about Trina, I had no doubt she'd want to hear what I had to say.

The phone rang twice before her groggy, but still alert, voice answered. "Detective Paxton. How can I help you this morning?"

"Sorry to call you so early, Sheila. This is personal, but I need you."

"Your kids okay?"

"They're fine. I'm actually in Atlanta."

"Not sure I can help you from here. You okay?"

"Yeah. I'm good. It's not me I'm calling about. It's Trina. Trina Mills...well, Wolf, now, I guess."

Just saying her last name had me grinding my teeth. She would *never* be a Wolf. Or at least she wouldn't stay that way. I'd get her home and erase any memory she had of that man.

The grogginess evaporated as she asked, "Oh...well, this is a surprise. You saw her?"

"Yeah. I'm at Atlanta Community. Long story how I knew she was here, but she's got a friend who's working on getting her out."

"If she's in the hospital, Cole, that's probably the best place for her." She chuckled like I was being ridiculous, but she'd change her tune soon enough.

"Not when it's her husband who beat the shit out of her and put her there."

Silence slammed into the phone with a heavy weight.

"I'm so sorry to hear this," Sheila whispered. Pain thickened her tone and then she was back to business. "What do you need from me?"

I explained what I knew, the minimal information I could give, along with Valerie's mystical and vague plan, and finished with, "They said they can get her transport. But Deer Creek's a long way away."

"Let me make some calls," Sheila said. No hesitation, no worry. "I might have connections near there who wouldn't be swayed by who her husband is, if you truly think that's a concern."

For the first time since I got the call from Valerie, I felt like I could breathe. Finally, someone I knew and trusted was helping. "Thanks, Sheila. I'd call officers down here, but if cops aren't doing anything with the alleged break-in as he's calling it..."

I liked to believe all cops were clean and honorable and joined their prospective forces to do a duty, but I also knew that wasn't purely true. Some joined for power and could be swayed.

"Leave it to me. I'll call as soon as I know more."

"Thanks, Sheila."

"Not a problem, for Trina, it's absolutely an honor. Chin up, Cole. We'll take care of her."

With Sheila on my side, I had no doubt we would.

It was now six fifty-five, the hope of sunrise barely beginning to make an appearance beyond the horizon, and I was standing outside a two-story building that looked part storage or manufacturing, part business.

As the time ticked down on Valerie and Kip's arrival, I was scanning the doorways and buildings and nearby light poles to ensure there weren't cameras recording me.

I was putting my trust in people I didn't know, and that could go either way, but I tried to trust Valerie had Trina's best interests at heart.

---

EXACTLY FIVE MINUTES LATER, two vehicles pulled up. I stood outside of my pickup with my hands on my hips. Hair unwashed and not giving a single crap about it, I'd stopped at a gas station on the way here, the most run-down one I could find in hopes their cameras wouldn't be as high-tech as brightly lit chain stations. And that was assuming they had cameras in the first place. Using cash, I'd bought a Snickers bar and a bottle of water and then used that water to brush my teeth in the stained and rusty bathroom that reeked of filth. Once I reached this building, I'd changed into a fresh, simple gray T-shirt, as unremarkable as the other one, and tugged on a different ball cap. Anything to make myself as unrecognizable as possible. Couldn't do much about my truck, but I'd parked and pulled out of the station in such a way my rear driver's license plate could never be seen.

Both cars stopping in front of me were black Mercedes, the emblems on the front of both grills glowing.

Valerie stepped out of one first and then waited at the front of her car for her husband to meet her. Kip Sutton followed and went to his wife, sliding his hand to her lower back.

"Mr. Paxton," she started, but I immediately corrected her.

"Cole."

"Right." Her lips pressed into a tense smile that had my

fingers digging into my hips. "Cole. This is my husband, Kip."

I nodded toward him but didn't move a muscle until they were in front of me. He was exactly like his pictures. Slick-styled hair swept to the side. Only a small hint of gray at his temples and hair part that showed his forty-two years of age. I'd done my research, seen dozens of photos of him, and although he was thinner than I expected, he was still a man who clearly worked out and did it frequently. Matching my six-two height, I was broader and bulkier, probably enjoyed more heavy beers than this man did. If he was a threat to me, he'd be difficult to subdue.

"Mr. Sutton."

"Kip." He smirked. "And it's nice to meet someone else in Katrina's corner."

I thought of correcting him, but let it go. We'd played the name-correction game enough already.

He held out his hand, keeping his left on his wife's back. "A pleasure, and I mean that genuinely."

I reached out and shook his hand. His handshake was firm but respectful.

A small knot of tension at the back of my neck loosened. "What's the plan? And how is she?" I averted my gaze to Valerie.

"In pain. A lot of it, so she's heavily medicated. She woke up, some, but not enough to speak to anyone really."

"And Jonathan?"

"I convinced him I could take care of her. Played up the home invasion part of his story and insisted he needed to ensure it was cleaned up for when Katrina returned home."

"He believe you?"

"We've worked hard to ensure he trusts us," Kip cut in. "And I assure you, he does."

"So how do we get her out of there, 'cause what I saw last night, that's not going to be easy."

"Easy is a matter of opinion," Kip said.

I scowled at him. How dare he trivialize my comment or talk down to me. My chest expanded with a heavy, calming breath.

"I assume you know who my father is, as well as my great-grandfather."

"I do." It was Kip's great-grandfather that started Sutton Community Bank in Savannah decades ago.

"If you do, then you may know that many years ago, my grandmother had a stroke. Her rehabilitation needs at that time forced her to go to Tennessee and my grandfather didn't like that very much. He also didn't like that people without the means he had wouldn't be able to send their loved ones all the way there, so he and my father donated money so Atlanta Community Hospital could create and build their own stroke rehabilitation center."

I'd known that. Read about it at least but hadn't made the connection.

"I'm following."

"Good." Kip nodded and continued. "There are a lot of people at that hospital who know us. Know my family. My mother has been a frequent volunteer there and it's a cause that's important to my family."

"Which means you know people inside who can help."

"Precisely. As soon as I heard what happened, and I'm not only incredibly sorry it did, but furious I haven't been able to help sooner, I made calls. In previous instances, Jonathan has sent Katrina away, more than once to Greece. He's had the decency to wait until she's healthy enough to travel, but considering the damage he's done to her, I doubt he currently sees it as a requirement."

"He needs her gone before she can talk."

"Exactly. Which is why, at nine o'clock this morning, there will be a hospital lockdown training exercise. Two orderlies from the rehab facility will be there to get Katrina's bed downstairs and into a van along with a nurse and everything she could possibly need. That vehicle will take her to my private jet, already waiting to go, and will take her wherever she needs to go to land somewhere safe."

I glanced at my truck. I hadn't considered how I'd get my truck back home because however Trina was getting to Deer Creek, I was going with her.

"You already have a place in mind?" I asked him.

"My brother has a mountain home in Colorado. Was planning to send her there. He'd take care of her and his land is gated. Plus, Valerie and I go there often."

Worry pinched Kip's brows together, and I worked my jaw back and forth as I considered this option.

It'd be the best for her. Somewhere difficult to get to, nowhere near anyone she knew to give her time to heal. Maybe, if I was a better man, I'd let her do that.

But I wasn't, and I knew exactly who to call.

"Give me two minutes," I told him.

I grabbed my phone and shot off a quick text to my mom.

***Things are fine. Will give you an update soon. Need the number of Philip Scranton.***

The seconds ticked by with every moment I had to wait. Time was ticking down. It was barely past seven, and in two hours Trina would be leaving the hospital. I still had no idea what was happening with Jonathan, or where he'd be. My gut said to trust the man in front of me, who was glancing at his phone, tapping on it. Valerie chewed her lip, nervous, and stared at my phone like it'd jump out and bite her.

My phone dinged, and I grinned as I saw the number.

I instantly dialed it and two rings later a sleepy and very unhappy voice came through the phone.

"Told you you don't have any trouble with me."

"Mornin' Philip. Nice of you to have my name programmed."

"Well I hear from you enough."

Philip Scranton was old and crotchety. He also liked to play his jazz music and host parties that even more crotchety and old people across the lake from him hated. Which meant we spent a lot of time asking him to turn it down.

The small, gated lake community he lived in also happened to have its own private runway, and Philip's own private plane sat in a hangar connected to his house. Part of the reason he had such large and loud parties. Pull the plane out and the hangar was one hell of a gathering area.

"I'm actually calling this morning because I need your help."

He might not have known Trina well, but he was born and raised in Deer Creek and anyone who was from there was one of our own. Without bringing up her name, I explained the rest of the scenario and when it came time to figure out if his neighborhood's private runway was long enough for Kip's jet, I handed the phone over.

"You have your own connections," Valerie said softly, while I kept one ear on what Kip was saying.

"It's a small town but it's not an irrelevant or dying town like others." We were a large tourist area in both the summer and winter. And while many towns were dying, our ski slopes kept people coming back year after year. Not only did we have a small, private college in town that had seen an increase in enrollment, there was a growing university twenty minutes away. All that meant even our shopping had grown over the years. But the people who lived on that lake had either lived there for generations or bought their second homes out there for privacy—the private runway being one of the main enticing factors.

"Promise me you'll keep her safe."

Her tone had such a thickness, held such guilt and worry I looked her dead in the eyes. "To my dying breath."

It was a vow. I'd swear it with my hand on the Bible if she requested. She must have understood how serious I was because she exhaled and went back to nibbling her bottom lip.

"I don't mean to keep questioning you, but Katrina didn't speak a lot about her past. And she only mentioned you a few times."

"But she mentioned me."

Valerie blinked slowly and nodded. "After I confronted her about Jonathan, the night she finally admitted to what he was doing to her. I kept giving her drinks and she kept talking."

I chuckled. "Nice. Get her drunk to steal all her secrets."

A quick flash of a grin appeared and then vanished. "She was a vault before then, one massive cement block that I'd been chipping away at for years. It didn't take much to finally have her crumble."

A 45mm bullet to the gut would be less painful than knowing how miserable she'd been for so long. Still, I forced myself to nod, like I knew.

I didn't. I suspected there'd been a lot of traumas in Trina's life since she left for New York. "It's good she had you."

"I know about the baby," she whispered on a hitched

breath. "You should know that. She hates herself for it, you know. Despises that choice she made and telling you she's still carrying guilt for it isn't a heavy enough phrase to use."

I'd despised her for it, too, for a while. And then I grew up. But I had a life to look forward to, a good one. And while it may have never been as full as I once wanted, I now had two little girls I couldn't imagine a life without, and Trina was sitting in a hospital bed. Any lingering anger I'd had about Trina's decision was gone years ago. I hated hearing she still hadn't moved past that.

"Thank you for letting me know."

"I figure you should. Just...go easy on her. I doubt the road ahead for either of you will be easy."

"A road smoothly traveled isn't one I have a lot of experience navigating," I assured her and cracked a smile.

It was small, but she grinned back.

Kip handed me my phone back. "It'll work. Mr. Scranton says he'll handle everything on his end."

"Then let's work out the details down to the second, shall we?"

Kip grinned. Valerie chewed on her lip.

And me? For the first time in a long time, I had an overwhelming sense of hope and peace that things were finally going to go exactly the way they should.

# FOURTEEN

## TRINA

**Then**

"HAVE YOU BEEN HERE BEFORE?"

I peered up at my escort, friend, and model, Matteo Laurent, and smiled. "I come to the Met as often as possible, but not like this."

A gala at the Met. *Not* the Met Gala, but this was as almost as prestigious. Where only the most famous were invited, Steven's entire agency had been so this year, and I was still floating on cloud nine. His requirements of me weren't getting me down this year. Mostly because the more money I brought in and the more popular I became, the less Steven bothered me. I would have figured it was because he was worried I'd finally say something and report him, but the truth was, it'd been three years since I started working for him. I was now twenty-one, and over the years, there'd been dozens of new models dropping to their knees for his approval.

The modeling industry was more painful and difficult

than anything I could imagine. I wasn't sure there was a woman I'd met yet who came through unscathed. Whether it was with a cocaine and or nicotine habit along with a diet of bone broth to say thin, or women who were in my position and forced to do the things I'd chosen, we were all injured.

Frankly, the men didn't have it that much easier, from what I knew.

"This is a beautiful sight," Matteo said, in his faint French accent. Born in Montreal, his parents were from France. He'd been in the States working for a couple of years and I'd had the good fortune to meet him at Fashion Week last year. We were now both models with Calvin Klein and not only did we run into each other frequently, but because he was gay, Stephen didn't mind if we spent time together.

"I'm sorry you couldn't find a prettier date," I teased.

Matteo chuckled and covered his free hand with mine that was wrapped around his other arm. "For a female, you are not too shabby." He patted my hand in sympathy like one would pet a pouting dog.

"You're rotten," I laughed as we were escorted up the stairs. Lights flashed and photographers asked for our names, both of which Matteo and I ignored.

We were known in the modeling world, and maybe by generations that still clung to magazines, but we weren't who the press was waiting for. We were small fries, and I was thankful Matteo was as humble about our successes as I remained.

All of this could be yanked out beneath my feet tomorrow and I'd lose everything.

Stephen threatened it enough, but without the threats I already knew it was true. As an agent, he'd grown in popularity even more so than he'd been when I first met him.

Because of that, I'd never fought our contract or left for another agency. If I ticked him off, he had the power to ruin me.

I had no doubt he'd do it.

We reached the top of the stairs and a whole new world of glittery lights and fashion made my jaw drop in disbelief. "Wow," I exhaled on a deep breath.

Matteo's back straightened. "This is... this is truly unbelievable. What do we do?"

I spied a waiter, with a silver tray in one hand filled with bubbly champagne flutes. "Drink," I replied. "We drink."

I slipped my arm out of his hold and followed the waiter carrying pink champagne, Matteo's deep laughter following my lead.

We drank. We snacked on the occasional appetizer that wouldn't ruin our diets or make my already skintight, silver dress any tighter. I'd had to soak in eight pounds of Epsom salt to squeeze into the thing and I was already a size zero these days.

Eventually, we wandered through the crowd, where dinner would be served, and we scanned the tables to find Cormack's agency and where we'd be seated. Matteo found his name, but as we searched the nearby tables, my golden nameplate wasn't anywhere to be found.

Dread crept its way into my stomach, making me set down my champagne.

"Where do you think I'm sitting?"

Matteo shook his head. "I don't know. This must be a mistake."

Steven wouldn't make mistakes. He would have had

someone here as soon as we could enter, ensuring every-thing for him was perfect. His agency hadn't just been invited, it was being recognized for some humanitarian effort. I'd stopped listening at the word humanitarian because Steven was most definitely *not* that in any way, shape, or form.

Was he not allowing me to sit and eat?

"Ah. There you are."

I froze at his voice, the slick tone of it as if he was truly joyful to see me. Turning, Steven was several steps away, weaving in and out of chairs covered with white, shim-mering seat covers.

"Good evening, Steven." I dipped my chin out of politeness.

He didn't return the greeting. At least, not to me. To Matteo, he turned and said, "Leave us for a few minutes."

Matteo's glance slid to mine. His gaze was a heavy weight at my temple, but I didn't dare turn my head or my attention off Steven who was peering at me with much the same intensity wafting off Matteo.

"Very well," Matteo said, "I'll be back soon." He brushed my fingers by as he passed, to which Steven hmphed.

"Truly, take your time. Our lovely lady will be more than occupied soon."

Matteo, smart enough not to ask questions, moved away but did it slowly, glancing at me once he was behind Steven with his brows raised in questions and marked concern.

"What can I do for you?" I asked.

Steven stepped forward and wrapped his arm around my bicep. His grip hurt, and I flinched as his thumb and finger met and pinched the soft, tender skin of my inner bicep.

He proceeded to drag me along, barely giving me time to keep step with him in my four-inch, needle-thin stilettos.

"I have someone who is interested in meeting you. Do not let me down."

The first came as surprise. The last came as a warning.

"Of course, Steven. Who?"

"Jonathan Wolf."

"Who's that?"

His grip on me tightened as he tugged me along. He also didn't answer, leaving me confused and more than a little worried. I should have known better than to believe tonight would be a celebration and a night of fun.

When it came to Steven, I was nothing more than a toy or a pawn.

The only remaining question was how he planned to use me.

---

JONATHAN WOLF WAS EXTRAORDINARILY HANDSOME, and that barely began to describe his good looks. He was older than me by at least a decade, most likely more, but he'd aged to perfection with a body that instantly stole my breath and a deep, rumbling tone that made my stomach flutter in wild ways I wouldn't have expected. As Steven dragged me closer to a small cluster of men and women, all far older than me as well, it was Jonathan who stood out the most.

We were in a large ballroom with some of the most beautiful people in the world, models and celebrities included, but seeing Jonathan, with looks like his, I figured he was often the most seen person in any room.

I knew it was true because he might have been in

discussions with those around him, but it was apparent he was the one holding court, and they were all fawning over him. I had no doubt this happened often when it came to him. As soon as Steven and I grew closer, almost close enough where I could call his name out loud, he turned, and our gazes met.

*Wowzers.* I trembled in my heels as that penetrating gaze landed on me. Eyes so dark they were the color of the night, his lips curled into a soft hint of a smile as his eyes scanned my face. Never once did they drop further down to my cleavage or the outline of body, obvious in my dress. Not even a flicker.

Classy. This man was beyond classy, and my unease at Steven forcing me to meet him dwindled as he excused himself from his group and closed the space between us in two quick strides.

"Steve." He held out his hand. The men shook hands while I played the part Steven had instructed.

"Jonathan. Allow me to introduce Trina Mills to you. Trina, this is Jonathan Wolf."

I leaned forward and forced my face to remain impassive. Hard to do with Steven's fingers still digging into my bicep, and the gorgeousness that was in front of me.

I spent my days and nights and life with models, men who were extraordinarily good-looking, but something about this man in front of me took it to a whole different level. Perhaps because he wasn't model pretty. Perhaps because he was definitely all man and masculinity wrapped up in a designer suit and a gold Rolex that appeared on his wrist as his hand extended to me.

"Jonathan," he said, and the rumble of his voice covered me like a warm blanket. My hand shook as I held it out to him. "Trina, is it?"

"Yes, sir. Pleasure to meet you."

His gaze skipped to Steven for a moment and his hand loosened from my arm. "I'll leave you two to get acquainted. Enjoy yourself," he said with a smile, but as he turned and met my eyes, his dark blue eyes went glassy in that way they did before he turned evil.

I swallowed and tipped my chin. I was to be good. Check that. I was to ensure I made Steven look good, regardless of what that meant for me.

With a lump forming in my throat, I turned back to Jonathan.

His coloring reminded me of a Viking. All hard edges and sculpted cheekbones. His hair was a sandy brown, longer and shaggier than most of the men in this room but his style still showed care and class. His lips were full, and his jawline had a sharp edge to it.

The man was far beyond anything I ever expected to see in a living, breathing male.

"Trina." He grinned as he said my name and his head tilted to one side. "Is that short for something?"

"Katrina," I whispered, my throat somehow unable to work properly. "It's short for Katrina."

"Beautiful, much like yourself. Why don't you use it?"

There was no way to explain to this man why. That where I came from, it was too much. Too everything. Too *large* of a name, too exotic. I had no idea what my mother was thinking when she chose it, but it was far beyond the simpler name of my older sister, Kari.

"Trina suits me," I replied.

That hint of a smile of his vanished and I had the strange sensation I'd disappointed him.

"I disagree. Trina is common and playful. Yet you are beautiful and so much more than something so simple."

It was impossible he knew anything about me beyond my looks, and yet the compliment still increased that flutter in my stomach. A heat spread to my cheeks, and I found I could no longer meet his gaze for fear I'd melt into a puddle of mush in front of him.

"Thank you." I looked away as I said it, but his hand reached up.

I cringed for a moment before his thumb pressed the sensitive flesh beneath my jaw and drew my gaze back to his. "Lovely. So lovely. Shall I show you to our seats?"

"Our seats?" My brows rose in surprise.

"I approached Steven earlier, informed him I'd like the honor of your company this evening while we dine. I hope that's okay."

I'd be a fool to do anything but agree. Not only would Steven have my head on a platter come Monday morning, I had the distinct impression this man got what he wanted. Always. Fortunately, his company appeared to be enjoyable.

"Of course. I'd be delighted."

Jonathan held out an arm, gesturing for me to precede him and when I did, his hand settled low at my back. Low enough, his thumb could brush on the upper part of my backside. I tried to remain calm as he guided us toward the table, but then he leaned in, close to my ear. "Don't be nervous. I promise you that it will be me who is delighted by your company."

My head spun as his quiet rumble wafted over me. The floor became uneven beneath my already shaking legs.

This man was something...something far more than I'd even been surrounded by.

He was intoxicating.

"Sit," he said, and pulled out a chair for me. "I'm

thankful Steven brought you here tonight. I've been wanting to meet you."

I couldn't fathom *why*, based on his age, and the fact he had to be wealthy given the table where he sat. The tuxedo he wore was Tom Ford, and the gold Rolex on his wrist would have been dead giveaways anyway.

"I'm afraid I'm at a disadvantage, and I apologize for what I'm about to say and don't mean to be rude, but I have no idea why or who you are."

His eyes flared and then a wide, boisterous smile broke out on his face right before he laughed. Not at me but amused all the same. "No offense taken. We don't run in the same circles."

He lifted his hand, and a waiter appeared. Jonathan plucked two glasses of champagne off the tray and slid one in my direction.

Pink.

Like what I'd been drinking all night. Had he been *watching* me? He must not have been lying. He truly had wanted to meet me. I shook off the strangeness and thanked him for the drink.

"What circles are those?" I asked.

His smile deepened and there was humor in his vibrant, rich dark eyes. "Technology, athletics. I've recently become General Manager of the Georgia Gators."

My lips rolled together. That had to be a big thing. And it took me a minute until I flipped through all the memories of my dad shouting at the television screen on Saturday and Sunday afternoons. "Football," I finally said. "You manage a football team."

"I do."

"That must be...fun?"

Again, his chuckle. I took a sip of my drink, tiny little

sips that barely wet my tongue so I could stay sober. This man was disarming enough. The way my body felt when he was near was something I hadn't felt in a very long time. I needed to keep my cool.

"It is. And a challenge. But yes, and the team is having a good year, so that's always a bonus."

"Congratulations." I tipped my glass out to him, and he clinked his flute against mine. "So you live in Georgia?"

"Most of the year. I own a place here in New York though as well. Which is enough about me. Tell me about you. What brought you to New York?"

I tipped my head to the side and gave him a smile. "How do you know I'm not from here?"

"That's easy." He chuckled and reached forward. For the first time in years, I didn't flinch and didn't pull away. Didn't even feel the need to wait for pain when his thumb brushed over my cheek, over the shell of my ear, and down the column of my throat. Goose bumps popped and made my blood sing at his soft touch and my lips parted. "You're too soft. Too beautiful and your eyes are too kind to have grown up in New York."

"Oh," I breathed. "Okay." My words were gone, my senses were alive. It was such a *vast difference* from how I'd been treated for so long.

Jonathan licked his lips and trailed that finger down my arm to my hand, linking our two ring fingers together. Like we were childhood friends making a promise. It was sweet. Enduring. So wildly different than the way I was currently feeling. He settled our linked fingers on my thigh, and it felt good. *Right.*

He leaned in then, close enough anyone watching would think we were far more intimate than we were, but he didn't kiss me, didn't do anything except whisper, "Plus, your accent is a dead giveaway."

He pulled back and took a drink of his champagne, humor and teasing making his eyes glimmer with joy.

I laughed and shook my head. "Right. Of course it is."

We talked more. I learned so much more about Jonathan Wolf that night. We laughed about how different the South was from the North. He told me how the Gators were having their first winning season in six years. And somehow along the way, he got me to open up more than I had in years. It was so easy to talk to him. He was quick to laugh. Quicker to ask me questions instead of only talking about himself. He was gloriously handsome, crazy smart, and undeniably wealthy and yet he talked to me like we were old friends.

Which was why I told him about my parents. My small town of Deer Creek. How it was stifling to be the daughter of the pastor at the largest church in town where every step I took was watched with eagle eyes, and how the city gave me the freedom to figure out who I was.

The entire evening flew by, and I hadn't laughed so much, enjoyed myself so much that when Jonathan asked me to go back to his hotel room with him...

I couldn't find a reason to say no.

# FIFTEEN

## COLE

**Now**

MY NERVES WERE RACING. The hospital's alarm for the training lockdown could be heard from where I was tucked and hidden in the blacked-out van that had somehow been fitted to look like an ambulance. Plan set, it included me trusting Kip to get my truck back to my place and to keep Jonathan exactly where he was supposed to be.

I focused on calming my nerves. They were rioting worse than they did on a call-out or an investigation, but then again, the cost was much higher.

"Come on," I whispered into the void.

The driver was already in his seat. Kip introduced us and then headed into the office. That meant I'd had a whole thirty seconds to grill Jim Bower on his intention and motive. Considering the man was larger than me, bald, and looked like he could kill a lion with his bare hands, I decided to trust him. Also, because he looked at me and in a voice that came close to scaring me, grumbled, "Men like him should be staked and then plastered on a pole for all to see."

I figured he wouldn't get that colorful if he was lying, so I nodded, climbed into the back of the van, and began my waiting period.

One that was lasting far too long.

I twisted my neck and asked Jim, "You know what's taking so long?"

"Subterfuge takes time." He glanced at me out of the corner of his eye and then went back to staring straight out the windshield. We'd pulled up to a private entrance to the hospital, one far less scrutinized and one where security personnel had been routed away from.

It felt like forever. Hours went by as I stewed inside the back of the van and considered every possible scenario that could go wrong. Ten minutes ago, Kip called Jonathan in for an emergency meeting, using the ruse of someone embezzling from the Gators' franchise as the excuse. He'd assured me Jonathan would be so furious at the thought of being stolen from, it'd take his entire focus away from Trina. It'd give us the time to get out of there. But if Jonathan didn't believe the reports Kip was going to show him, or if he decided his wife needed constant vigilance...or if she woke up and refused to leave, things could go sideways in a millisecond. Fortunately, Jonathan was thirty minutes away so even if it didn't go perfectly, we'd still hopefully be able to get to the air.

The doors opened and I cursed, relieved to finally see a woman with her back to me, hair piled on her head, bending down.

"I'll help." I moved from my seat to the other side of the bed as the woman and another man at the other end of Trina's hospital bed went to lift it.

"On three," the woman said, her attention on the man across from her. Neither acknowledged me so I stepped back, balling my hands into fists so I didn't reach out to Trina, and run my fingers down her bruised and mottled cheeks. She looked worse in the daylight than she had under the harsh hospital lighting.

"You're good," the man said. "Be safe."

With a dip of his chin and no introduction, not that it was necessary, the doors slammed closed behind him.

"You must be Cole," the woman said to me. She still hadn't glanced at me, but that was fine. Both of our focus was on Trina, anyway.

"I am. And you are?"

"Heather. She's doing really well today." Her eyes were working on hooking up clear bags filled with a clear liquid to a pole at the side of the van.

I glanced at her and then back to Trina. Her lips were swollen, and there were multiple cuts on her cheeks. Her leg was still braced. The cut at her forehead that had left smeared blood in her hair had been cleaned, and the stitches were now visible.

Fury rose like a rushing tide I choked down. "Has she been awake?"

"Some. Overnight and very early this morning, but she was disoriented. The pain meds should keep her sedated for most of the flight."

That'd be good. I didn't want her feeling any pain at all, but mostly I didn't want her asking questions until we were safe and secure.

"Any word from Mr. Wolf?"

"He's called and been told all is well."

There'd be a fight on the hospital's hands for this. He'd hold someone accountable, I had no doubt. I still held out hope that given her injuries and his fragile story, he wouldn't push it too far.

A wave of relief washed over me, and my shoulders relaxed as the van pulled away from the hospital and onto the main roads and then the interstate beyond.

Thirty minutes later, we were aboard the plane, taxiing down the runway, and Trina was safe and secured in her hospital bed, locked in place to give her the smoothest flight possible.

"Thank you," I told the nurse again. It must have been my twentieth time I'd thanked her.

"No woman should live like this." She swiped her hands down her dark blue scrubs. "If only we could save more."

I couldn't agree more. But for now, I'd give my gratitude for being blessed to save one.

---

I STILL COULDN'T BELIEVE it. Too afraid if I blinked, she'd disappear, which was why I still couldn't take my eyes off Trina. She'd been carefully moved and was now resting in my guest bedroom downstairs.

In my home.

Thank God for Sheila who'd not only come over and set up the room with everything she thought Trina would need, but she'd also met us at the plane and then ridden with us in one of the Sheldon County ambulances back to my house.

Now she was here, in my bed, strapped to monitors like in the van and on the plane, still wearing the same brace and hospital gown and yet I swore she already looked better.

Twenty-four hours after getting the phone call from Valerie, I now had Trina back exactly where she belonged.

And if she didn't see it that way, at least she was safe.

"Thanks again," I muttered to Sheila, helplessly watching while she rechecked vitals and triple-checked to make sure her IVs were set.

"You say that every thirty seconds."

"Yeah, well I mean it." I rocked backed on my heels, and shook the tension out of my balled-up fists.

Like Heather had predicted, Trina slept the entire plane ride. She was still out, and while I wanted to stay in this room until she opened her eyes and woke up, my mom was also upstairs, probably pacing a worn path in my living room carpet, and I needed to call Marie. Check in with Valerie and Kip.

"Go," Sheila said, glancing at me like she heard my racing thoughts. "I've got this. Ten minutes away from her isn't going to hurt anything."

"Is there anything you need?"

"No." She grinned at me. "And if I did, I'm fully capable of taking care of myself. Now go. I can hear you fretting from there."

"Right. If you change your mind..."

She scoffed and went back to reading the files the nurses had gotten copies of and brought with us.

Good news out of this was that Sheila didn't think her cheekbone was broken. Her knee was swollen, and she believed it'd been stepped on, but at least not hard enough to do any serious damage. It was swollen and there'd be pain as it healed. She wouldn't know until the swelling went down if there was ligament or tendon damage, but for now, she was okay. It brought no amount of joy to learn Jonathan hadn't broken anything in her body, just bruised her from head to toe.

Something told me that wasn't luck, but years of experience of an abuser knowing exactly how hard he could hit to bruise and damage but not break, and that part made my blood boil.

Jonathan Wolf deserved to be treated exactly like he'd treated Trina, and possibly every woman he'd known before.

My phone buzzed in my back pocket, and I yanked it out.

Kip's name flashed on the screen, and I answered the call. "This is Cole."

"How's everything going? I heard your delivery arrived safely."

"It did. And my truck."

The man chuckled through the phone. "Good. That's good. How is she?"

"Still sleeping. Our doctor here expects her to wake up soon, though. And there?"

"Good news is nothing pisses Jonathan off more than the idea of someone getting one over on him, so he hasn't left his office, nor has he checked his phone."

"Sounds like a man really concerned about his wife's injuries."

There was a slight chuckle that held no humor. "Good for us. He'll be in the office for a while, and I'm hopeful the rabbit chase I've put him on keeps him focused for days. In the meantime, Valerie and I are headed out tonight for some dinner and dancing and drinks in town. I've been assured he'll get a call later, and if he answers, he'll finally learn she's gone, but strangely enough, no one will know when she vanished."

"And you'll be in public after being in the office all day with him, so there's nothing to suspect."

"Let's hope it continues that way. I should go, just wanted to check in. Let me know if you need anything."

"Will do. Keep me posted on your end."

"As soon as I hear if anything's changed, you'll be the first I call. Stay sharp, Mr. Paxton. He might be distracted today, but tomorrow could birth an entirely different kind of animal."

"Of course. Thanks again for the call."

I slipped my phone back in my pocket. He was right. Today was a distraction, and it worked in our favor, but our luck wouldn't hold forever. I just needed to keep hoping that Kip did everything he needed to in order to make Jonathan's search for her as difficult as possible.

That call down, I blew out a breath. "Shout if you need me," I muttered to Sheila and left my room.

Left Trina.

But this time, at least she wasn't alone.

I'd make sure she never felt that way ever again.

## SIXTEEN

### TRINA

**Then**

TIME FLEW. Days and weeks were suddenly spent traveling to a host of exotic and luxurious locations for work. More vacations and trips were taken for leisure and fun with Jonathan. During the football season, he spent most of his time in Atlanta, Georgia, but he also owned a penthouse in New York where I now lived full-time.

It was easier, given the way our schedules crisscrossed frequently, so when he'd suggested it and I was still living in the tiny little apartment with Stella because I never got around to finding anything else for us, I accepted.

Which reminded me...

I pulled my phone out of my clutch as my heels clicked on the wood floor entrance to our penthouse. Behind me, the elevator doors slid shut and Jonathan's shoes made a heavier thump.

His arm wrapped around my stomach, and he pulled me back to his chest. Peppering my throat with kisses, he murmured, "Have I told you how gorgeous and stunning you are tonight?"

"Several times." I dropped my clutch to the floor and with my phone in one hand I spun around so we were facing each other and draped my arms over his shoulders. "But you can tell me often, as many times as you'd like."

He slid his hand up my left arm and tugged it down so my palm was flat to his chest. His fingers spun the gold band he'd set on my ring finger at dinner two hours ago. I was still blinded when I looked at it. Four carat, princess cut, something or other. He'd explained it to me, but I was in far too much awe at the ring, at the engagement to pay attention.

Truthfully, after a year, I was still far too in awe of the man smiling down at me to pay attention to much of anything.

"The ring is so beautiful," I told him, whispering like the spoken word would shatter the beauty of it. Man, it *sparkled*.

"It's salt and stone compared to its owner."

His lips came down and brushed against mine, and like every time he kissed me, I leaned in and craved more. But tonight there were people to call. Plans to start making.

Jonathan could wait a few more minutes.

"Wait," I whispered and pulled back, cupping my phone to my chest. "I just need to call Stella and my parents."

I'd already texted them but hadn't heard a word back. For my parents, that was becoming more common. With Stella, I shouldn't have been surprised.

She was still waiting tables but had gotten her degree, so she was also working full time. Our lives had taken us in radically different directions. In fact, as I stared at my phone screen, I couldn't remember the last time we'd talked. Or seen each other.

Jonathan's fingers wrapped around the edge of my phone, and he plucked it from my hands.

"Hey." I reached for it but he pushed me back so it was out of my reach.

Confusion knitted my brows, and I laughed softly. "I want to call my parents."

"Later." The softness in his expression dimmed and his nostrils flared as I frowned up at him. "They can wait."

"They're my parents, silly." I reached for my phone again, but he held it out of my reach. "Jonathan, come on. I want to tell them the good news."

His free hand wrapped around my wrist and yanked it down to my side with such force I stumbled a step forward. "Hey...careful."

"You can call them later. Besides, it's not like they'll come to the wedding."

He let go of my hand and began unbuttoning his suit coat like he hadn't just knocked the wind out of me.

"That's not nice. They'll be happy for me. For us." I spun on my heels and then kicked them off. The move put me a good eight inches shorter than him. "Why would you say that?"

He tossed his suit coat onto the counter and began unbuckling his cufflinks. He barely spared me a glance as he said, "Because they don't like us together, and because they're too simple. You're too good for them."

I gaped at him. Jonathan could be ruthless. I'd seen it at business dinners and with some of my contracts his lawyers now always looked over, but he'd never been so rude to me. Not once.

"Hey." I set my hand on his shoulder and pressed my front to his side. "Be nice."

He dropped a cufflink and began working on his tie. "Get me a bourbon, would you? I need a drink."

I blinked at him. Blinked again. "Please?" I teased.

He turned to me, brows arched. "Get yourself a glass of wine, too."

What the heck? I dropped my hand from his shoulder and stepped back. Whatever was going on with him, whatever came with the sudden change in mood I doubted a whiskey would fix but whatever.

I grabbed his drink, poured a glass of white for myself and brought both back to the island where he still rested, scrolling through his phone. Mine was on the counter so once I slid his drink toward him, I reached for it.

His hand slammed down onto mine, and I jumped. "Jon—"

"What did I say?"

"You're on your phone."

"Drop the sass, Katrina. I told you that you can call them later."

An icy sensation tickled the back of my neck and my spine.

This wasn't just rudeness. He was being *mean*. My chin wobbled and I swallowed the thick lump growing in my throat. His fingers wrapped around mine until I flinched in pain.

"You're hurting me."

A sneer scrolled across his face, twisting his features into something unrecognizable.

"And when you tell me you'll listen when I tell you to do something, I'll let go."

I scanned his face, trying to find something that resembled the man who had slid my engagement ring onto my finger and kissed me so tenderly only a few hours ago when I was the happiest woman in the world. "They're my *parents*, Jonathan. I've dreamed of getting married my whole life. I *have* to call them. Please." I tacked it on at the end and hated the pleading in my tone. But his fingers were still pinching mine and his face kept contorting into something ugly. Sinister.

I stepped back but he only squeezed my hand harder. "Ouch."

"Did I say you could leave?"

"What is going on with you, honey? We should be celebrating..."

"Tell me you'll listen to me. You're mine now."

I was his in all the most beautiful ways but now an oily sensation covered my skin. "Jonathan."

"Say it," he demanded and squeezed my hand so hard I thought my fingers would break.

"Ouch. Fine." I flinched and yanked on my hand again. "I'll listen. Whatever."

He let go of my hand, and I brought it toward my chest.

I blinked at him, only to see a blur of movement. A stinging pain slammed into my face, knocking me backward. I twisted as I fell, and my head slammed into something hard. Cold.

The fridge.

He'd just *slapped* me. Tears came immediately as I stood, hunched over, cupping my injured hand to my chest. A shriek rang out. Delayed reaction? And then a cry. That was mine.

*Dang.* Something warm and wet slipped down my cheek. I reached up and came back with blood on my fingers.

"What is wrong with you?" I gasped.

I couldn't look at him, couldn't bring myself to see the look on his face. Would he regret this? Maybe something on his phone upset him. Surely something had to be wrong. He'd never done this. He'd *never* do this to me.

And yet my cheek was throbbing, something was bleeding, and my fingers burned hot as I forced myself to stand.

"Jonathan," I cried. "What are you doing?"

His shoes appeared, and then his fingers were at my chin. I cringed away but he pinched my chin between his thumb and finger and forced me to meet his gaze.

"You're a mess, and you've made me ruin your pretty face."

Ruin.

Ruined.

I *was* that. I'd been that for years but thought I'd hidden it from him. He'd never mentioned Steven to me, and while I still worked for him, he hadn't touched me since the night Jonathan and I met. Just one more reason why I loved him so much. He saved me from hell.

At least, I'd always thought so. But now?

I blinked up at him and wiped more blood from my cheek. It wasn't much.

"I'm sorry," I rasped, and what? The words came out of my mouth before I could think. I wasn't sorry. I hadn't *done* anything.

"I forgive you." Jonathan grinned, and all the ugliness on his face was now gone. *This* was my Jonathan. "Now, promise me you'll listen, right? You'll do that from now on? And you'll do it without talking back."

I'd do or say anything to get away from him. "Yes. Of course."

"Good." He leaned forward and kissed me. "Now go

upstairs, clean your face, and get ready for me. We have celebrating to do."

My body froze and turned straight into a block of ice. "You can't be serious."

He'd *hit* me, and *now* he wanted to celebrate?

He reached out his hand and pressed his thumb to my cheekbone. The same cheekbone that had slammed into the fridge until I cried out in pain. "You promised to listen, right?"

Oh god. He meant this. More tears fell, and he grinned as they slid right down to his thumb. He brushed them away and then brought his thumb to his mouth, tongue darting out to lick them away. "Right, Katrina? You've promised to listen."

"I have." There was nothing left to say. I couldn't get away from him. Couldn't leave. I *lived* here.

"Good." His hand dropped to my throat, and he leaned in. His warm breath skated across my lips as his fingers squeezed until my lips parted in surprise and pain and fear. Who *was* this man in front of me?

A pained squeak escaped my parted lips, and he kissed me, shoved his tongue inside my mouth and pressed his lips against mine so forcefully they'd bruise. His fingers kept squeezing and my breathing turned ragged. "Now, Katrina. Go do what I said. You don't want me more disappointed in you than I already am, do you?"

I shook my head. It hurt. My breathing was shallower.

He pushed me away and let go of my throat. "Then do what you're told. You agreed to this life, Katrina. Might as well get used to it."

I hurried around him, ran upstairs and when I got to the bathroom I crumbled to the floor and sobbed.

I'd thought he'd saved me from Steven.

But like a wolf in sheep's clothing, he'd bided his time until he could turn on me.

He hadn't saved me at all.

He'd waited until the perfect moment to complete my ruination.

Still, somehow, I stood.

I washed my face and did as I was told, and by the time morning came, I knew exactly what I'd signed myself up for...

A lifetime of unending pain.

# SEVENTEEN

## COLE

**Now**

"HOW IS SHE? AWAKE YET?"

As predicted, my mom was pacing and worrying her knotted hands together when I reached the kitchen. Instead of worthlessly pacing in the living room, she'd moved to the kitchen where pots and pans filled all four burners on my stovetop.

Stress cooking. Couldn't blame her, and I wasn't at all surprised.

"No. But she's here."

"I still can't believe...she's so hurt...what kind of monster..." My mom shook her head as she started and stopped a half-dozen more sentences. Couldn't blame her there, either. There wasn't much to say and certainly no explanations to give where anything made sense.

"Dr. McElroy says nothing is broken, so that's a good thing. She'll heal, Ma. And she's here and safe. Be thankful for the small things."

"Right." The edges of her lips curled up. "You're so wise."

"Had wise parents. What are you cooking?"

"Soup. Figured broth would be good for her, and she always liked my rolls so I'm baking some of them, too."

A memory of eating dinner with Trina's family came to mind. Sunday family dinners were a big thing around here and Pastor Mills, Trina's dad, always insisted on having a potluck at his house. Mom always made sure to bring her rolls, and Trina, the picky eater she was, would have half her plate piled high with them, the other half usually macaroni and cheese.

"She did." I chuckled at the memory and kissed my mom's cheek. "Thanks for helping out and doing this. I appreciate it."

Her warm, soft palm pressed to my cheek. A good eight inches taller than my mom, I'd towered over her since I was fourteen years old and in eighth grade. Being disciplined by a woman I could pick up and move out of the way had been unsettling, but lucky for Mom, she'd done a good job raising me to be respectful.

Plus, Dad woulda had my hide if I'd treated her any less than the good and sweet woman she was.

"I'm glad she's here. Her face, though..."

I couldn't think about how bad she looked without wanting to punch something. Which was why I kept trying to focus on the positive. "Good thing is it'll never happen again. Not to her."

Tears swelled in her eyes as she smiled and stepped back. "I still can't believe she's here, after all these years. Her parents will be so thrilled."

"Don't call them. Or don't tell them. Not yet."

"Why not?" Her shocked eyes jumped to me as she tasted her soup.

"That'll be her choice, her timing and her decision."

She'd had enough of them taken away. This wasn't one I would push on her too soon.

"But—"

"Don't, Ma. I know what you're going to say, and I know they'd love to hear from her, but you gotta keep this quiet. At least until she's awake and we can talk."

Her lips worked back and forth before she finally nodded. "All right. I get what you're saying."

"Thank you. How were the kids and Marie?"

"June was upset you weren't here. Ella didn't seem to react. I told Marie you got called in for a case, so she happily took them."

"Good." I patted my back pocket and pulled out my phone. "I need to give her a call, let her know what's going on."

"You're going to tell her?" My mom froze as she took bowls out of the cupboard and peered at me over her shoulder. "All of it?"

I couldn't very well hide the fact I had a woman in my home from my kids. And that was if Marie was okay with them being here in the first place. "Of course not all. But this messes with her life too, right now."

I dialed her number and while I expected her voice to be the one who answered, I wasn't at all upset by the tiny little voice that did. "Daddy!"

"Hey Junie bug." I grinned into the phone and headed downstairs. "You having fun?"

"Where were you today? I missed you, and I didn't get my hug."

"I know, kiddo. But things came up with work. I'll get your hug soon."

"I don't like it when I can't hug you." Her little pouty tone started to shake. My heart hurt hearing it even if I knew she'd move on in a moment.

"I know, kiddo. It's okay though, right? It'll just make the next one extra special."

"Mommy said I can only say hi and then I have to go to bed. Can you sing to me really quick?"

"Really quick, June." I sang off a hurried tune of "Twinkle, Twinkle, Little Star," and then managed to coax June to get into bed and listen to her mommy.

When Marie's voice came through the phone, I said a silent thanks that June's tantrum didn't explode. "You doing okay?" Marie asked. "Long day for you."

"Yeah. Listen. We gotta talk."

"You hurt?" Panic infused her tone. I should have known it would. For as bad as a husband I'd been to her, she'd been an incredible wife, and was always there. Always understanding of my job and role and risks.

"No. No. I'm good. But there's something that's happened that we're gonna have to talk about. Sit-down style."

"Oh gosh. This sounds bad."

"Not bad. But I think it's going to hurt you, and for that I'm sorry, but I need you to know it, think through it, and then let me know when you're ready to talk about it."

"Cole..."

"Trina's here," I told her, ripped off the pain like a band-aid and like I knew it would hurt, her quick gasp said it all. Before she could say anything, I continued. "Please, *please* keep this to yourself. I know it's gonna be hard, but it's not what you think."

"She's in your home."

"Yeah."

"She's in your home and you sent your girls away so you could what...spend the day reconnecting?"

"No. Shit, Marie, no it's not like that, and you know I wouldn't do that. Not to them or you. Listen." I lowered my voice before I continued and gave her a moment to get her panic under control. "I can't get into specifics right now, at least not until you swear you won't tell anyone a thing, but I sort of...well... I sort of stole her from her husband."

"You..."

"Who's been beating her." I finished it quickly, on a whisper, and prayed she'd be the woman I knew her to be.

A thick, heavy silence hit the phone and then a rush of breath, followed by a quick chuckle.

"Only you. Only you would do that."

"It's worse than that. Swear it to you, Marie, but she's here. And she will be for a while. Her injuries are *bad*, bad."

There were a thousand reasons why I liked Marie. So many reasons of why I thought she'd be the woman to truly get me over my lingering obsession with Trina. It wasn't just that our values aligned, and it wasn't because of how whip-smart she was and how passionate she was about causes she believed in. She was also a woman filled with kindness and grace, a woman who tried to understand others' perspectives before jumping to conclusions, and a woman who genuinely cared about people.

"That's horrible," she whispered. "I'm sorry to hear that."

And just like that, I remembered all the reasons why I married her. Logically, she was my perfect match. It was just that my heart had always been shelved for the broken woman a floor away from me.

"I know. I'll give you the full story when I can, but since she'll be here for a while, with the girls and all..."

"I'll keep them. Of course I will. It's fine. And you can come see them or take them at night or whatever. You know that."

I licked my lips and stared down at my feet. "Thank you. I'll see the girls tomorrow after school and let them know I'm taking care of a sick friend if that's okay."

"Just tell me what you need, and I'll do it. Within reason of course."

"Of course." I didn't miss the warning. She'd help, but she wouldn't be happy about this. "I should get going."

"I'll give the girls kisses from you."

"Thanks, Marie. I appreciate it."

There was a hitch in her breath and while I expected a goodbye that wasn't what came.

"What happens after?" she asked, and I flinched at the pain in her voice. "When she's better. Are you planning on having her stay...there? I mean?"

I wanted it more than my last breath, but I couldn't tell her that. Not then. "Too early to make that call, honey."

"But you want that...never mind. Don't answer. Good night, Cole."

The line ended before I could say a thing, although truthfully, what was left to say?

She'd found the pics of Trina, and she'd heard the stories. Getting her to move to Deer Creek and live in the same town when half the folks knew my high school girl-friend and soulmate vanished on me and her family wasn't a thrilling prospect for her. Then she'd found the letters, and everything went downward from there.

She stayed in town for the girls, to give them the life in a small town she wanted for them.

This was already hard enough for her, and now I'd made it even harder.

"Cole?"

I tore my gaze off my phone and my regrets and failures and turned to face Dr. McElroy.

"Yeah? Everything okay?"

"She's awake. I'll let you two talk and then I'll fill you in before I leave."

Trina was awake. Alert. *Thank God.*

———

THERE WASN'T a word to describe the void in Trina's expression as I entered the room. She looked exactly the same. Somehow, I'd expected color to return or for her to look happy or something when she finally woke up, but the darkness in her eyes could have blanketed the entire town. And that darkness had nothing to do with the discoloration and swelling on her face.

"Hey," I said, and stepped further toward the bed.

Her eyes were on the window, curtains and blinds open. There wasn't much to see but trees and maybe a hint of the afternoon sun peeking through them.

Hard to believe it was still afternoon. Considering the day, I felt like I'd aged a decade in twenty-four hours.

"You're awake."

Trina's eyes strayed to a picture on the nightstand table. It was a photo of June, Ella, and me at Oak Island over the summer. Both of them were clinging to my shoulders. A nice mom who'd been grappling with her own three kids all day had offered to take our picture. My trunks were soaked and clung to my thighs, my hair an absolute mess from being in the water all day. June and Ella's weren't any better, but they'd thought it was hilarious that I bought swim trunks that matched their yellow and white hibiscus flowered ones, so there we were.

Thrilled.

Happy.

Joyful.

Smiling and sun-kissed and laughing.

Slowly, Trina's head twisted, and she met my gaze straight on. With no change of expression in her eyes, no light whatsoever, she deadpanned, "You have kids now."

It was absolutely the very last way I expected her to start a conversation.

"Yeah." I choked down the words climbing up my throat. The comments I'd usually make bragging about them, giving her their names and ages, and telling her everything about how awesome they were.

The look in her eyes stopped me.

"Good. That's good you have that now."

There was no happiness in her tone that said she meant it, only the same chillingly blank tone and expression.

"Did Sheila tell you what happened or where you are?"

"Deer Creek. Your house. You were at the hospital." She said it like an accusation.

I hadn't known if she'd remember or not, if she was ever truly aware of my presence. "Valerie called and said you needed help." I took another step toward her bed. "Do you want to talk about it?"

"No." She closed her eyes and turned her head away from me. "You weren't supposed to see me like that. You were never supposed to see me."

Her words gutted me. So did her dry tone.

Trina was anything but dry and lifeless. Hell, she'd left Deer Creek because she had a thirst for adventure. She'd always been quick to laugh, quick to plan something that was guaranteed to get one of us, if not both, grounded.

Maybe I had to start thinking of the Trina as I knew her as gone, but I couldn't. I'd do anything to bring that part of her back to life.

"Trina—"

"Katrina." She flinched as she said it, and I bit my tongue to keep from snapping that she wasn't that. She would never be that again because I had no doubt she didn't choose it but was given it.

The fight for that could come later, along with so many I figured were coming.

"Ma's upstairs with some soup. I can bring it to you."

"I don't want to see her."

"You don't have to. I can go get it."

"I'm not hungry."

"You need to eat, Trina...you need..."

Her head shifted, eyes popped open. "Don't even think for a second you have any idea what I *need*, Cole."

She closed her eyes again, turned her face back to the window and went silent, breathing so slowly her chest barely rose and fell.

I'd give her that. She'd probably had many years of not having many choices, at least none that were truly hers in the first place.

"All right, honey. I'll let you sleep."

She had no reaction to me calling her honey, and even though her eyes were closed, there was no way she was sleeping. She could fake it, sure, and I'd let her have that play, too. But someday, as the bruises and bones and ligaments and muscles all started to heal, she'd have to face what happened.

Figure out what she wanted, who she wanted to be now.

I went to the nightstand on the other side of the bed, grabbed the bell Sheila had left out and moved it closer to her. Setting down the bell, I opened the drawer to the nightstand and knocked the photo of my kids into it. It clearly wasn't helping her any.

"There's a bell here," I told her softly. "Ring it if you need anything, but I'll be checking on you. I know you're angry, probably feeling a whole lot of things. But I worked with Valerie and Kip to get you safe and away from him. Be pissed at me for a lot of things, if you need to, but don't be pissed that I couldn't bear the thought of you being hurt like that anymore."

She didn't say a word, which wasn't unexpected or surprising.

She might think she was Katrina now and Trina didn't exist, but the Trina I remembered had always been a gold medalist in winning the silent treatment.

Looked like that asshole hadn't beaten everything out of her after all.

# EIGHTEEN

## COLE

Days went by. The doctor came by multiple times a day and not only checked Trina's wrapping and swelling but also maintained her pain medicine and helped her in the bathroom. For as much as I wanted to be the one shouldering the weight of that activity, Sheila made it known Trina didn't want my help.

Not that it was a surprise. I brought her food, asked her if she wanted to sit outside and get some fresh air. I tried to make conversation. She ate—barely—and she kept silent.

The bell never rang.

Dr. McElroy tried to encourage me, telling me I needed to give it time. She needed help. Therapy. Sheila was working on a list of doctors and trying to find some who would do virtual appointments, but Trina hadn't yet agreed to any of it, and we couldn't make her.

The only time I saw barely a hint of happiness was when Valerie called, and I handed my cell phone to Trina. That conversation lasted over a half an hour, and through my stalking and pacing on the other side of the bedroom door in the guise of giving her full privacy, I'd heard more than one soft laugh. Her voice was dry and scratchy from lack of use and pain, but even then, that laugh had been exhilarating.

After the call ended, and I went to grab my phone back, I got a mumbled *thank you* in response, and while her gaze held no emotion, her eyes seemed to be softer.

I took it as a win, as pathetic as it was.

When I left to get some work done and spend time with my girls, Mom and Dad came over. Even though Valerie had a bag stocked full of comfortable clothes for Trina on the plane before we headed back to Deer Creek, Mom had also gone out and bought a bunch of lounge sets and soft pajamas for Trina. She kept cooking and baking up a storm, but considering how Trina had treated me, Mom didn't head downstairs. They were just there in case she rang the bell, in case she ever gave any indication she wanted help from us.

By day five, Marie wasn't thrilled Trina was in no shape to leave my house, and we'd made a short-term decision about the girls. They'd stay with Marie another week for her week of time with them, but after...

Well, *after* another week and a half, there'd be explaining to do.

Trina's leg brace wasn't required unless she moved around too much and it caused her pain. As painful as it was listening to her fumbling around, I tried my best to stay back and respect her wishes. I heard the water run when she was showering and using the bathroom, and by day seven, I decided she'd had enough silence and seclusion.

Nothing good could be going on in her head with all the noise she had to carry, and not only was she fine to move around, it'd be good for her.

The sky was bright blue, the temps were going to hit the

low sixties so I decided that when I took Trina's breakfast down to her that we were getting out of the house.

I'd carry her myself if I needed to.

A quick knock on her door got me a quiet, "Come in," and when I entered, I was surprised as hell to see her.

She wasn't in bed like she'd been. Her hair was wet and air-drying even though she had a hair dryer she could use, and she wasn't lying there, doing nothing but staring at the window.

Instead, she was using her bed as a stabilizer and doing elevated push-ups on them.

"What are you doing? Your ribs." I caught myself and the bark in my voice and scaled it back. "I brought you breakfast."

Trina stared straight ahead, down slowly, up slowly.

"Get tired of laying down?"

"Need to stay in shape."

The hell she did. And she definitely didn't need to do it *now*. "You can relax, Trina. Take your time...you don't have to—"

"When Jonathan comes to get me, it'll be worse if I've let myself go."

She spoke like a robot, cold and plastic, and I hated everything about it. About the thoughts she had.

I *knew* she hadn't been alone down here, planning a new vibrant future, with the entire world at her fingertips.

No, she'd been down here thinking of Jonathan's retribution.

"The hell he will." I gripped the serving tray harder and set it down on her bed. "He's not coming here, and you're sure as hell not going back to him."

She scoffed, like I was the fool. "Of course he'll come here. Don't be naive."

Okay. So maybe he would. "Even if he does, he won't get to you. I'll never let him lay a hand on you again. You're safe here. I swear it."

She speared me with a glare, and there was nothing kind of shimmery or hopeful in that look. It was so dark, so ugly, I sucked in a breath. "I think I've believed enough promises that have been broken. I know who Jonathan is, and if you think he'll just happily be okay with his wife going missing, you're an idiot. Besides, I didn't ask for this."

All the breath fled my lungs and my brain.

Did she...was she *mad* at us for getting her away from him? Did she *want* to go back?

Trina turned back, all that long blond hair of hers fell over her shoulder blocking my view of her face. She did two more push-ups which I was certain she did to make her point and then climbed back into bed. Tray situated on her lap, she shoved the bacon to the side and began using the side of her fork to separate the egg whites from the yolks on her fried eggs.

I was still frozen, trying to understand and yet it was beyond my capability. As the words clawed up my throat to ask her what she meant, I choked them down.

"I'd like to take you somewhere today," I said instead.

She blinked at me. "No."

"It'd be good for you to get out. I'm not saying go walk around in public, but I'd like to take you for a drive. See something outside these walls."

"Is this a trick?"

"No." I shook my head and took a step back closer to the doorway. I'd like to tell her I'd throw her over my shoulder and haul her out there if I had to but had to remember what she'd been through. A joke right now about doing something against her will would be the least respectful thing I could say, no matter how badly I wanted to make her. "Choice is yours, but be warned...I'll keep pestering you every day until you agree."

Trina bit into a piece of toast and chewed. The bite was the size of something a mouse would eat and yet she chewed on it like she'd shoved the whole piece into her mouth. I should probably stop giving her bread and bacon altogether. All she usually ate were the egg whites, anyway.

"A car ride." She stated it like fact, and I nodded.

"Thirty minutes. No tricks."

"And then you'll leave me alone for the rest of the day?"

Goodness. We were bartering like I was making her doing something painful—like try oysters—and I'd never forget the expression she made, or the color she turned, when she finally did. But hell, maybe this was how she survived.

I really needed to see if she'd called any of the therapists yet. Doubted that too, but it was the reminder of how hurt she'd been that had me keep my tone light.

"Sure." I'd try, anyway.

"Okay then."

She speared the last bite of egg whites with her fork and set that back on her tray. "I'm done now."

Two egg whites. A nibble, if it could be considered that, of plain toast. No bacon. This wasn't a *meal*, and there was no way she could be full.

"Fine." I moved toward her, caught the tightening of her arms as I reached across her and grabbed the tray, and picked it up. She did that every time I came close. Was it because she thought I was some threat? Or was it habit? Either way, every one of these small reminders were stark realizations she wasn't the same vibrant, adventure-seeking girl I used to know.

I needed to tread carefully, and that sucked when I'd spent the rest of my life bulldozing through everything else I wanted.

"We'll leave in an hour. Is that okay?"

"It's fine."

Trina wasn't looking at me, not surprising. She rarely did. She was looking at the blank television screen. As far as I knew, she hadn't yet turned it on even though the remote was on her nightstand. She just stared at the black television screen all day.

Maybe the exercise she was doing was at least something good for her. Or would have been, had it not been cloaked with the thoughts that Jonathan would come back and beat the shit out of her again.

"Okay then."

I headed out of her room, up the stairs, and to the kitchen. As much as I wanted to take out my anger and frustration on my plates and slam them into the dishwasher, I didn't want to alarm her, so I stayed quiet, grabbed my phone and went out to the back deck where I stood, staring off into trees and did nothing until my temper cooled.

# NINETEEN

## TRINA

The world around me was a fog, darkening and pressing into every side instead of lifting with the morning sun and heat. Ever since I opened my eyes in the hospital and saw Cole, everything was different.

Not better.

Not worse.

Dreamlike.

If I allowed myself to believe I was free of Jonathan, my reality would come crashing down on me and I'd be back to my forever torment.

No. I needed to stay smart. Think ahead. Plan and figure out how to make it through this so when Jonathan arrived—and I had no doubt he would—I would not be the one at fault in any of this.

It didn't matter if it made me cold for being so willing to throw Cole, and perhaps Valerie and Kip, and their part under the proverbial bus, but they hadn't lived my life.

They hadn't had to do what was necessary to survive.

I wasn't getting out of this without more scars.

The only thing I had a chance at determining was how deep those cuts went before they scarred over.

Was I thankful to be away from Jonathan? I couldn't even say. I knew him. Knew how to read his moods and respond appropriately. I knew my limits and my boundaries. At least, I did until he changed them without notice. Here, back in Deer Creek, there was no safety. No boundary.

I had been whisked away and snuck into Cole's house, and in the few conversations I'd had with Valerie, I hadn't let her explain what happened. The less I knew, the better.

One thing for certain, Jonathan wasn't just going to come for me.

He was going to come for Cole once he figured it all out.

That he had a part in my disappearance wouldn't be far-fetched considering the business card. The card our cleaning lady somehow found in my underwear drawer and stupidly left on the dresser.

The card that had fueled Jonathan's rage.

The card that started it all.

My fault for keeping it. For wanting one tiny, insignificant reminder of when life was good and I wasn't trash.

"Enough." I climbed out of the bed. I'd lingered long enough and the quicker I went along with Cole's plan for fresh air and sunshine and absurdity, the sooner I'd be back in this bubble in the strange empty room with the smiling little girls who brought tears to my eyes every night.

Happy tears for Cole who had what he'd always wanted. He'd wanted children. Now he had them.

Sad, tortured tears for me. For every choice I had made in this life that had led me to being broken beyond hope, ruined far deeper than any bruises would ever show.

If Cole was planning some massive rescue operation, he

had to realize it was a failure before it ever began. He might have temporarily saved my body, but he'd never find and rescue all the parts of my shattered and tattered soul.

I was already dressed and while it probably wasn't necessary for a car ride, I clipped on the knee brace. You never knew who was watching. Who could see me. It'd be better if he saw me as the still-healing wife, forced here against her will...waiting for when she could be returned.

And perhaps that's what I should do.

Go back. Explain.

Maybe...

I limped out of the bedroom and into the downstairs bathroom. Cole's house wasn't large, but it was homey and a normal-sized home for Deer Creek. Clearly a split-level, I'd been stashed in the downstairs bedroom, right outside what looked like a movie watching area and a toy room. Everything was neatly put away. If I hadn't already seen the pictures of him and his girls, I'd know he had daughters. Pink and purple toys and books and buckets and baskets lined one large wall.

I yanked my gaze back to the carpet.

The pain was too much to see. The regret too large to face.

Had I been smarter that could have been mine.

Cole must have heard me coming. As I started up the stairs, thumps came from my right. His body cast a large shadow over where I hobbled up the stairs, and then he met me in the entryway space. It was small, and he was too close. His presence too large and his scent too memorable.

I kept my gaze on the floor.

I'd thought of him every minute since that day on the street. When I cried myself to sleep, once I was assured Jonathan's snores meant he was sleeping, I thought of Cole.

The easy smiles he gave, the boyish charm, the stubborn set on his features. All of it came mixed between memories of the boy I used to love and the man he'd become on that sidewalk.

In reality, all of him was harder now, more jagged, but no amount of maturity or growth could eviscerate the joyful glimmer in his eyes he'd always had. Like life was one big party and he was along for the ride. There was a time I'd followed along on that ride, hands up and enjoying every moment of it.

I now knew different.

"You ready?" Cole asked.

I glanced at my hands, empty of any belongings, and shrugged. "Not like I have anything to bring with me."

It wasn't a cut at him, and since I couldn't bear to look at him any more than necessary, I had no idea how he reacted, but there was a beat and then a heavier pause before he sighed. "I can get you a phone. You're not a prisoner here. Valerie and Kip thought it'd be better for you."

That didn't take a genius to figure out, and having my wallet or phone or whatever else was in my Hermès bag, an apology from Jonathan for a bruised rib last year, wouldn't do me any good anyway.

"Whatever."

Like I needed my failures thrown in my face. Who cared if I had a phone? I had no one to call. No one to miss me. No one to talk to. Other than Valerie, I no longer had a single person in my life who cared about my existence.

Cole had offered me his, along with suggesting I could use it to call the therapists Dr. McElroy left for me.

That list was in the trash, and his phone had gone unused outside the two talks with Valerie.

I didn't need therapy. The last thing that would be good

for me would be to *talk* about my decisions. I wasn't an idiot. I had made choices. Born of greed and fear and worry and dreams and fantasies, but I'd made them all the same. There was nothing to discuss.

I was a stupid person who made worthless and destructive choices. No amount of therapy could change who I was at the core.

"Let's just go," I mumbled. I hadn't been this surly since I last left Deer Creek. "The sooner we go, the sooner you can get rid of me."

"I don't...never mind. Truck's in the driveway," Cole said, and he stepped toward me, reached around and opened the storm door. My body locked as he moved and didn't release until he stepped back.

He saw that.

I knew he did, and yet he never said anything.

Of course he wouldn't.

I was now the woman he pitied, and that's all I'd be to him. A pitiful excuse for a woman.

Who could blame him?

---

THE TOWN WAS DIFFERENT. So vastly different I could barely recognize many of the streets we drove through. Cole lived on the northwest side of town, in an older neighborhood I *did* recognize because many of my friends had grown up in the area, but as we drove south toward the old downtown, there were vast differences.

Additional lanes and stoplights at intersections that had once been two-lane, four-way stop signs. Gas stations that had never existed. There were rows of townhomes going up on my left that used to be trees we'd spend all day exploring as kids. A new YMCA sat across the street from at least four baseball fields.

It was unnerving. As much as I'd quit believing I'd ever be able to return to Deer Creek, a small part of me had hoped I would and that it would feel like home.

Cole's truck had a country music station playing at a low level, something easy to talk over, and yet my gaze was stuck outside my window.

"It's different, huh?" It was the first thing he'd said to me since we got in his truck and pulled out of his drive. If he was expecting me to answer, he didn't act like it because he kept talking. "Town's growing. Doubled in size, at least, since we were kids, and our old high school is the new middle school. New high school is on the other side of town off Mountain Road, and all that side of town that was Traventine's farmland is now school and homes and businesses. We've also got a new library finished last year so we don't have to drive all the way to Boone."

As he spoke, he turned left on the main road that went east-to-west through town. We took a bridge over the lake that had my already stressed nerves tighten further.

We'd hung out at the small beach at that lake, bemoaned the lifeguards that kept us from having too much fun, we'd laid on the grass as close to the private airstrip as we could get and watched the small private planes fly overhead. We snuck off onto worn mountain trails and made out in the woods. Some of that land backed up to homes...one in particular I knew too well.

"Don't," I rasped, as we came to the turn that would take us there.

I couldn't. Couldn't bear to drive past my own neighborhood.

Without missing a beat, Cole turned in the opposite

direction. Years ago, this had been a dirt road that led to land and homes that had enough acreage for horses or small, family homesteads. It was now paved, like the rest of the town, but as he turned away from my childhood home, the church that'd be nearby where I spent as much time in as my home, my lungs released like a valve.

"Thank you," I whispered.

"They love you, you know. Never stopped. They were never angry with you. Worried maybe, but never angry."

*I'm not angry... just disappointed.* I couldn't count the amount of times my dad or mom would say those words. It'd be followed by Bible verses about how we should live, a teaching moment and a quick prayer and then all would be forgiven. It hadn't been a bad childhood...but it'd been a small one.

At least, that was what I thought back then.

"Do they know I'm here?"

"No. Some men at the station know, Mom and Marie, my ex, and that's because they had to. Mom and Dad said they'd keep it quiet until you were ready."

"I don't want to see them." I doubted I'd ever be ready, and I wasn't sure there was a point. Jonathan would find me. Why give them hope I was home if it was only temporary?

"Okay."

There was a shrug from him in my peripheral vision and I turned, barely enough to face him. "That doesn't bother you?"

"They've waited a long time to have you back. They'll wait forever."

The last thing I wanted was to give them hope when it would only be torn away. Truth was, he was probably right. My parents, Mom especially, still reached out to me. Not often, and I wasn't brave enough to return her calls, but when Jonathan had told me to block their numbers so I couldn't talk to them, I'd changed both of theirs to *Spam Risk* in my phone's contacts. Amazingly, he'd never searched my contacts and found them, but it allowed me to occasionally, usually around my birthday or holidays, hear my mom's voice.

Karen Mills was soft-spoken but bold. She was kind and loving and never showed a hint of fear. And she loved me despite myself. Which was why I always listened to her voicemails in the bathroom with the shower running...so no one could hear me cry.

"It doesn't matter," I told Cole and faced the window as he drove by the new library he'd mentioned. "My life ended the day I left town. I've been nothing since."

Maybe if he finally saw the truth of who I was, he'd move on from trying to save someone who couldn't be saved.

# TWENTY

## COLE

Whatever I'd been thinking was wrong with Trina came to a crashing halt the moment those words left her mouth and hovered in the space between us like a weighted bomb.

She thought she was *nothing*? Truly, completely believed she had nothing to offer this world?

I must have been naive, thinking she'd be grateful for us getting her away from Jonathan. Maybe I'd been too hopeful she'd be excited to be free of him. I'd worked with enough victims, heard their stories and how they consistently returned to their abusers that I should have applied that to Trina.

But man...I hadn't expected this level of self-hatred and worthlessness to come from her.

Knowing nothing I said would make a difference in her current state of mind, I made a left that would take us away from the lake, toward the highway. If she'd been awed by the changes in town she'd already seen, nothing would surprise her like the businesses along that strip of road.

"You've always been everything to a lot of people," I said, because I still had to try. Still had to speak the truth against the lies she believed. "You still are, especially your parents."

I caught a quick flinch, and then she turned back to face the window. I turned and took us toward a new shopping strip that was packed. Who knew so many locals would go ballistic over a Home Goods and TJ Maxx, but the parking lot was always packed with cars.

"Tell me about your girls," she said so quietly I almost missed it over the rumble of my truck and traffic.

"June and Ella. They're four and five."

She didn't want to know about my girls. That was obvious with the way her lips scrunched up like she tasted something sour. This was a distraction to get the focus off her. I'd give her that, but if what Valerie said was true and she still hated herself for her choices when we were kids, I wasn't sure it'd help.

"Their mom?"

"Marie. She lives in town. We split custody."

"How'd you meet?" Her questions came by rote, with no joy, but considering she was talking instead of staring out the window with an empty expression, I told her.

"Through friends at the academy. She was the sister of another candidate's girlfriend."

Her fingers twisted together in her lap as she considered that. She was no longer looking at the window but down at her hands. "You said she's your ex."

"Yup."

"Why?"

Of course. Of course that was the next question, but how could I explain it to Trina in a way that wouldn't make her want to jump out of my truck going fifty miles per hour?

Screw it.

She had to know *someone* cared about her. That she wasn't *nothing*.

I pulled off into the parking lot of the new strip. She tensed in the seat next to me, but I parked near the back where there was less traffic.

Truck in park, I turned to face her, willed her to lift her head and meet my gaze.

Slowly, like she could feel the weight of my words bubbling in my throat, she looked at me.

"In the end, Marie realized she wasn't you and never would be."

She blinked. Did it again and then her lips parted in surprise. As they did, color flushed her cheeks enough that she finally looked alive and not knocking on death's door, and her blue eyes brightened like the sun.

"That's stupid," she finally said and looked away. "I was never anything special."

"Trina—"

"Katrina," she quietly snapped, but her point was made. She'd had enough of a walk down memory lane. "And I'd like to go back now."

My nostrils flared, and a rebuttal burned the tip of my tongue. How could I help her see the truth when she was so focused on believing made-up lies?

---

I JUMPED up the final stairs to the home I used to live in where Marie was waiting for me behind the storm door. Dressed in wide-leg jeans and a mint green crewneck sweater Marie looked as relaxed and calm as she always did.

I was still in my uniform, coming over as soon as I got off work which had been delayed due to a tourist who decided drunk driving down the mountain was a great idea. He was drying out in our holding cell, pissed as a smacked hornet's nest, but he should be grateful we stopped him before he tumbled his car down the side of the mountain.

As I got closer to the door, she pushed it open. "Hey. Thanks for being willing to stop by tonight."

"Glad to do it." I glanced up the stairway. "Girls asleep?"

"Yeah. Thought that'd be less chaotic."

It was a good idea, but it also still sucked to be so close to them and not be able to see them.

When Marie decided she wanted a divorce, I moved out almost immediately and let her have the home in our divorce because I wanted her to stay in it with our girls. It wasn't like the small and cozy split-level I lived in, but a larger two-story home in one of the newly built neighborhoods out by the new high school I'd mentioned to Trina three days ago.

We'd bought a small, fixer-upper three-bedroom ranch when we were first married and then moved into this home when she was pregnant with Ella.

"Sorry I couldn't make it earlier. Work's been busy."

"So has your personal life." It wasn't a deep dig, but it cut nonetheless.

"Marie..."

"Sorry." She had turned her back and was headed toward the kitchen. I hadn't been in the house much after I moved out. I usually met the girls at the front door. Occasionally, I'd carry a sleeping June upstairs and to her room. Which meant I hadn't seen the differences she'd made to the downstairs, certainly not to all the picture frames she had covering the walls.

The pictures were only of the girls. Some of her with

them. Mostly the girls. Their entire lives, from the newborn stage to now, were framed all over the house that had also been repainted from a light gray to a cream color.

Like she had tried to sweep every single living, breathing memory of me out of the space. Not that I could blame her for it.

"I didn't mean that," she said when we reached the kitchen. She went straight to the fridge and pulled out a beer, sliding it across the island to me, and then grabbed a bottle of white wine from the fridge.

"You keep my beer in the fridge?" I asked.

"Yes," she deadpanned. "On the off chance you show up to hang out with me, I make sure your favorite refreshment is available." She rolled her eyes. "I bought it today. Figured you'd want one after work."

That was thoughtful of her. It also shouldn't have been a surprise because that was simply the kind of woman Marie had always been.

She poured herself a glass of wine, and since she'd called me to meet with her and talk, I let her take this conversation at her pace. Her time.

It came after one sip of wine.

"You told me when you called me that first night that you'd tell me more details about what's going on when you could. I decided to stop wondering and worrying and simply ask you."

She was on one side of the island. I was on the other. We were facing off against each other like enemies, but it wasn't lost on me there'd been a lot of *good* times with us on this very surface.

And since Marie wasn't only my ex-wife, but the mother of my kids, and the one who'd been pulling double duty and single parenting a lot more than usual lately, what she was asking for wasn't wrong.

It'd been three days since Trina and I went for the brief car ride and nothing had changed. Trina was alone at my place. Since she preferred to stare into the void in the bedroom even though most of her physical wounds were healing enough for her to move around and get what she needed, there was no point in Mom being there with nothing to do but twiddle her thumbs.

I was still anxious to get back and check on her, make sure she was okay even if I doubted she'd tell me the truth.

Hell, I wasn't even sure she knew what the truth was anymore.

"Remember that police conference I had to go to back in October?"

"I do."

"I ran into Trina." Her brows rose in surprise, and before she could wonder, I continued. "Walked right out of a coffee shop and ran straight into her, or rather, she ran into me, but whatever. That part doesn't matter nearly as much as what happened after."

Marie's jaw worked back and forth, and I could practically see questions gathering in her brain like a tiny cartoon bubble above her head.

"She had bruises then, Marie. Her cheek. Her wrists. Covered in a way it was obvious she'd been doing it for a while and had a lot of practice."

Marie frowned and her eyes slowly closed as she tilted her chin downward. "That's horrible. Truly, it is."

"I gave her my card. Told her to call if she ever needed help. She had a friend with her. That friend called me the night she ended up in the hospital. Apparently, and I don't know how yet because Trina won't talk about it, but she kept my card, and her husband found it."

"That's not your fault."

Of course she'd move to protect me. "I know, and yet I still blame myself for it. I've worked with enough women to know how risky that was. But, regardless, Trina's friend called me, asked me if I really was the kind of guy who'd help her."

A soft, well-known teasing smile stretched her mouth. "So of course you had to be the hero."

I grinned back and then took a drink. "I know this hurts you, and this is gonna hurt to hear, but it's Trina. Of course I would."

"I know. And yeah, it hurts, but not so much anymore, it's more of a bee sting compared to a copperhead bite."

"Comforting," I muttered. "Thank you for that."

"How's she doing? Healing wise?"

Marie nipped at her bottom lip, a show she was worried. She also did that when she was uncertain. This was one of the reasons it was so easy to care for her, to even think I truly was in love with her. Despite her own fears, she was worried about someone else. If I were a better man, I'd work to set her free from more of that pain.

"Physically she's getting better. Emotionally...mentally..." I paused and shook my head. There were stories that weren't mine to share. Things that weren't mine to give, but this was Marie, and out of everyone I knew, she'd be a tightly sealed vault. "She's saying some scaring things, and it worries me."

Her self-hatred topped the list. The fact she was so sure Jonathan would come and get her. I shook my head. There was only so much Marie needed to know.

"And you plan on helping her through all of that."

"Marie..."

She held up a hand and swallowed. "I get it, Cole. I do. I wouldn't have married you or fallen in love with you if you weren't exactly how you are, it's just...she can't stay at your place forever. And the girls..."

"She wouldn't even let me drive past her parents' home earlier this week, Marie. Her own childhood home. She's not ready."

"Maybe not for them, but she has friends in town, right? Like Ashley and Heather? Someone who can help her."

Heather worked at Max's Tavern for the fun of it but made her living being a social media creator and influencer. Ashley was married to her high school boyfriend. Robbie was an electrician and owned his own business. Ashley taught Honors English at the high school. All three would jump in with both feet to help.

And the fact Marie knew they were her best friends, and she'd spent *years* spending time with them...

"You must think I'm an asshole," I told her. "All those years you had to be around us. Hearing her name." Because she always came up. There wasn't a way to prevent it when you had the same friends you'd had since you were practically born.

Marie's sad smile told me I was right. "I knew what I was signing up for when we moved here, Cole. It hurt sometimes, but you were always honest."

Not always. And certainly not enough. Either with her or myself.

"I can try to talk with her. Something needs to change, so yeah, you're right, maybe I need to take a pushier approach, at least in getting her to talk." I finished my beer as I considered my options. Ashley would be the kindest. Heather would probably force her to a stool at Max's and shove drinks down her throat until she puked. "I'd like her to stay at my place though. She's downstairs. Girls can just think she's a friend. And she is, Marie. She's just a friend I'm helping."

She rolled her eyes. "Stop lying to me, and yourself. It's a sad, overly replayed song."

Crap. She was absolutely right. I tried a different, and completely honest one. "It's safer at my house than anywhere else."

"If the girls aren't safe..."

"Don't," I warned. "You know I wouldn't put them in danger. At least let me try it. I'll keep an eye on the girls. The way Trina is now, I doubt she'll even come out of her room when they're there. Hell, she doesn't do that *now*, Marie. She just stares at a wall all day. But you're right. It's not fair to you to have this all thrown in your lap. Try it my way, and if it makes the girls uncomfortable, we'll change it."

I saw her point, I did. Truly. But the thought of giving Trina up when I didn't even have her was hard enough.

Marie's jaw worked back and forth. "Fine," she said, which really wasn't fine at all, and we both knew it. "But be smart. With everything you're saying, she might need more help than you can give her, as much as you want to save her."

"I'll be careful."

She snorted. "Please. You have *never* been that, and we both know it. Current predicament proves it."

Well, sure.

She had a point there.

MARIE HAD A POINT. Trina needed time to heal, but she also needed company. She needed to start talking about what happened. Or at a minimum, start talking about how to heal from all of it. Being alone with her thoughts could only be detrimental to her.

I paused at the landing in my front door only long enough to ensure the house was quiet, that things were good.

The deadness in her eyes and the lack of any kind of hope or life in her tone every time we spoke worried me.

But that was why I was doing this.

She needed help. Someone to talk to, and if it wasn't me, I'd get her someone. I kicked off my boots and hurried down the stairs. Like usual, it was dark, only the soft light coming from the downstairs bath to light her a path if she got up.

It wasn't that late, just hitting nine-thirty. I expected to open the door and find her staring at that wall. Maybe at her lap.

A quick knock and silence followed. Sleeping. She was probably sleeping.

We could wait until the morning if she was. That wouldn't be the worst thing.

I turned the knob and opened the door. It squeaked softly, and I braced to see the pale, lifeless expression on her face she wore like armor.

My heart sank to my feet. A made bed, slightly rumpled covers. A glass of water on the nightstand.

Nobody in it. No Trina anywhere.

# TWENTY-ONE

## TRINA

"Trina!"

There was a thundering. A shout. I jolted up in the bed in the small dark room and panic clawed its way up my throat.

Oh no. *Oh no, no, no, no.* He was not supposed to see me like this. Not supposed to—

The thundering stopped and the light switched on, blinding me so badly I shirked back from him, closer to the white wicker headboard, and squeezed my eyes closed.

This was bad. So very, very bad.

He wasn't supposed to know I did this. Wasn't supposed to know I came here...

How *pissed* was he going to be?

"I thought you left," he finally said. And there wasn't anger in his tone, something that sounded more like relief.

I forced my eyes to peel open and stared directly at him.

Cole had both hands braced against the sides of the doorframe, confusion making his brows rise and the *what the hell is going on* expression on his face was clear.

"I'm sorry. I'm so sorry." I clambered out of June's bed,

and stood, patting down the rumpled covers as I rushed to get away. "I'll just... "I'll..."

I'd go back to my hole. Go back to ignoring him. Go back to living in fear and waiting. There were a million things I could *just* go do so easily, but as I stood in that tiny little beautiful room, with the fluffy pink bed coverings on the beds and the ladybug nightlight and books on the shelf, all I wanted to do was collapse and cry.

Cole *had* this. A beautiful life with everything he'd always wanted. The career he dreamed of. Girls. I'd thought it so bizarre the day he told me he wanted daughters and not sons. How something about being a *girl dad* made him excited.

I sold my soul, my morals, and my body until I was a shell of a human being, nothing like the girl he remembered, and Cole had everything he always wanted.

In a way, I'd given him that.

"What are you doing in here, honey?"

"Don't," I rasped. "Don't call me that. Or Trina. I hate them." I shook my head and edged away from him. Desperate to flee and hide, but he was standing in the doorway now and I was stuck with no escape.

"Why are you in June and Ella's room?"

I shrugged. No answer I could give could make sense other than it felt *safe. Clean.* I never should have put my dirtied body in it.

The bright-colored, daisy-shaped rug beneath my feet blurred. "I'll go back to my room."

There was a beat... then... "We should talk about this."

"It won't happen again."

He was never supposed to know I did this in the first place. Wandered through his home, soaking up everything I could see, hints of treasures of pure beauty.

"I'm not mad you're in here. I'm curious as to why."

Because it was pretty and clean and beautiful and had pops of vibrant color that made me, in glimpses, remember the little girl I used to be.

I'd never intended Cole to find out I did this. I'd never fallen asleep before. *This* was a mistake I'd ensure I never made again.

I shrugged and kept my blurred vision on the adorable little rug. It was so soft and thick my toes wanted to curl into it. "I'd like to go back to my room now."

Another heavy, weighted silence hit and then there was the ruffle of something. I glanced up, hoping he'd backed away, but that wasn't what was happening at all.

Cole was moving closer, slowly, and I had nowhere to go to get away from him. He stopped in front of me, chin dipped down.

It was the care in his eyes, the cautious way he held himself back even while being so close that had a sob lodge itself in my throat. He was *scared*, and I'd done that to him.

"You can talk to me. You can tell me..."

I shook my head. Absolutely not.

"You need to talk about it, Trina. You need to heal."

There was nothing to heal. I was broken beyond repair and the sooner he learned that the better off we'd both be. Cole had always been a protector, a fixer. But he couldn't fix me.

He couldn't back then, and he definitely couldn't now.

"If not me, then you need to call one of the therapists. Or someone else. Valerie or *someone*. This isn't healthy. *You're* not healthy."

I scoffed and found the strength to look him directly in his eyes. "I know that."

He blinked. Surprised I was self-aware? Please.

I was well aware of my faults and my mistakes. They were blinking neon lights in my brain every time I tried to shut it off and since being *here*, in his home and in this town, I could no longer find my weapons for dimming them.

And because of that, because I couldn't find my reasons or ways to *hide* them, anger rose. Fast, furious, so quickly and so powerfully my body trembled, and my fingertips burned as my hands curled into fists.

"He wasn't the first you know."

Cole jolted, head snapping back as I spoke. For once, he needed to know. "What do you—"

"Jonathan. He wasn't the first to beat me. He wasn't the first to force me to do other things. He wasn't the first to *hurt* me, Cole. There were many before him. And I did it all. *Willingly.* All to get what I wanted. All to get my dream. I had choices in front of me and I made every single one of them knowing exactly what I was doing. Don't stand there and feel sorry for me. Just stop it. I'm not a wounded victim who needs to heal. The person you knew *died* the moment I left town, and there's nothing you or anyone else can do to help bring me back. So just...stop!"

Rage made my voice shake. Shame made my tears fall. I skirted around him and ran down the hall, down the stairs, slammed the door, and dove into the bed.

Covers yanked up over me, I shoved my face into my pillow.

He was so wrong.

No one, not a single person, could help me... especially when I'd never been able to help myself.

I was still crying when the stairs creaked. Stupid of me. Stupid of me to think he'd leave it alone. Leave me alone.

There was a quiet knock and then the squeak of the door.

"You don't have to look at me. And I'm sorry, for tearing you away from your life, for trying to help. It's just...you might think you died that day, but I think you're still there. You're just too afraid to come back out."

A quiet thud landed on my nightstand, and my breath hitched.

"If you want..." He cleared his throat and there was pain ripping through him. I'd done that. Brought him more pain. God...what a *loser* I was. "If you want to go back to your husband, I can't force you to stay here. I know I can't, even as much as I want to protect you from him and more pain. But if that's what you want...I'll call Kip. We'll figure something out."

My tears froze and my blood turned to ice. Send me back? To Jonathan? Did I...did I want that?

"If you want to stay, if you want to be safe, I can make that happen. Other people can, too. You still got friends in this town, both Heather and Ashley are here. I bought you a phone today. Call someone, if you want, but maybe try considering something else."

He paused, and I waited for him to continue. When he didn't, I couldn't resist temptation, and I pushed the covers off my face. I rolled to my back and peeked up at him.

My room was dark, and the lights from the playroom shadowed his figure, but there was no hiding the defeat in his curled shoulders and the way his head hung.

I couldn't quite tell if he was looking at me, but I wasn't sure that mattered. Cole *saw* something in me, he always had.

"Maybe you can't go back and correct your mistakes or get over the things that happened. But if you want to *stay*, only you get to decide what kind of person you want to be moving forward. There are lots of people around who would help you figure out who that new person is. Including me."

"The day I got rid of our baby..." I started and pushed through the wretched pain and memories in my throat and forced the words out. He had to know who I was now. The monster I'd become.

"I don't hate you for that anymore. I don't."

That didn't matter. It also wasn't my point.

"If I could go back and do it all over again, knowing what I know now...I'd kill myself right along with it." His entire body flinched and swung back, but he couldn't be surprised by that. "Thanks for the phone. I want to sleep now."

I rolled to my side, closed my eyes, and pretended he didn't stand there silently watching me for a long time. Pretended I didn't give him a glimmer into the kind of person I truly was.

"You give me a chance, you have any inkling of a desire to be happy, I'll get you to a place where you want to live again. I swear it."

The door closed. The stairs creaked.

I doubted with every fiber in my being that would ever be possible again. But as I fell asleep, there was a glimmer.

A tiny shimmer of a thought floated by on a breeze that asked, *but what if you did?*

# TWENTY-TWO

## COLE

I tossed and turned all night. Probably slept in thirty-second increments before Trina's words came back to haunt me, over and over again.

*I would have killed myself.*

*I died that day.*

*He wasn't the first.*

That one. Among all the others. The fact she couldn't see how she'd been used or taken advantage of, that she didn't truly go into whatever happened to her with her eyes open and *choose* it. I'd been in law enforcement long enough to see the ugliest sides of people, to see abusers at their worst. Men who took what they wanted either through power exchanges, coercion, or force—or a combination of the three.

All through the night, her words rattled my brain, leaving me exhausted, *furious*, and ready to fly to New York and Georgia and have my vengeance on the men who beat her down so badly she was terrified of taking one single step to get back up.

Eggs bubbled in the pan, fried egg whites only since

Trina had yet to eat a single yolk. Bacon sizzled and even though I knew she wouldn't eat the toast, that too was in the toaster. I had coffee ready, orange juice on the counter. I'd get her eating. I'd get her smiling. I'd get her finding a single shred of hope inside of herself to cling to, and I'd work on it for as long as it took.

A woman like Trina, a girl who'd had such huge dreams, an even larger heart for people, and a foundation that was built on everything good and pure and sweet deserved to crave a life that was at minimum, filled with peace and not despair or self-hatred.

Bacon done, I used the tongs and gathered the slices on the paper towel-lined plate. Turning to put it on the plate next to Trina's breakfast tray, I froze.

Tongs in one hand, plated bacon in the other, I stood there, unable to say a single word. Too afraid if I moved, she'd disappear.

Trina stood on the other side of the counter, hair brushed, eyes sleepy but alert.

At least one of us got some sleep last night.

She was also dressed in an outfit Valerie had sent with us. And I knew it was one of Valerie's because it was far too high-quality to have come from Target or TJ Maxx.

"Hey," I finally said, startling myself back to life. "Morning."

She pushed her lips to the side and scanned my kitchen. "I thought I'd eat up here if that's okay."

It was far better than okay. It was a miracle considering her state last night.

"Of course it's okay."

I set down the bacon, and turned back to the eggs. Once hers and mine were done in separate pans, and the toast had popped, I gathered everything and plated it at the counter.

I stayed on my side of the counter while Trina hesitantly slid into a stool across from me. She sipped her coffee. I added cream to mine. She played with her egg whites while I devoured my entire plate.

"Where are your kids?" she asked, moving her eggs around her plate.

"Their mom's house."

"Marie?"

So she had listened. At least to some of the things I said. "Yeah. We share weeks. You should know I get them back Sunday after church."

"I shouldn't be here when they get back then."

She should be here with them, every day, for the rest of our lives together, but I was desperately trying to keep that from unfurling into anything larger.

"Marie and I talked. She knows what's going on, and she's okay with the girls coming back. You're a friend in town visiting. That's all they need to know."

She stabbed at her egg whites and then pushed a slice of bacon around. "You told her about me?"

"Not too many specifics of why you're here, but some. She'll keep it quiet." After all, I got all the friends in the divorce, which again made me an ass and Marie a saint. She could leave town and start over, but she stayed to give the girls stability. "She's a good woman, and I screwed her over. But she's okay with trying this, letting you be here with the girls. You'll like them, Trina. They're sweet. They have school in the morning and usually go to my parents' afterward on the weeks I have them while I'm working. Well, Ella's sweet. June's on the race to give me as many gray hairs as possible."

For the briefest moments, I swore her lip curled, but she tucked her chin closer to her chest and it was gone.

"I really hate it when you call me that."

"I don't know what else to call you. And I won't call you Katrina, no matter how many times you snap at me too."

"I don't snap," she said, and her head lifted, eyes rounded, and the color washed from her cheeks. "Sorry, that was rude..."

"Stop." She clamped her mouth closed. "There's nothing to apologize for, so don't do it. In this house, you are free to say anything you feel like saying, *however*, you feel like saying it, but do not ask me to call you the name he did. That, I can't do."

Tears pooled in her eyes, and she looked away, shaking her head. It'd been a guess until then that it was Jonathan who forced her to go by Katrina, which *was* her birth name, but she'd never once used it. Said it was too stuffy and too classy for a small-town Southern girl.

"Do you hate the name or the reminder of who she was?"

She shook her head and for the first time, chomped down on her bacon. "You probably need to get to work, don't you?"

"Yeah." I was dying to do anything but that. Dying to ask her what changed. Why she was in my kitchen, not appearing completely hollow. Dying to know if she wanted to go back to Jonathan.

But those answers had to come on her time.

"Is your mom coming over today?"

"She can, if you want that."

She shrugged, but somehow managed to finish the entire piece of bacon while she didn't answer. "I think... maybe...? Maybe it'd be nice not to be alone today?"

The day would come when she wouldn't turn every-thing into a question. I'd make sure of it.

"Then she'll be here."

The edges of Trina's lips twitched. "Thanks, Cole."

God, I wanted to kiss her. I wanted to brush my thumbs over her cheeks and wrap her in my arms. I wanted to hold her tight and fight her demons for her, and I wanted to do it all, all at once and all the time.

"You're welcome."

It took effort to hold myself back, finish my breakfast and load my dishes. By the time I was done and had filled my to-go mug with more coffee, Trina was still picking at her own plate. But she hadn't moved, and she hadn't run away, and she'd asked to spend the day with Mom, and all of that was good.

So I was going to make sure this ended on a good note.

"I'll be back around five, assuming nothing wild happens. Have fun with Mom."

"Okay."

I wanted more than that. I wanted to see the light in her eyes shine again, see any hint of a spark in them, but that too, I'd have to wait for.

I grabbed my keys on the wall at the top of the stairs and headed down them. I had one hand on the garage door, the other holding my keys and coffee.

"Yeah?" I turned and found her at the top of the stairs, chewing the inside of her cheek.

"I don't...I don't want to go back to Jonathan."

Thank *God*. "Then you won't."

"I don't know if I can do the rest, though."

She sure as hell could.

"Then we'll get you to a place where you think you can."

"I don't know if I can do that, either, anymore." More tears swam in her eyes and *damn*. Her pain was my new hell, and I couldn't do anything about it. Couldn't take it from her. Couldn't slay the darkness she had living in her.

"Then we'll start there. We'll start by getting you *thinking*, and that's all you have to do."

She worked her lips back and forth, blinking back tears. "You're being too nice to me, and I don't deserve it. Not from you, most of all."

Yeah, well, she was wrong about that.

"You remember what I told you that day you broke up with me?"

One shoulder lifted and fell. "Mostly."

"Then you'll remember I said I'd hate you for a day, but I'd always love you."

"But—"

"No buts. I don't think you're ready to hear why, but it's still true to this day. You don't feel the same, but that doesn't change the way I do."

Her lips parted, full and pink and tears were running down her cheeks, and if I didn't leave *then* I'd do something dangerous. Something stupid and reckless and I could ruin everything.

So, I flung open the garage door, climbed into my truck, and left with that look on her face in my memory.

Which was a lot better than how I left her last night.

# TWENTY-THREE

## TRINA

*But what if you did?*

The question haunted me through the night. It came to me in dreams, where I ran through heavy thickets of brush and trees, lost in a forest. Every time I spun in a circle, a tiny glimmer of light sparked and faded and whenever I shifted, the light moved and disappeared making it difficult to find.

But it was there. Sparking. I woke drenched in sweat and filled with regret, but whatever that ridiculous thought was lingered.

It was that driving force that moved me straight to the shower, that urged me to get dressed and not crawl back into bed and rethink every miserable thought I constantly lived with. And it was that ridiculously naive question that guided my feet up the stairs straight to Cole's kitchen.

His back had been to me, giving me a moment to drink him in. Something I definitely shouldn't have been doing, but I couldn't help myself.

He'd always been the best-looking guy in school, and that wasn't my sole opinion because I'd once loved him. It was a fact, and every girl in the school and town knew it...

and sure, two thousand people wasn't much as far as the world went, but it was still fact. Even if the town had grown, I doubted that had changed.

He'd barely shown his surprise at my appearance and carried on like it was normal, and somehow, that had settled me quicker than if he had asked why I was there. Or if he started questioning me about last night. Why was I in his daughters' bedroom? Did I *want* to go back to Jonathan?

The answer to the question was no. Absolutely not. I'd long since given up hope of leaving him though. With his money and connections he'd come get me. I was certain of it.

*But what if....*

There it was again. It kept jumping into my head, making me think, urgent almost in its need for an answer.

*What if...*

What if Jonathan didn't care? What if Jonathan left me alone? What if Cole could protect me? What if I *could* leave Jonathan?

The questions kept coming, long after Cole left for work, leaving me alone with nothing to do other than wander.

I cleaned up his kitchen. I made my bed. And then I sat, phone cradled in my hand as it powered on.

*Call someone.* There was only one person I could talk to, and even then, it wasn't like I'd ever memorized Valerie's number. I'd programmed it into my phone and never looked twice.

But what if...

Cole wouldn't leave me helpless and stranded. Sure, he said he'd call his mom, but it could be hours before she got here.

The screen on the phone lit up, and my finger

hovered over the internet icon. I could find Kip. It'd be a risk, but no one *had* to know who I was when I asked for him. No...

Cole wouldn't leave me helpless.

I hit the contacts icon instead and for the first time in weeks, a genuine smile stretched across my cheeks. A water drop hit the screen, and I brushed it away. Then my cheeks. This was crazy. So he was helpful and gave me phone numbers. I was being ridiculous.

Still, I couldn't stop crying as I scrolled through the few numbers he must have programmed in. Ashley. Bridget. Cole. There were so many. He hadn't given me just his mom's number but his dad's. *My* parents' numbers. Even my sister was in there. I ignored them all as I sniffed back more tears and scrolled to the end, past Kip's name all the way to Valerie's.

I hesitated over the phone icon. I hit the message one instead.

**Me: Hey it's Katrina. Can you talk?**

There. Now she'd know.

My phone rang almost immediately and more tears, bigger ones that burned my cheeks fell as I answered it.

"Hey." My voice shook and I couldn't hold back my cries.

"What's wrong?" Valerie snapped. "Are you okay? Why are you crying?"

I sniffed, and it came out more like a snort and a laugh. Another laugh. That had to be two in a single day.

"I'm fine, I'm good. Or, well, I think?" Another snort-laugh fell from me. Valerie called my name, quieter this time, and this time I flinched at it.

"Please. I can't bear that name anymore." Odd because I'd snapped at Cole for *not* calling me it, but I liked the idea of this. Not being who I used to be. Not who Jonathan turned me into.

This time...today at least, I got to decide.

"Okay, honey," she muttered. "You're really okay?"

I sniffed and looked around the room with its bare walls and television I had never turned on. The only life in the room were the pictures of Cole's girls that as much as it hurt to see, I kept pulling out of the nightstand drawer and staring at.

"I don't know if that's the word I'd use to describe me right now."

"But you're safe, right? And getting better?"

That one took longer. Was I?

"Physically, I'm getting better, yeah."

"Okay," she breathed out through a sigh. "That's good, real good. And I'm glad you called. I've debated whether or not to call Cole, and I know he and Kip have talked, but you should know Jonathan's mad. And I don't want to scare you—"

"How mad?"

"Well, he's not going to the cops, and he's been questioned more by them since the good ones don't believe his story for a minute, so there's some suspicion *he* did something with you. People who helped you get out are staying silent though, and no one really knows what happened so if Jonathan takes the fall, I'm not sure I care, but you should know he's looking."

It came as no surprise, but that didn't help the fear. So much fear chilled my spine I jumped off my bed and rushed to the windows. I didn't dare peek out, just yanked on the cord that tugged the blinds closed and darkened the room.

"He won't let me go."

"He'll have to," Valerie quipped back. "That's not his

call to make. It's yours, and there's not a lot he can do when you're there. You're safe right? With Cole...he's been okay?"

Another round of emotion flooded me. The way he'd looked at me that morning. The care in his eyes along with the pity every time I flinched from him. The fact he wasn't backing down in trying to help. Or his honesty.

*Safe* wasn't a word I'd used to describe the way I felt around him at all. But the danger alarms were definitely muted.

"He'll come for me," I whispered. "I know he will. And I don't want Cole to get hurt."

I didn't want him hurt because of me for Jonathan's revenge.

"You know he will, too, Val. Especially with that stupid card I saved."

"Yeah, but you wouldn't have saved it if you didn't want that lifeline, as scary as it was. My advice?"

"You give crap advice," I muttered.

She did, most of the time. It usually ended up with me having one more drink than necessary. Her thinking a color would look good on me but it turned me into a clown.

"Shut up." She chuckled. "Listen to me and listen good. That man you're with would walk through *fire* for you. He'd take everything Jonathan swung his way, no matter the danger he was in to keep you safe. We wouldn't have let him go with you if Kip thought for a second he'd fall down on the job doing it. Take that lifeline you had the hope to reach for and hold on with all your might. I miss you like hell, but I'm super-duper proud of you. You deserve this chance."

I wasn't sure I deserved much of anything. But that stupid lingering question made me consider otherwise.

*But what if...*

"How's Kip?" I asked. "Jonathan doesn't suspect you guys?"

"He does. He's pissed and has shut Kip out on anything other than absolutely necessary, but Kip has feelers out for a new job, and he's started working on ways to get Jonathan removed by the board. Don't worry about us. We'll take care of us, you take care of you, and when I can, I'll visit, okay?"

I hadn't realized how much I'd absolutely missed her until the thought of seeing her again was a possibility. "I keep freaking crying," I muttered as more tears fell and I sniffed and brushed them away.

"You've got years of holding it all in, my guess is it needs to come out so let it. Take a bath in your tears if you have to and let them wash away all the ugliness you've survived. But don't forget that, Trina. You've *survived*. And now you have a chance of something new."

"Okay, maybe you don't suck at advice."

She laughed into the phone. "Tell me about your hometown. You never talked about it much. You've ventured out yet? Seen anyone?"

"No, not really." I still told her about the drive Cole took me on. About the town as far as I could remember it, anyway. It'd changed and there was new growth all over. I told her about our talk, about not being ready to see really anyone else, and then I jumped on the bed when Bridget opened the door and popped her head in.

She waved and ducked out, same friendly smile that had more lines around the edges than I remembered.

When she was gone, I told Valerie I needed to go. "Cole's mom is here."

"Okay, but think of something for me?"

"What?"

"Your town is changing. It's growing. That's life. We change and we grow and sometimes we have to bury the rubble of what came before, but you can do that. You get to choose what you bury and how you grow and change from here, okay?"

I wasn't sure my mountain of rubble, as she was implying, was possible to bury.

*But what if...*

"I get you," I told her instead.

"Good. Then chin up, friend. We'll talk soon."

---

BRIDGET PAXTON HAD BEEN AS MUCH of a mother to me as my own had been, minus putting me in timeouts and groundings that came with being a real parent.

Now that I knew she was there, I debated whether to even face her.

And now I'd asked Cole to invite her here? To spend time with me?

What was I *thinking*?

She'd also be patient. She knew what happened. She was keeping secrets from my own family and my mom had been her friend since they sat next to each other at a women's Bible study way back when Mom and Dad had just gotten married and moved to town to take over the dying Baptist church. Not the easiest assignment for a new pastor from what I heard, especially with the town so small and people in the church so old, but somehow, from the time my parents moved to Deer Creek and by the time I left, the numbers in the congregation tripled and the ages slowly grew younger. Even the college kids who went to the small, private college nearby would cross the street to listen to my dad speak.

I'd heard the story so many times I could write it in my sleep.

So, I owed her, I guess? At least she deserved my politeness.

Inhaling a deep breath, I headed out of my room and up the stairs. Kitchen cupboards clunked closed and there was rattling of silverware, or someone digging through drawers and like this morning when I entered the kitchen, her back was to me as she dug through a drawer.

Mrs. Paxton had always worn dresses. I couldn't remember a time seeing her in pants. They weren't old-school matronly dresses, either, but they were cool. Usually sweater-like in the fall and winter, they always managed to look stylish and warm.

Apparently, nothing had changed, because her camel-colored dress floated around the tops of her feet. The long-sleeved arms were dolman-shaped, and she had a gold belt wrapped around her waist.

I cleared my throat, letting her know I was there and slid into the same stool I'd taken earlier.

Mrs. Paxton stood slowly, her dark brown hair now had slips of white and silver at the temples and her part. The rest of her was as pretty as ever. Her makeup, her skin, the curls in her hair and the way it shined. Time had aged her, but it had done it well. She had to be fifty-five by now, around there anyway, and only showed small signs of aging.

The smile she wore as her kind, shimmering blue eyes met mine was as sweet and joyful as it'd always been. "Hi there. Good to see you up on your feet."

My fingers tapped on the counter. "Thanks, for um...well...helping."

She blinked and pushed her glossy red lips to the side like she had a decision to make. It must not have taken long before she smiled again and gestured toward two reusable shopping bags on the counter. "I thought I'd do some baking today. Want to help?"

So we were going to ignore the fact she knew enough of my shame. The fact she must have seen me in the days when I barely woke and Dr. McElroy came frequently.

"I haven't baked in a long time," I admitted. Whatever ingredients were in those bags might as well have been foreign substances. Jonathan insisted I cook dinner, but dessert was out of the question, at least for me. He'd sometimes come home with cookies or pie from a bakery, but the first time I reached for them after thinking he was joking they weren't for me was a memory I never forgot after. "I'm not sure I know how anymore."

My mom and Mrs. Paxton had frequently baked for the church. Pies, cookies, all sorts of things around the holidays. Sometimes we'd made cupcakes for weddings.

Mrs. Paxton's look softened. "I'm quite certain there are things we never forget in our lives. Baking is one of them."

I had a feeling she had a whole bunch more lessons than baking to imply in that, but I wasn't delving too deep.

Not today.

Getting out of bed was enough.

But still...I could try.

"I'm not sure how much help I can be. But remind me? Please?"

"It'd be my pleasure." I figured that was for a whole lot more than baking, too.

"Thanks, Mrs. P." I blinked back tears.

Her eyes shined with her own, and she turned away and sniffed.

When she turned back, her watery eyes were gone, and her joyful expression was firmly in place.

"All right then," she said. "Let's get baking."

# TWENTY-FOUR

## COLE

I prepared myself for the same eerily quiet home I'd returned to for the last two weeks. Sometime between getting in my truck this morning, chasing down a couple teenagers who decided to skip school and throw their families and the school into a panic, and finishing up paperwork on a couple other call-outs, I'd convinced myself that this morning had been a dream.

There was no way Trina sat at my kitchen counter eating an entire, single slice of bacon. She hadn't smiled at me, and she hadn't stood at the top of the stairs asking me why I was being so nice to her.

So it pretty much shocked me back on the heels of my feet when I opened the door from the garage to the sound of laughter and the scents of sugar, spices, and what could only be Mom's homemade lasagna and bread. Her own SUV was still outside, so I knew she was still there, I'd just expected to find her quietly knitting a new sweater for the girls or something.

Not laughing.

Not laughing *with* Trina...because that was definitely the second voice I was hearing.

"Hello?" I called out, as I slipped out of my boots.

"Up here, dear!" my mom called back. "Dinner should be ready soon and your dad is joining us, too."

I skipped a couple of stairs in my hurry to get up there. Was this really my life? My reality? Trina sitting at the table with both my parents again?

I blinked a couple of times when I reached the living space, and sure enough, she was there.

Trina was sitting with her back to me, on the bench at the dining table Elle and June usually fought over, peering at me almost warily over her shoulder. But her color was good. Her cheeks flushed. There was some kind of... glow... about her.

"Hey," I said, and hung up my keys.

Her eyes flicked to my belt, to the gun at my hip and then down to the floor. "Hi."

*That sound.*

It was so much better. Not boisterous, and it was only two tiny simple letters, but there was a timid life to it.

Heaven. It was better than anything I could have imagined after last night.

"Dinner will be ready in fifteen. Trina and I made pies and cookies so don't eat them before the girls get back, and your dad will be here any minute. He's stopping at the store for some more drinks."

"More?" My brows rose. "How much have you already had?"

"None. Yet." My mom chuckled and tossed down a playing card. There was a face-down deck between them and a stack of cards in each of their hands.

I had no idea what they could be playing, but they were

doing something. Trina was out of her room and smiling, as little as it was.

And soon, I'd be with my family and her, enjoying a meal together.

"I'm changing. Be back in a second." That was said to Trina, who nodded and then quickly turned back to the cards in her hand.

I reached my room, closed the door, and shortly after, my mom shouted, "WAR!"

"Well, that explains the game," I muttered.

Still, I was grinning.

Hope bubbling.

Maybe it was a foolish hope, built on the dreams I had as a teen, but knowing my dad was coming over, my family and Trina were going to all sit down and eat dinner together. The only thing I could figure that would make that day better was if the girls were there to join us.

Soon.

Soon they would be.

___

AS MUCH AS I'd wanted to slide into the bench next to Trina, I took my normal spot with my back to the kitchen at the head of the table. My mom stayed across from her, my dad at the other end.

He'd showed up with a couple bottles of wine, some light beer, and managed to say hello to Trina like it wasn't the first time he was seeing her in twelve years, looking healthy, smiling, and sitting at my table.

Bless them for being able to act so normal when I knew they were feeling anything but. They kept it up all through dinner, too, sneakily tossing in news of town that we all already knew, brief mentions of people, and who was running what these days. No one too close to Trina, and no mention of her parents, but it was clear they were trying to make things as normal as possible for her while also filling her in on how the town had changed.

Like in the truck with me last weekend, she mostly stayed quiet, but there was interest in her expression versus the deadness I'd seen before.

I still had a dozen, if not a hundred, questions for her and still wanted to know why she'd fallen asleep in June's bed, but the questions could wait.

They could wait a lifetime if she kept giving my mom that soft, timid smile.

Trina stood from the table and began gathering and stacking plates. "Thank you for dinner, Mrs. P. It was lovely."

She reached for my plate, but I set my hand on her arm. "Don't."

Instantly, her face paled, white as the snow, and the plates in her hands began to shake. "I was going to clean up."

I shook my head.

"I'll clean," I told her. "You two have spent all day in the kitchen."

She opened her mouth to say something back, possibly to insist, but the light dimmed in her eyes, and she flicked her gaze toward my parents. "Umm..."

She swallowed, hands still trembling until I finally slid the plates from her before she dropped them. When I had them in my hands, she stepped back. Trina glanced at my parents, then me, and rolled her lips together. "I'm supposed to clean."

Her voice had gone quiet, and in my periphery, Mom's brows tugged closer with concern.

"You don't have to," I assured her, and I tried to quiet my voice, but when she got like this, my ire spiked. Seriously, what did that monster *do* to her?

How had she been treated?

I had a killing urge to know, and yet it was probably better I didn't. Not if a simple touch and correction from me had her shaking like a leaf.

"Trina," I rumbled her name, low enough to get her attention, hoping I didn't scare her. "You can do anything you want in this house, but *nothing* is expected okay? You and Mom spent hours in the kitchen today, and you know her rule."

"Whoever doesn't cook cleans," my mom said, but even she was quieter, worried.

Trina blinked. Glanced at my mom and then nodded.

"Okay." She turned back to me. "But I still want to help."

"I'll let you help," I told her. But she wasn't doing it alone.

I wanted her to learn she never had to go it alone again if she didn't want to.

"But I'm doing it with you," I said, so she knew I'd be with her. Close. My kitchen wasn't huge and the space to rinse and load was tight.

"Okay," she finally whispered.

From his spot at the table, Dad stood. "I'll get you ladies more drinks. Bridget isn't cackling yet, so she's not nearly done for the night."

It was a joke to lighten the mood. My dad was good at that.

"I don't cackle," my mom cried out, laughing. But there it was...the hint of a cackle.

My lips twitched and I grinned at Trina. "She totally cackles."

Her grin fought for its appearance, and then she turned to my dad. "I'd like to hear this."

There she was.

My brave, beautiful, *fighting* girl.

---

IT WAS after my parents left. A quick hug from my mom and a gentle pat on the back from Dad shortly after the kitchen was cleaned up, and then they were out the door. I half expected Trina to head back to her cave downstairs, but instead, she curled up into a corner of the couch. Glass of wine nearby, I noticed she drank them slowly, and by the time she got a refreshed glass, what had to be left in it was too warm to drink.

Which meant she wasn't drunk by any means, but maybe loosening up and relaxed a bit.

"I forgot how nice your mom was," she said.

I took the chair on the far side of the room near the fireplace. We'd be getting snow soon and it'd be on every night, but for now it was off with a cool draft coming from it. It was also the farthest away from Trina I could get, but I was too afraid if I moved closer, I'd move *too* close. So there I sat, across from her, and yet she hadn't run and that alone was progress.

I sipped my beer, my second and last of the night. "They're good people."

"She told me your daughters are a handful and a half and that June's just like you."

Of course she did. Bragging came with becoming a grandmother. At least it did in Mom's world. But the last few times she'd brought up my girls, it hadn't exactly gone well. "Ella's quiet. She takes everything in. She's soft-spoken like her mom, but June... she's..." I sighed and spun the beer in my hands. "She's having a hard time with the divorce. But she's only four, so she doesn't get why I don't live with Mommy anymore. But yeah, she's more likely to paint the walls with nail polish or kick a soccer ball through the house window."

Which she'd done already.

"You get them back Sunday."

We'd briefly talked about this. "I do."

"You said only your parents and Marie know I'm in town."

"That's true."

"But you have kids...and kids don't really keep secrets."

Ella was a vault. June, on the hand...June had a loud voice that currently had a lot to say about everything. Which made me realize where she was going with this. "Not really, and not well. No."

She reached for her wine, and her fingers tappity-tap-tapped on the glass. "That means my parents will learn I'm here. Probably quickly."

Her top lip curled, and then she blew out a breath. "I don't know if I can do that. I don't know if I can see them. I'm not...I don't..."

Screw the distance. I stood and made my way to the coffee table in front of her. I wasn't touching her, but I could, and I also realized she didn't jerk back from my quick movement which was a win in itself.

"My mom called me, and I never, not once, called her

back." Tears. More freaking tears slipped out of her eyes and onto her cheeks.

I worked my jaw back and forth. There was only so much assurance I could give before she needed to start learning truths for herself. "You wrote me letters and I never wrote you back. Do you hate me?"

She blinked in surprise. "You...what?...You remember that?"

Better than remembered...I kept every single one. I kept pictures and mementos and movie stub tickets and all the dumb shit she and I had ever experienced together. "I was still in my angry phase then," I said, and a slow smirk curled my lips up.

She blinked at me. Twice. Then huffed. "It's not the same."

"It's not," I agreed. "But your parents are the same people too. Just like my mom was. The only thing that hurts them is not knowing where you are and how you're doing. I can guarantee you that."

"I'll have to do it. Won't I? Get brave enough to go see them?"

Or have them come here, but I doubted logistics were her question. "If you plan on staying, yeah. And I know you're going through a lot, but you get it done quickly, and it won't weigh on you so much either."

I hoped it brought her some relief, some healing. She'd already come so far in a day. The fact she was even *considering* seeing them was huge.

"I'll think about it."

I relaxed back onto my seat on the coffee table. "Did Mom mention Ashley to you at all?"

"No. I didn't ask, either."

"She married Robbie. They're foster parents too.

They've adopted one child and currently have three siblings with them in their care."

"That's amazing," she whispered. "Ashley would be good at that. She was always so...soft."

"Still is. She teaches at the high school with your sister."

"You're still friends with all of them then?"

"Yeah." I scratched the back of my neck. "Robbie and I, definitely. We see each other all the time. The four of us... Marie and I and them used to hang out pretty regularly."

"Oh." Her lips formed a perfect O. "Is she...what does she think about all this? Me...and well..."

"She's a good woman, like I've said, and I wasn't all that great to her, and some of those things are only now becoming clearer, like hanging out with Ashley and Robbie so much with her. She was hurting for a long time, and I'm only now getting how hard being married to me was. That's my fault, though, and if she gets mad at anyone, guarantee it'll be me, but even then, Marie's a good person, and she's not bitter or anything."

Her eyes trailed to my large windows. Outside was dark, pitch black except for the occasional twinkling of house lights through the branches. Soon we'd be seeing ski lifts moving and their lights shining bright until the lifts closed at night, but for now, those were dark, too.

"You all did exactly what you wanted. And are happy."

"We all have our days." Before she tunneled back into the empty void, which I could see flickering at the edges of her eyes, leeching away the color in her skin, I held out my hand. "Can I show you something?"

Her head turned to me; eyes wide. "What?"

"Something. Come with me." I wiggled my fingers.

Slowly, she set her glass down on the table next to her and stood.

It didn't escape me that she didn't take my hand, and I let it fall to my lap before I stood.

"Where?"

"You been outside much yet?" Since I now knew she lurked, at least in my daughters' room, she probably had.

"No. I didn't want to be seen."

As if that could happen. Not here.

I led the way to the sliding back door and flicked on the lights. A string of white Christmas lights lit up outside, draped and wound all over the deck railings and from poles settled equal distances apart. They created a soft glow, but not bright enough to take away what I wanted to show her.

Thank goodness it wasn't cloudy.

Trina's laugh was as bright as the lights as we stepped outside. "What are we doing out here?" She crossed her arms over each other and rubbed away the chill. "It's cold and dark."

"Maybe." I gestured to the sky. "But see that? You've spent so much time in the city, I bet you forget what the stars look like."

Her smile faded. I didn't let her linger on her years living in cities. "I come out here at night. Morning. Doesn't matter when, because I think you've forgotten this, too, but that's okay. The point is, I come out here to be amazed. To think. To be reminded of my rightful place in the world."

"And what's that?"

I spun, head tipped to the dark sky, millions of flickering stars in the distance. "That we're small. We're insignificant. We're vapor in the span of time."

"How uplifting," she muttered, but I swore there was a tease in it, so I turned to her, stone serious.

"We'll all be gone in a blink, the good, the bad, the happy, the miserable. Life and fulfillment come from the decisions you make with the choices in front of you. You've had a lot of corrupt and wicked and horrible choices in front of you it sounds like, and I'm not judging you for that. But today, tomorrow, the day after—all you have to do is step onto a different path, make a different choice."

I stepped toward her, careful not to reach out, not to take her hand, not to do anything that could wipe away the oddly-focused expression on her face. "You can *choose* something that brings you happiness. It's just one simple choice in the moment. That's it."

"I'm not sure I'm the best decision maker."

"Then lean on the people who love you to help you."

She blew a breath into her hands and then scrubbed them together. I barely felt the chill, but it'd been years since she'd lived in the cold, so I didn't blame her. "You think I should call my parents."

I shrugged. "Not sure there's anyone out there who loves you more than them."

Except for maybe me. But I'd pressed that enough.

She turned toward the railing, her profile to me, head tipped up to the sky, and I decided to give her all the time out there to think about what I said.

But I left her with a lifeline, and hopefully, she'd choose to grab on to it.

"No one hates you, Trina. No one's mad at you. They're all worried and sad, but anyone in this town you reach out to for help, they'll break their backs and their necks to help you heal. I think if you take a second to truly remember the community and family you came from, you'll stop being so scared about how they'll react, because you already know."

# TWENTY-FIVE

## TRINA

I chickened out. I stared at my phone after Cole left for work again. After I joined him for another breakfast. After I didn't bother offering to clean up once he started to do it himself like the *last* place he wanted me was in his kitchen. After I asked him if his days were busy, and he responded with a look that said it all. Deer Creek might have been growing, but it wasn't exactly a metropolis, overflowing with constant crime. Still, I sensed he adored his job.

Who could blame him?

He was doing the very thing he'd dreamed of doing since he went to Deer Creek's Spring Time Daze festival and not only got to go for a ride in one of our town's cop cars, but went home with a shiny police badge sticker.

I couldn't dwell on the fun we had as children though. The intimate moments we shared as we grew older. The distance that separated us before I left.

The days were counting down until his kids returned. The days were counting down on my ability to avoid everything, but changing course wasn't always as simple as turning around.

The road behind me was paved with craters I couldn't avoid. It was lined with destruction and darkness, so thorny and jagged, one wrong turn could slice the remaining parts of me in two. The path ahead wasn't much brighter. Riddled with fears, a single misstep and I'd be thrown right off a cliff.

Which was why I couldn't call my parents.

Not yet. Not until I made other calls first.

Which was why I was still staring at my phone, the contact number pulled up. Spending time with Mrs. P hadn't been bad. It'd actually been enjoyable. Sure, there'd been moments of awkwardness and times when I caught her looking at me like she had something to say, but overall, I'd had fun.

Logically, I believed Cole. I doubted people hated me. That wasn't my largest hurdle. The problem was I still hated myself, and that was a root I'd let burrow so deep inside of me no shovel could dig it out. I could tear off the stems and offshoots, but that root would remain.

It'd taken years to stop having nightmares of the decision I made when I left Deer Creek, and by then, my nightmares were plagued with more horrifying memories. They still came, yanking me from sleep in a cold sweat almost nightly. Somehow, when I'd been living my nightmare with Jonathan in the bed next to me, they hadn't come. But now, almost every night they clung to me. I couldn't shake them, and it didn't matter that my bruises healed a little more every day, or that my knee was improving and the pain in my ribs didn't feel like a stab to my gut with every cough or sneeze.

The injuries inflicted on me by Jonathan were the least of the things I needed to move beyond.

Before I could talk myself out of it again, I pressed *Call*.

It rang twice, before she answered. "This is Dr. McElroy. How can I help you?"

"Doctor, hi, this is Katrina...Trina. Actually, it's Trina." Good grief. Even I didn't know what to call myself anymore.

A whole new flood of nerves and fears crashed into me as the doctor's soft sigh came through the phone.

"Good morning, how are you today? Is everything okay?"

At least if she noticed my nerves she ignored them. "No, well, yes. I mean, I'm *fine*, but I guess I do need your help."

"What is it?"

"I, uh, well, I threw away the lists of therapists you gave me, and I guess I'd like to see if I can have another copy?"

There was a brief pause, followed by another pleased sound. "Of course, Trina."

"I think maybe I'm ready, or closer I guess."

"Well, that's lovely to hear, sweetheart. And there's no rush, you know. Your physical health comes first, but of course it'd be good for you to talk to someone who can help when you're ready. Or when you think you might be getting there. I'll get the list to you as soon as we're off the phone. I assume you're calling from a cell?"

"Yes. I am. Cole got it for me."

"Good. I'll text it right over, but while I have you, how about we talk about the rest of your injuries. Are you doing your therapy? For your knee?"

We spoke for a while. She went back over the exercises, movement, and pain I should be experiencing and reminded me to wear the brace as much as I felt comfortable, but not to rely on it. She skipped over the reason for my call so smoothly, I almost forgot I'd even asked for it until we hung up, and a few minutes later my phone dinged with a text.

I jumped at the sound, and then laughed at myself as I pulled it up.

There it was.

Lists of doctors as close as the first neighboring town, and then more in Boone, and some even further away who could do virtual.

A step.

I'd taken a step, and somehow, it felt like a leap.

---

THE DAY CRAWLED BY, but it wasn't the same kind of crawl it'd been for the last couple of weeks. Or the last few years, really. There wasn't dread in the waiting, and somehow, there'd been a lightness to it. Once I got off the phone with the doctor, I did my exercises like she'd suggested. I spent the rest of the day in front of the television. My days with Jonathan hadn't been extremely busy, but I'd always had certain things to do that were expected of me. Long since retired from modeling at his demand, he'd insisted the house was spotless and that I managed everything else. There were days I'd spend with Valerie, and time I'd spend attending events for him. Exercising was always planned into my day, and without all the structure and the fear of him jumping out of every dark corner, I wandered around Cole's house lost.

He clearly cleaned, so there wasn't much to do. I did a load of my own laundry, and though his mom offered to come back and spend time with me, I declined. Surely, she had things to do other than babysit me.

Which was fine.

But it left me alone all day, and without a whole lot else to do, I helped myself to a canned soup for lunch, and then scoured his fridge and pantry for something I could make for dinner. Last night's heavy lasagna dinner meant I had to take it easy the next few days, but he had spinach and chicken, so at least there was something.

I prepared that to thaw and then turned on his television. I flipped through his streaming services, thankful I could figure everything out on my own, and was in the middle of an episode of *Bridgerton*, when my phone rang.

Cole's name popped up, and I grabbed the phone.

"Hello?"

"How's it going? Having a good day?" he asked, as if it was impossible for anyone to have a bad day.

I shook off the weirdness, the fact I hadn't had a good day in a decade. "It's okay. I...um... I called the doctor earlier—"

"What? What's wrong? Did you get hurt?"

Of course he'd assume the worst. "No. It's that I um, I threw away the therapist list a while ago, so I had her resend it to me."

"Oh." At first, I swore there was disappointment, but when he spoke again, his voice was deeper. Softer. "Good, Trina. That's really good. Proud of you."

"Thanks." A lump swelled in my throat, and I bit down on the inside of my cheek. "How, um...how's your day?"

"Not bad. Things will pick up soon with tourists and snow. Listen." He cleared his throat in a way I knew he wasn't gearing up to share good news, and my chest tightened. "I forgot about this, but Robbie called me today. He and I were supposed to go hang out tonight."

Robbie. I could picture the man...at least the eighteen-year-old version of him. Probably dressed in work boots, tight jeans, and a thick flannel, he'd been close to Cole's size, but had a more boyish, rounded face when we were kids.

"Oh. Well, okay." Because he could hang out with Robbie whenever he wanted.

"I was wondering how you'd feel if they came over. I haven't said anything," he said quickly. "But I thought, dinner with my parents went well, and one of their parents can watch their kids. It'd be chill. Pizza or something, and there's a football game on, so..."

I let him trail off and clung to the silence through the phone. He wanted this. It was obvious. And yet if I said no, he'd meet Robbie at a bar, probably Max's Tavern or somewhere newer. Maybe at a place I didn't know existed and held no memories for me, but a lifetime for both of them.

"I almost called her today," I admitted to Cole. "Stared at her number for the longest time, and then I couldn't..."

I'd thought of her though, so many times over the years. She was furious with me when I broke up with Cole and didn't understand why. She was only one in a hundred people who would never know my darkest secrets.

"She'd be happy to see you," Cole said. There was that soft tone again. Coaxing.

He wanted this. He wanted this so desperately, and yet I froze. My fingertips clung to the phone. Twelve years of memories I had with all of them flashed through my mind.

"It's hard," I admitted. "And scary."

"I know it is. It'll get easier."

Shoot. My vision was blurry, and I could hardly see the screen across from me. I reached out and paused the show and sniffed. What would I *say* to her? To friends I abandoned and whose lives I vanished from with no explanation.

"Does Robbie know?" I asked Cole. Because they'd *really* hate me then. For sure.

"Told him a long time ago, back before Marie came along. I assume he told Ashley, yeah, but I never asked, and she never brought it up."

"They foster kids," I whispered. "They'll…"

"They won't," he assured me. "They might have, back then, but they're the same good people you've always known."

"If it goes bad—"

"It won't, but if it does, they're gone. Trust me on this, like you've been doing."

I hadn't been actually. I just had no other options and no choices considering I'd gotten the crap beat out of me in my home and then woken up in a strange bedroom. The hospital was a blur, and I still couldn't remember the plane ride.

But I was trying. The last twenty-four hours I'd tried a lot.

Maybe I could do this too.

"Okay," I rasped. "I'll try."

"Proud of you, Trina."

And there it was again—that sensation that wasn't quite right, but it wasn't entirely wrong, either.

"Thanks, Cole."

# TWENTY-SIX

## COLE

She'd agreed. I still couldn't believe it.

"Everything okay?" Eddy asked. I glanced at him and then back to the phone still in my hand. The call had ended, but I was still gaping at the app-filled screen.

"Yeah. I have a quick errand to run."

"Where we headed?" He pulled his feet off his desk to the floor.

"Not *us*, me."

"Oh, come on. It's so dang slow today." Eddy waved his hand in the air, but the gesture was unnecessary. It *was* slow today.

It was also a Thursday at two o'clock in the afternoon, and we were a town of four thousand.

"It's always slow this time of day, unless we're in the middle of some kind of storm. I have something personal to do, and then I'm picking up the girls and taking them to Marie's."

"Fine," he huffed, crossed his arms over his chest and pouted. The move was so similar to June's I had to tell him.

"Screw you," he muttered, and stuck his tongue out at me.

"See? You two have clearly spent too much time together."

I pocketed my keys and phone and stood from my desk chair. "I'll be back by four. Stay out of trouble until then."

Eddy picked up a pen and spun it in his fingers. "I make no promises, partner."

That didn't surprise me. He was as likely to end up neck-deep in a barrel of trouble as he was to be the one pulling people out of it.

I jogged out of the small station and since this was a personal mission, I jogged past our SUV and went to my truck. Five minutes later, I was pulling up to the new high school, and our SRO was opening the door for me. "Something wrong?"

"No, Bill, I'm good." Since the middle and high schools were right next door, Bill Thomas spent his day moving between both schools. We'd tried to petition the county for more resources, due to school safety, but so far that hadn't happened. "I'm here for personal reasons. Need to talk to Ashley."

"Get a visitor sticker and check in at the front desk. Mable will help you out with that. You know where her room is?"

"I'm good. Thanks."

I'd been in this school dozens of times, for both minor offenses and scares and athletic events. I checked in with Mable, a woman who went to church with my parents and Trina's, and after a brief, socially polite conversation, headed toward Ashley's room.

Mable had checked her schedule, and she wasn't in a planning time, but this didn't matter. I had to drop this news to her, and there was no way a phone call would suffice. I could have gone straight to Robbie, but this was news Ash needed to hear from me.

Mostly because Trina wasn't entirely wrong. Ashley *was* pissed at her, had been for a lot of years, and while I never knew if Robbie told her about Trina's abortion, the fact that Trina took off and ghosted us all was still painful for Ashley.

I knocked on her door, and a few seconds later, a student opened it, eyes turning large and round as she saw my badge. "No one's in trouble," I murmured, the first thing I *always* found myself saying to people and ducked my head in the door. Ashley was sitting at her desk, laptop in front of her, and all the kids' heads were bent to their own on their desks.

As soon as I entered, she glanced my way, and her face paled. "Robbie—"

"He's fine. It's all good. Everyone's all good." I smiled at the entire classroom. "Need to talk to you for a few minutes, okay? But swear, it's all good."

Ashely shook her head, blinked a couple of times, and then scanned her classroom as she pushed her rolling chair away from her desk. "Keep working on the test. No cheating. I'll be right outside, but don't forget that I've got eyes in the back of my head."

I chuckled. Spoken like any mom, and I didn't doubt her. Ashley knew *everything*.

She met me outside her classroom but kept her foot lodged in the door. School safety protocol said all doors had to be locked, and while I knew she had a key on her somewhere to get back inside, this was to ensure the kids did, in fact, not cheat like she'd said.

"What's up?"

"I only have a minute to tell you this, and you're going to have to process everything really quick, so I'm sorry to do it here, but I couldn't wait. You with me so far?"

"Yeah, Cole. Sure. What is it?"

"Trina's here."

"What?" she shrieked. "Why? *Here* here? Like *home*?"

"Calm down." I chuckled. "And yeah. She's at my house. Has been for a couple weeks now."

"Weeks!?"

I glanced through the glass part of her door and saw several kid's head whip back to their laptops. "It's a long story, but yes. She's *here* at my home, and you have to know the reason she is because some friends of hers down in Georgia helped get her out of a real bad situation."

"How bad?" Ashley's face, like I predicted, turned from shocked to worried and then scared. "How bad, Cole?"

"Real bad. Let's just say if my gun happened to accidentally discharge around her husband, soon-to-be-ex, hopefully, I should get a medal and not a citation bad."

Her chin wobbled, and her pale blue eyes darkened. "Stop. That's not funny."

"I'm not kidding. It's *bad*, Ash. But she's getting better, too."

"She's here? Home?"

Tears fell down her cheeks, and her chin trembled. Damn. Maybe I should have had Robbie tell her. "She's been through a lot. More than I can even imagine, but I think she's been hurting and lost for a long time, and I need you to know that because I think she's getting better. Or trying to, and I think, well, I don't know if she's going to stay here, but I think she's definitely not going back."

"When you say it's bad." Ashley's voice quaked as she

spoke. "Do you mean bad, like the things you know that go on in this town you won't talk about, bad?"

We had domestic violence and all the other kinds of violence that all other towns in the world had, but still, yeah. "Worse," I confirmed. "But she's here. She's safe, and tonight, Robbie and I were going to go out and watch the game, but I thought maybe the two of you would want to come over. Pizza and drinks and football at my place."

Maybe not the football part. Not with Trina around. At least Georgia wasn't playing, not like I ever watched them anyway. One glance at Trina next to her husband in the owner's box had been enough for me to ban those games from my presence.

"She's there," Ashley whispered and wiped tears from her eyes. "Your girls?"

"They've been with Marie."

"Dang. How'd you keep this all quiet?"

Carefully. She didn't need to know it all. "I can't stay, Ash, I've gotta pick up the girls to see them for a minute, but I just needed you to know what's going on. And to see if someone can watch your kids. That is, if you want to see her."

"Wow. Of all the things I thought you'd tell me when I saw you, this isn't it, at all."

"I know."

"We'll be there. I'll call Robbie when I can. You okay? I mean..."

I scrubbed a hand through my hair. "It's Trina, and she's in my home." Where I hoped she'd stay, and that hope kept growing even while I tried to strangle it. "I'm good, mine-fields I have to sidestep around, but I'm better than I've been in a long time."

She blinked, and the sweet, caring friend I'd known almost my entire life reappeared. "I know, you know... Robbie told me."

"Don't bring it up. Don't even let her think you know."

Ash's chin wobbled again, and she sniffed. "I've missed her. Been really mad at her, and then angry, but mostly I've just missed her."

"And tonight, you'll get to see her."

She scrubbed her eyes, and I gave her that time to collect herself. Get it out. Eventually, she stopped, opened her eyes and smiled. "Tonight. I get to see her. Finally."

I leaned in and kissed her cheek. "You're the best, Ash. Have Robbie text me your pizza order."

"We'll pick it up and bring it with us. Think she'd still like Scalecki's?"

Scalecki's Pizza had been around as long as Deer Creek existed. Had to go up the mountain to the base of the ski slopes to get it, but it was worth the trip even in the snow and ice, it was that good.

Personally, I doubted Trina would eat something so heavy with carbs and crap from the way she ate like a bunny rabbit, but whatever. She had to get free of that, too, and Scalecki's could probably help.

I never met anyone who could resist it.

"Get all her old favorites. We'll see."

"Thanks, Cole. You're a good man. I hope she appreciates it more this time."

"We'll see." I shrugged, like I wasn't hoping for the same thing. Like I wasn't hoping her eyes would be open and she'd finally see the life I could give her, the life I'd worked to earn and have but had always felt like something was missing even with my girls.

THERE WERE few things brighter than the babbling of my girls in the back seat of my truck. I'd stopped at Mellie's on the way to get them and set aside two of the dozen cookies I bought for my girls.

Ella's face had melted chocolate on it, and June was still devouring her frosted and sprinkled sugar cookie.

Sending them back to Marie on a sugar high might not have been the nicest thing, but I was trying to soften the girls up to what was coming. There was no doubt Ella would be nice and roll with it.

June was the one I was worried about.

I pulled off into the parking lot of the town's park and threw my arm over the passenger headrest.

"Girls. I need to talk to you about something."

"You get hurt at work, Daddy?" As Ella asked, her eyes trailed over my face and the parts of my body she could see. "You look okay."

"I'm good, Ella. Something else. I have a friend staying with me at my house for a while."

"A friend!? Like Mr. Robbie or Eddy? I *love* those friends," June cried. "Eddy brings the best candy."

"He does." I chuckled and then shook my head. "No, it's not Mr. Robbie or Eddy. It's not someone you know, but it's someone who was friends with Mr. Robbie and Miss Ashley and me all the way back when we were little kids."

"Little like *me?*" June pushed her frosting-coated fingertip to her chest on her shirt. Whoops.

"Kind of. We were all young when we were friends."

"What's his name?" Ella asked. I glanced at her, the quiet way she asked the question as if she *knew*. And heck, maybe she did. She was always smarter than most kids her age.

I made sure to look her right in the eye. "Her name is Trina."

Ella, definitely my quieter and more thoughtful one, took a second. But when she spoke, she shocked me.

"Is she like Mommy's friend, Zack?"

"Who?" And I'm sorry...*what?*

"Mommy's friend, Zack. He stayed at our house once, too. But he didn't stay in the guest room. Mommy said sometimes friends like to have sleepovers."

"I think that's fun," June said. "I can't *wait* until I'm old enough for sleepovers."

Over my dead body would June have that kind of sleepover.

Words stuck in my throat and clawed their way out as I finally realized what they were saying. Marie had *friends.* Maybe that was why she wasn't as hurt as I expected her to be about Trina. When she told me she was doing well and moving on, I hadn't thought of exactly how *far* she'd been moving on, but this was good. Better than. Even if the awkward factor was skyrocketing.

"I think it's good your mommy has friends, too," I told both girls, choking down my surprise. "And right now, Trina's just a friend to me, too. I wanted you to know because you'll see her Sunday after church when I get you back, okay? And I didn't want her to surprise you."

"But I like surprises," June said. Her bottom lip pushed out into a pout, and I really wished I had my phone to snap a pic and send it to Eddy. I was right.

*Identical.*

"Don't worry, June. I'm sure there are lots more surprises coming your way some day."

"Goodie." She sucked the frosting off her fingertips, and I turned back to the front of the truck.

This had been easy.

Far easier than I expected.

Was it possible we were *all* moving on?

Lord, I hoped so.

---

IT WAS normal for Marie to meet us at the door when I pulled up to the house. It wasn't normal for me to follow the girls up, and as I did, with them barely stopping for hugs and kisses from their mom, her brows rose with a questioning look toward me.

"Everything okay?"

Oh. Everything was good. Just fantastic.

I smirked and leaned in, teasing her. "I hear you have a *friend*." Her cheeks paled, and I kept going. "And *sleepovers*."

"Oh." She huffed. Chuckled, and then her pale cheeks turned flaming pink. "Cole—"

"With a friend named Zack," I finished, and leaned back, smirking.

Clearly flustered, Marie stammered out, "I was going to tell you. It was an accident how they found out, I swear it, and they haven't seen him since."

I held up a hand, chuckling and making sure she could see I wasn't mad. "This is gonna be awkward for us all, but you're a good woman and deserve a good man. I'm just giving you a hard time."

"He's really nice," she said quietly and rolled her lips together. "I like him."

"Then he better be the kind of man deserving of you.

And if he's not, let me know. I know all the good hiding spots in these mountains."

"Shut up." She laughed and reached out to slap my shoulder. I let her have that and watched as she nibbled her bottom lip and glanced back toward the house. "You told the girls about Trina, I take it?"

"June seems pretty sad that we don't think sleepovers are nearly as fun as you do."

I stepped out of the way before she could slap me again.

"And before you tell me to shut up again, yeah, I did. I wanted you to know Ash and Robbie are coming over tonight. To see her."

"Oh." All previous humor left her face, and she blinked, then frowned. "That's good, right? I think, I guess?"

"It's a step." I didn't want to hurt her. Didn't want to tell her how excited I was about this and how it didn't feel like a step at all, but after voluntarily spending time with my mom and getting the names of therapists, it felt more like a giant leap.

"Good, Cole. That's good. I'm glad for her."

"I need to get going and head back to work. I'll see you Sunday?"

"Afternoon like always."

"And will I see Zack?"

She rolled her eyes and shook her head. "We're not there yet. Like I said, it was an accident the day the girls saw him. I'm moving slow."

Slow didn't sound like sleepover territory, but Marie was an adult, and after being married to me she deserved all the fun she could have. Besides, I trusted her and her judgment.

"You don't owe me explanations."

"Okay then. Sunday."

"Have a fun weekend with the girls."

"Have a good night," she said, turning to open the door. "I hope it goes well."

That made two of us.

# TWENTY-SEVEN

## TRINA

This was a mistake. Had to be. Nothing good could come from this. My head was a mess, my heart was racing. I couldn't get my conversation with Valerie out of my mind and now was *not* the time to be panicking, but there I was.

"You keep pacing in my kitchen, you're going to end up wearing a hole in the floor, and I'll be ticked if the fall breaks my projector screen."

Leave it to Cole to be so calm.

"I'm worried," I told him.

He kicked his feet up on his coffee table and grinned. "Really? Couldn't tell."

"Ugh." Of course he'd be calm. These were his friends he saw all the time. These were friends who loved him.

Sure, they'd once loved me, but he didn't know about the last conversation I had with Ashley.

*"I hope you go to New York and are as miserable as you've made Cole. You'll never find someone like that up there. I hope you fail and live a long, lonely, and painful life."*

She'd spat the words at me at graduation, when

everyone around us had clearly taken Cole's side in the break-up. Who knew Ashley had been so clairvoyant?

Not me. Not then. But that didn't mean the weight of her words hadn't hit me like a two-ton truck slamming into me, running me over, and then backing up to make sure I was done for.

Perhaps that was why I'd fought so hard when I got there. I'd wanted to prove everyone wrong. I'd wanted to return to Deer Creek a star. I'd wanted everyone, especially Ashley, to eat their words and be jealous of me and all I'd accomplished...

And look at me now...

My eyes burned and I spun, intending to take off down the stairs, but a warm hand wrapped around my arm.

"Hey," Cole said.

I froze at his touch, the surprise of it, and the strength in his hold.

He let me go and cursed. "I'm sorry, Trina. I didn't mean to scare you."

"I don't think I can do this," I whispered. "I can't face her again, and there's no point. Val said Jonathan is pissed and looking for me and if he doesn't know I'm here, he will soon. She said he already suspects it, and you're not hard to find, and now I'm putting you at risk. Your girls...."

Everyone. I was putting everyone at risk.

"Hey. Hey there." He reached out again and took my hand.

Warmth flooded my fingertips as soon as he entwined our fingers together and rushed straight to my rapidly beating heart.

"Come here, Trina. Look at me." He tugged on my hand, gently but firmly, and kept tugging until I was forced to turn.

I stared at his floor. It was clean because I'd spent hours making sure his house was perfect even though he'd come back home and told me I didn't have to clean for them.

I couldn't help it. I'd needed *something* to do to get rid of the anxiety choking me.

The floor and my sock-covered feet blurred in my vision, and I shook my head. "I can't, Cole. I can't do this."

His hand fell from mine and reached out. I forced myself not to flinch as it came up, and his thumb pressed to my chin. "Look at me," he repeated and pushed against my chin.

I shivered and fought against meeting his eyes as he lifted my face.

He was in front of me, so close. So handsome and as *good* as he'd always been, and I was... tainted.

I'd bring him nothing but ugliness, and it was so frustrating he couldn't *see* that.

"You're safe, and you're okay." He proclaimed the words like he believed them to the depths of his soul. "Jonathan can't hurt you. I won't allow it. And *no one* will hurt my girls. Absolutely not."

"You don't know him." My chin wobbled and his fingers brushed along my jaw. Another shiver sent shock flames to my chest.

Handsome wasn't strong enough to describe him. Beautiful too feminine, but as I locked eyes with his deep russet eyes, it felt like I could get lost in them. Lost in his promises and proclamations.

For once, I had the desperate desire to see what he saw when he looked at me. What made him treat me with such tender care and be so kind.

And that was maybe more terrifying than anything else.

Even Jonathan.

I sniffed and stepped back. His hand fell, but the warmth in his gaze only heated me further. "You're *safe* here, Trina. To do anything you want, be anyone you want to be."

He'd told me that before. I didn't believe it any more or any less this time. And that lingering, hopeful *what if* I'd spent all week pondering was suddenly nowhere to be found.

Doubts and fears assailed, and it had everything to do with the visitors who would be arriving any minute. Visitors I *had* to see. Maybe if Cole finally saw what I knew I would, he'd see the truth, too.

Everyone hated me and knew I was as worthless as I'd become.

"I need a second," I told him and wiped tears away.

"If you need more time, I'll call Robbie right now and let him know. They'll understand."

Please. That'd make them hate me more.

"It's fine," I mumbled.

Soon. He'd see the truth soon enough, and then maybe he'd finally stop his foolish hope I was something better than he believed me to be.

---

MAYBE I WAS WRONG.

Ashley's arms were around me, and I was crushed against her. She looked different but the same. Older but happy. As soon as she and Robbie entered Cole's house, Ashley ran up the stairs and threw her arms around me. Her purse slammed against my hip, and her tight embrace shot pain to my ribs, but she held on.

It took a while before I hugged her back, so shocked by

the smile I'd glimpsed on her face right before tears poured from her eyes.

"Hi," I finally managed to mumble, getting her hair stuck on my lip gloss.

She squeezed me tighter and cried. "You're here," was all she mumbled, hiccupping over her tears, and somehow, I found myself needing to comfort *her*. When I'd been so sure she'd want nothing to do with me.

There was only one explanation.

Cole told her why I was there.

I opened my eyes and found him and Robbie setting pizza boxes on the kitchen counter.

I'd recognize the green, red, and white boxes anywhere. Scalecki's was a local favorite, and where I'd had my first part-time job one summer.

One glance at the boxes and not only did my stomach rumble, but I could envision the kitchen and all the home-made spices and Louie Scalecki's boisterous Italian voice.

It smelled like *home* and heaven and peace and happiness and now, darn it... my own eyes were leaking tears.

I squeezed Ashley back and held on. "I thought you hated me."

She nodded against my shoulder. "I did. For a long time," she admitted, and I was thankful to hear the truth of it. "But that was a long time ago," she whispered, her voice nothing more than a rasp.

"Any chance you're going to let her go tonight so I can say hi?" Robbie's voice was a laugh, but there was a warning tone in it too, and when I glanced back at him, he was watching both me and his wife with a wary expression.

"I don't think so," Ashley said and then she pulled back. Her hands pressed to my cheeks and it was so *sweet*, so kind, I almost collapsed to my knees.

There was no anger at all in her eyes, just concern, and it didn't skip my attention that her eyes lingered too long on my yellowing bruises I'd tried so hard to hide. "I'm glad you're here," she finally said. "So glad to see you again."

"Me too," I mumbled, and maybe for the first time since I'd been back, I truly meant it.

"All right, all right," Robbie said and gently guided his wife to his side. "My turn."

He held out an arm, and I went to him, fell against his chest as he one-armed hugged me. Robbie was larger than he'd been in school and definitely stronger. His arm, draped across my back, holding me against his side, felt like a steel bar.

"Good to see you, kid. Good to see you." He held me tight, kissed the top of my head and then stepped back.

For once, I hadn't flinched at a touch or an embrace, and I'd let myself think of all that later.

"I'm a mess!" Ashley cried. She half-laughed and sobbed and headed down the hall. "I'll be back. Give me a second to get my face put back together."

She vanished into the hall bathroom and Robbie chuckled, watching his wife go. He smiled down at me. "Don't know what she's so worried about. Makeup, no makeup, smeared makeup, she's always beautiful."

What a lovely thing to say. "You're a good man, Robbie."

His smile turned cold and then wary. "It's good you can still recognize them."

"Robbie." Cole's voice was a warning shot.

Robbie kept his gaze on me, and it didn't soften in the least, but it wasn't scary. It didn't make me tremble with fear. He was honest, and I appreciated that.

"Let me get you ladies some drinks," he said and turned to open the fridge.

I followed more slowly, uncertain on my feet, of my position in this group.

Years ago, it would have felt so normal, but that was before.

In the time in between, they'd all grown up together and stayed close. They had kids. Cole had had a *wife*. I wasn't part of the crew anymore, and I wasn't sure I could slide right back into it.

But for now, the moment, the dinner...

It felt good to be included in something clean and pure and good again.

What was the harm in trying to enjoy it?

# TWENTY-EIGHT

## TRINA

What a wild few days it'd been. Dinner and the evening with Ashley and Robbie had gone so much better than I'd anticipated. Like dinner with Cole's parents, it'd been awkward. Memories were shared that had made me laugh along with them, but for most of the evening I sat back and watched. It was clear their bond had tightened in the last twelve years, and there were moments I wasn't included at all.

The only dark moments came when the football game came on. I should have known they'd want to watch, considering Cole had said that's why they'd planned on getting together. Cole and Robbie had loved football. But for some reason, it had taken me by surprise.

I'd frozen, watching the television screen across the table from me in my line of sight to the open living room as the announcers and Thursday Night Football music started. That it wasn't Georgia playing helped some.

But when I hadn't been able to relax a few minutes into the game, Cole reached over and hit the remote, blanking out the screen.

"Game isn't important," Robbie had said, watching me again with that wariness. "Teams suck anyway."

He'd flashed me a gentle smile, and I'd excused myself. The kindness, plus the pity, was almost too much to bear.

But dinner hadn't sucked completely. I'd eaten what felt like my weight in pizza, something that had made Cole smile at me in a strange way. The pizza might have been days ago, and I'd probably eaten since then, but considering what I was doing now, I swore everything I'd eaten in the last few days settled like an anchor in my gut, forcing my feet to stay in place.

And that place was on the sidewalk, wrapped in a thick, heavy coat in the icy cold breeze, arms wrapped around my stomach, unable to move another step forward.

"I can go first," Cole said, next to me, taking in the house in front of both of us.

Was he remembering the things I was? The afternoons we spent bike riding around this neighborhood all the way to the gas station to grab candy? The snow forts we built by the sidewalk that the plows would eventually smash as they went by and cleaned the roads after a snowfall?

Was he remembering the first time he kissed me? The night he and I went to Boone for our first solo date, and he'd driven me home in his old truck. One hand holding on to mine, the backs of my thighs sticking to his worn leather seats beneath my cutoff jean shorts. His air conditioner hadn't worked then, and it was the height of summer, so my hair was sticking to my neck, and the hot leather seats had burned my skin when I first sat down, but I'd smiled at him almost the entire way back to Deer Creek, his hand in mine, his smile occasionally flickering in my direction.

He held my hand as he walked me to the door and then stopped me before I reached for the handle. And it was there, at the door right in front of me now, where he bent his head, brushed his lips over mine, and told me wanted to be my boyfriend.

"What?" I swore he said something, but I was lost in memories. Good ones this time.

Ones I'd thrown away and forgotten until I was forced to face them again.

"I can go first," he said. "Talk to them if you need me to."

"No." I shook my head. "I have to do this."

Cole was getting his kids back tomorrow. My dad would probably be at the church working on his sermon. Kari could be anywhere, and it was because of her I hadn't called to give my parents a heads-up.

I needed to see them, but Kari would be too much. She and her perfect life and her own kids and husband. She and I had never been close growing up. She was older than me, our age separated by multiple miscarriages my mom had, so she'd been too old to be my friend, too old to share clothes and yet she was too young to babysit me like other older siblings. We were separated by that perfect gap where I was always the annoying little sister who invaded her perfectly clean room and irritated her when she had friends over.

She got straight A's and went to a small Christian college.

I struggled to get B's and wanted nothing to do with school after college.

She wanted to stay in this town forever and have babies and raise them in the church she grew up in.

I murdered mine and fled town to worse decisions.

No, I couldn't see Kari. Not yet.

"Are we going to do this today?" Next to me, Cole bumped his hip against me.

"Yeah." I laughed and shook my head. "I'm surprised neighbors haven't called or shouted at us."

Who knew how long I'd been standing on the sidewalk after getting out of Cole's truck? Granted, it wasn't like anyone could recognize me with the coat and my hood pulled up, but they'd undoubtedly recognize Cole.

"I'm scared," I muttered and started walking forward.

"Keep being scared and keep moving. The fear will go away."

He'd become wise in the years since I was gone, and I wasn't always sure how to handle this new, bigger, manlier, and calmer version of Cole, but right then, as I started up the sidewalk, I was thankful he was next to me. So thankful I reached out and grabbed his hand. He tightened his grip on me immediately, and I let that warmth rush through me again.

"Thank you," I rasped. "Thank you for saving me."

He tugged on my hand, and I glanced up at him. "I helped get you out of a bad situation, Trina. You're the one saving yourself. Take the credit where it's due and own it, okay? You're *strong* enough to do all this. You're brave enough to move on."

Great. Just what I needed. To be crying before I even saw my mom. "Sometimes you look at me, and then I look in the mirror, and I'm so confused because I don't see anything you do."

"Then you're not looking close enough." He bent down, got his face close to mine. Close enough I could count the whiskers growing on his unshaved cheek. Close enough I could see the gold flecks that rimmed his pupils. "When I look at you, Trina, I see *everything*."

"Oh my...God! Praise the Lord!"

I whipped my head toward the front door. The now

opened door. Only a glass storm door separated me from the woman who had her hands clasped in front of her mouth, her hair much grayer than I remembered with grooved lines around her eyes, but they were the same eyes.

It was the woman who'd always loved me beyond reason. The woman I'd turned my back on out of fear and shame.

I flashed her a shaky grin and held onto Cole's hand with all the strength I had.

"Hi, Mom."

And then I burst into tears.

---

I WASN'T sure how it was possible to have more tears in my body. I was certain I'd poured them all over my mom's shoulder as soon as Cole opened the door and guided me into her arms. Without him there, it was possible we'd both still be crying on opposite sides of the glass partition.

It felt like a lifetime ago, but only minutes, and yet between the time lapse, my father had walked in the back door, jolted at the sight of me and then more tears fell.

"My daughter has come home," he kept repeating, murmuring it while he held me in his arms.

"Dad—"

I was definitely sure that was the only word I'd spoken. Mom. Dad. I could say nothing but who they were. No explanations. I hadn't even gotten around to the apologies yet, or why I was there.

Cole was never far away, keeping an eye on all of us, bringing me tissues. Refilling waters.

My mom cupped my cheek where I was sandwiched so tightly in between them it was like they were afraid to give

me an inch of space for fear I'd vanish. "You're so beautiful," she whispered, "and you're *here*."

"I'm here," I repeated.

I was in my childhood home. Wrapped in the loving
arms of my parents, and I closed my eyes, believing that if I
opened them, all the stains of my past would be wiped
away.

If Mom could see the still-fading bruises beneath my
smeared and wiped-away makeup, she didn't show it. If she
knew the horror I lived with for so long, she didn't balk at it.

I'd hated Jonathan for many years, despised the lies I'd
believed and the foolish and disgusting choices I'd made to
prove something in my life, but it was in this moment,
between my parents, that my anger with him rose to the
surface.

I clenched my hands together in my lap and forced
down that searing pain rushing through me.

He'd taken me from these people. From people who
loved me and wanted the best for me. I'd let him, but he'd
done it.

He'd sliced off all the good things in my life, even if I'd
put up the blockade years before we ever met. He'd
completed the task.

All so I'd have no one to turn to when I was ready to be
free of him.

And I'd *let him*.

"I'm so sorry," I rasped and shoved my face into my
mom's shoulder. "I'm so sorry for everything."

"No apologies, sweetheart." I was wrapped in her arms
again and squeezed tight. I wanted them to keep squeezing.
Squeeze all the ugly, tarred regrets right out of me.

"Someday you can tell your story," my dad whispered in
my ear. "But today is not that day. Today is a day to cele-

brate. Our daughter we've missed so much and felt so much worry for is home, and we're so thankful."

My mom pulled back, eyes shimmering with more tears. It was a wonder we hadn't flooded the house.

I laughed at the thought and bit down on my lip.

"You are home, right?" She brushed wet, stuck hair strands off my face and her chin trembled. "You are *home*, right?"

I nodded, swallowed a ball of tears in my throat and glanced at Cole before looking back to my mom. "Yeah, Mom. I'm home."

Something warm rushed through me, trickled down my spine and spread through my veins.

I was *home*.

Now, I had to figure out what to do next.

# TWENTY-NINE

## COLE

The last forty-eight hours had been exhausting, and I was only a witness to the healing taking place. For Trina, I was certain she'd had too much. Falling asleep during the five-minute drive from her parents' house yesterday back to mine drove the point home to the point that once she'd taken a nap, I'd gotten food in her. After she'd had a chance to relax, I asked if we needed to push back today's round of mayhem and chaos and difficulty.

She shocked me to my core when she blinked, looking cutely confused by the suggestion, and then asked, "Why?"

Which led us to now, where she was downstairs blow-drying her hair, and I was restless with waiting for Marie to drop off the girls.

This could go so bad in so many ways. With June's insistence Mom and Dad should live together and Elle's cautious and always-seeing approach to people, they could take one look at Trina and love her to pieces because she was beautiful and sweet, or they could see how I felt about her and take off screaming, never to return.

My phone buzzed in my pocket, and I grabbed it. It was the station and since I rarely got called in on my off days and considering this one was from the chief, I took the call.

"Good morning, Sir. You've got Cole."

"Hey, Cole. Got someone here who needs to talk to you. Can you come in? Won't take long." There was a tightness to his tone that made my hackles rise.

"It's Sunday. This about a case?"

I'd had a couple DUIs over the week, one home break-in, but nothing too out of the ordinary.

"Think we should talk here. Can you come in?"

It could be anything, or nothing... or it could be the worst thing, given the fact I could read our chief like a book, and he wasn't giving me anything. "Need to get Trina somewhere safe," I told him.

He grunted, and it told me all I needed to know. "This gonna go bad for me?"

"Can't say. We'll talk once you get here."

"Be there as soon as I can."

I ended the call and inhaled a calming breath. It was Wolf. Had to be. Chief didn't hide things from me like this, and my guess was he couldn't talk freely. There was no other option.

I texted Marie. They'd still be at church, but I knew her well enough to know she'd see the text. **Getting called in. Keep the girls until I say otherwise. Thx.**

I headed downstairs, phone in hand, calling Robbie. My parents would be at church, too, and while Trina's visit with her parents had gone better than I'd expected, there was no way she was ready to head there after a service, not when half the church usually hung out at their house for a potluck lunch. But like me, Robbie and Ashley weren't weekly churchgoers, especially with all their kids, so I took the chance he'd be home.

Outside of my dad and my partner, I trusted Robbie more than anyone.

Besides, he had guns. Lots of them.

"Hey, what's up? Aren't you getting the girls today?"

"Need to bring Trina to your place. Can you keep an eye on her for a little bit?"

"Yeah. What's up?"

"Think her ex is in town. Chief called me into the station and was cagey on why."

His voice dropped, and acid came through the line. "That man is *here*? What for?"

The blow dryer turned off on the other side of the bathroom, giving me only a minute. "Can only think of one thing he wants and she's not getting anywhere close to him until I have a chat with them."

"Bring her here. I'll keep an eye out."

"Thanks, man."

"Anything for you two, you know that."

The bathroom door opened as I ended the call. Trina took one look at me, the phone in my hand, and her softly done, beautifully made-up face paled.

"What's wrong?"

I tucked my phone into my back pocket. "There's been a slight change of plans."

"Marie changed her mind, didn't she? She doesn't want me to see the girls." She came to me, sorrow and apology stamped all over her, and it didn't skip my notice that this was the first time *she* approached me. "I'm so sorry."

"It's not Marie." I shook my head and reached for her arms. Wrapping my hands around her biceps, her eyes widened. She also didn't flinch or tighten as I held on to her. "I got called in to the station. Chief needs to talk to me about something important."

No way was I telling her what I suspected.

Her large, vibrant blue eyes ping-ponged back and forth between mine. "It's work?"

"He didn't say." I might not tell her what I suspected, but I wouldn't lie, either.

"You're worried, though."

"Yeah. A bit."

"Okay. Can I do anything while you're gone? Get lunch ready or something?"

I shook my head. "I'm taking you to Robbie and Sarah's. We'll talk to Marie about getting the girls later.

"You're... why... *Jonathan*." She breathed his name, and her voice shook with the fear of simply mentioning him. "He's here, isn't he? And don't lie."

"I'm not sure it's him," I admitted. "But I need you somewhere safe in case."

"I should go with."

"Absolutely not."

"Cole—"

"No, Trina. Absolutely not. You're not seeing him unless you've called a lawyer and had divorce papers drawn up, and I know you haven't done that, and you're absolutely not seeing him at all, in person, if I have anything to say about it. And honestly, Chief didn't say who was there so I need to go and get it figured out, but in case he knows where I live, I don't want you alone right now until I can get things figured out. So just...trust me. Please?"

I was asking a lot considering a week ago she'd been exercising in case Jonathan came back for her and took her, but that was all the more reason not to leave her here alone, too.

I wasn't exactly hidden and difficult to find.

"You'll tell me everything that happens after?"

As she said it, she stepped back. I let her go, hating the doubt in her eyes. "You'll know what you need to."

"No." She shook her head and ran a hand through her long, straightened hair. "I need to know everything. Every word or I'm coming with you."

"That's not safe for you."

"It's not safe for me to not know what's going on. Please…I can't explain it, but I have to know. Every word."

Panic was rising, making her breathing come ragged and color her cheeks.

"Okay. I promise. I'll tell you everything."

------

IT TOOK ME TWENTY MINUTES, and while I'd hurried to get Trina to Robbie's and then double-backed to the station, I'd kept one eye on the road and one eye on my rearview mirror to see if anyone was following. I'd moved quickly to get this done, but hadn't rushed enough to make whoever was waiting for me think I was scared of them.

Screw Wolf and his money and his southern prestige and all the things he had and the parts of him that made him evil.

I pulled into the station, taking note of the few patrol cars that were there and a black, nondescript Tahoe. The urge to slide my own truck's keys down the side of it hit hard and fast and I quickly quelled it. Wouldn't do any good to damage a car that was probably a rental anyway. And I didn't need Wolf any more upset.

I'd dressed in jeans and a Carolina Ice Kings hockey T-shirt for the day, intending to be relaxed and normal for my daughters' introduction to Trina and had only thrown on my Carhartt coat on over it along with my own personal 9mm handgun. That might have been overkill, but when it came to this man, I wasn't taking chances.

The roads were quiet, the town gloomy. More snow was on the way and the slopes would be open any day. This was the calm before the tourist storm, but there was another storm rising inside of me as I opened the doors to the office and was buzzed through the secured door in the front entryway by Eline, our weekend office assistant.

"Chief's office," she said as the buzzer sounded, and I yanked open the door. Considering the size of our town, our station wasn't large. In fact, I could see the empty desks for all the officers and the offices for Captain and Chief on the far end.

My lip curled as I went straight to Chief's office. His door was closed, but the wall around it facing the bullpen was all glass so while I'd normally notice his mess of piles of first, this time it was the enraged look on his face while he leaned on his desk, arms crossed over his chest and the back of the man facing him.

A man dressed in a suit, hair well-styled and side-swept, and a body I'd seen before, not only on television, but right before he stopped into an elevator at the hospital.

This monster had nearly beaten the life out of Trina, and for him to have the *nerve* to show up in this town, demanding time with me, forced every single one of my de-escalation tactics to the surface.

It was either that or end up in one of my own jail's cells for assault. I had no doubt this man would press charges to the fullest extent of the law. Men like him who got what was coming to him always believed they could do no harm and didn't deserve a moment of pain.

I didn't bother knocking but went straight to the door and opened it. Keeping my eyes focused on our chief's face, I didn't spare Mr. Jonathan Wolf a single look.

"Chief. You wanted to see me?" I should have been given an award for how nonchalant I sounded.

"Mr. Wolf here has come because you have something that belongs to him."

"Huh." I settled my hands at my hips and shrugged. "Can't say I do."

The man next to me bristled, and I turned to face him head on.

There was no life in the man's steely and oily gaze. If this was how he'd looked at Trina for so long, it was no wonder she felt so beaten down. The problem was, he was the one covered in filth, not her.

"I believe you have my *wife*."

"Ah...my mistake. See, Chief here said I have something of yours, and your wife is a person with her own thoughts and attitudes, so I don't have *anything* that belongs to you."

"She is my wife, and it's time for her to return to where she belongs."

*Screw him.* "She is not a dog you bring to heel, Mr. Wolf. And Trina is perfectly happy where she is, so that's where she'll stay. And make no mistake, that choice is *hers* to make, not yours to demand."

I wasn't quite sure that was the full truth, but based on his assessing examination of me, I'd definitely struck a chord. "Not smart, Mr. Paxton. Leaving her alone."

At least he thought she was alone, but the fact he knew where she was at all was disconcerting.

"Bold of you to threaten me in a police station."

"What was the threat?"

Smooth. He was smooth. Good-looking for sure, and his suit cost more than I made in a year. In shape, lean, and built. He could have been a wax model in a museum he was so shiny and perfect.

Too shiny.

Everyone had flaws, and I knew his biggest one.

With a sigh, like I was a child, he tugged on one of his dress sleeves. "I would like to talk to my wife."

"I assume if she hasn't called you, she doesn't feel the same."

His lips pursed and he glanced back at Chief. "I believe I'll leave you to relay the rest of my message."

He faced me with a sneer I wanted to punch off his face. "You'll see me again. And soon. And I'm sure by the time of our next meeting, you'll have had a change of opinion."

"Or what?"

Jonathan glanced at Chief, back to me, and grinned. "Test me and find out. Tell Katrina to prepare herself for me. I'll be seeing her soon."

I stayed frozen while he opened the door to Chief's office and strolled right on out the front door. A few minutes later, the Tahoe in the parking lot pulled out and turned left.

"Where's he going?"

"Said he'll be staying close to town until his wife comes to her senses and quits her tantrum. I'm assuming he's got a rental somewhere nearby. We'll start searching for him, keep men on him."

"He'll have his own men somewhere." Man like Wolf wouldn't go up against the law, he'd have someone do it for him. "What's the rest of the message?"

"You should have told me more about what was going on and what you were involved in. Would have been nice to be prepared, Paxton."

"Probably," I admitted and stayed quiet. Waiting. I'd told them I had Trina and she'd been beaten, and I was taking time to help her out, but I hadn't gone into the specifics of how I'd *gotten* her.

Chief sighed. "He plans to press charges against you for kidnapping, trafficking an unconscious adult across state lines. And alienation of affection."

The last one made him smirk, barely.

"You got anything to say against the first two?"

"Technically, her friends set the plan up, I was just along for the ride. So...an accessory at best? But she is an adult, capable of making her own choices."

"Not if she was unconscious and drugged."

A muscle twitched in my jaw. She'd been both, definitely.

Chief scrubbed a hand over his thinning hair and grimaced. "Man like him won't give up until he gets what he wants."

"Yeah, but a man like him doesn't usually show up and make those threats, either. He must have something else at play."

"Where's his wife?"

"*Trina,*" I stressed, because I was *never* going to call her that when it came to him, "is safe at a friend's house."

"Robbie's?"

"Dad was still at church and Robbie's the best shooter I know."

Chief sighed and looked at his booted feet. "Know you care about her, and I'm not the only one who's happy she's back in town, Cole, but this could cause problems."

Big problems, especially if I was arrested and left Trina unprotected. "How much help can I get ensuring she's safe?"

He pushed his lips to the side. "I'll call Boone's chief and see if he has any men he can spare. Would call the county but we're turning the corner into an election year, and you never know how politics play into decision-making."

Our county sheriff's office was filled with good men, but Jonathan Wolf was powerful, and even the best men could fold under the right kind of pressure.

It was still a risky call. Which meant I'd be calling Kip as soon as I left the station.

"That all?" I asked.

Chief gazed out the window, lingering on nothing and finally brought his gaze back to me. "Folks in town are starting to whisper. Word's getting out. How's she doing?"

"Healing, I think," I told him. "But she's got a long way to go."

"People heal quicker with loved ones around them."

"Think she's taken all of that she can get for a while."

"I think what I'm trying to say is, you keep her hidden away too long, and the gossip that starts won't help her any. Besides, you get her out and around people, that's more eyes on her. More of our own looking out for another."

"Right." I got it loud and clear.

It'd be a lot easier for something to happen if she was tucked away on my mountain. Something that could put me in the line of fire, too, and while that was the last thing I cared about, it'd bring more questions to our office, and no one wanted that. He had a point, especially if Jonathan stayed close. "Anything else?"

"Enjoy the day, sorry to drag you in here when I know you got a long one ahead of you."

I held out my hand and shook Tim's, and with that done, hurried out of the office, barely sparing Eline a wave as I left.

Kip's number pulled up, it was already calling him before I climbed into the truck.

# THIRTY

## TRINA

My heart was racing, and I couldn't sit still the entire time Cole was gone. Now that we were back in his truck, everything was magnified. My fears. My memories.

All the things I'd done before that had somehow led me right back to this man driving me through a town I remembered so vividly and yet was so different.

Growing.

Maybe, somehow, in the last week, I was starting to do that, too.

"You need to tell me," I whispered. My hands were tangled and twisted together, knuckles aching on my fingers. I couldn't sit still. He picked me up from Robbie's, said we'd talk soon, and then took me in a direction that wasn't at all back to his house.

"Later, Trina. I want to pick up the girls before they get worried. But things are okay."

"You promised," I reminded him. "You said you'd tell me everything."

He glanced at me quickly and then went back to the

road. But there was a tic in his unshaven, stubbled jaw. "I want to give you a good afternoon with the girls, first."

"Then tell me. I won't break. I can handle it, but not knowing will make it worse."

He must have heard the pleading in my tone because he pulled off the narrow, two-lane road and into the parking lot of a small shopping area. Five wood peaks all showing the names of different businesses and cafés and a bakery were printed in a scrolling scripts, colors all individualized to their own company's branding. A financial planner and insurance salesman on one, there was Mellie's Cakes on another, The Café on another, probably as simple as the coffee and food offerings inside. It was a new part of the town where I didn't recognize the names or the places.

I faced Cole instead of the unknown. I had enough of that. "Tell me. Was it Jonathan?"

He jerked his jaw up and then worked it back and forth. "He's here. Somewhere. Chief Lannister is working on figuring that out and we're getting some extra men in town to keep a close eye on him."

"He's *staying?*"

"Said he was sticking close until I returned what belonged to him and for you to stop throwing your tantrum."

"What else?"

Because all that was *bad*, and if he thought this was a tantrum, I was in some serious trouble. There could still be a way to get him to believe I hadn't wanted any of this. It'd involve throwing Kip under the bus, but better Kip go a round with Jonathan's fists than me.

Wouldn't it? I'd never asked Valerie for her help. If she had stayed out of this, I'd probably be in Italy, in solitude.

I shook the image out of my head. I'd probably be

tucked away in some villa and my bruises and scrapes would be well tended to, but I wouldn't be healing.

I'd be hiding in a forced seclusion, and not a single second of that time would be peaceful, even if it was quiet.

No...I wouldn't throw Kip under the bus.

And I would never go back. Valerie and Kip risked their necks to give me freedom for the first time in well over a decade, and I had no plans to squander the gift I'd been given.

No. I wouldn't do that.

"Tell me," I said to Cole, when he didn't answer my question. "There's more to this, and no offense, but out of the two of us, I'm the one who knows him better. I know how he works."

His lip curled up. "There were threats of charges, kidnapping, trafficking..." He glanced in my direction, and a smirk twisted his lips. "There was maybe the mention of alienation of affection."

"Alienation of...is that a thing?"

"It is."

I didn't know exactly what that meant, but I could figure it out close enough. The fact he was threatening it was absurd, which I blurted out to Cole who chuckled.

"It is. It's also a bunch of nothing that won't go anywhere. There's not a judge in this county, or this part of the state, that doesn't know you or your family. Or me, frankly, or at least my department. Jonathan might think he has the upper hand up here, with all his money, but if he tries to buy off anyone, I won't be the only one who puts him out of town with a thirty-two aimed at him. You know that, right? No one would let anything happen to you here, least of all some smug, manipulative stranger who thinks his money's more important than character."

"It is, though, Cole. For a lot of people that is what matters."

"Not here. You know that."

He had a point, but so did I. He might have wanted to believe that everything would be smoothed over easily if we only believed enough, but life worked differently. Especially life wrapped in Jonathan's bubble.

There was more Cole was hiding. His hands hadn't relaxed, and he was no less strung tight despite trying to brush off Jonathan's threats as a small annoyance.

I shifted in my seat and waited. "There's something else, isn't there?"

Cole pushed out his lips and dipped his chin. His rich, beautiful brown eyes that had once made me feel like the most special girl in the world swirled with indecision.

"Tell me."

There was another grimace, curl of his lips, and I figured it was bad because he was having to force them out of his throat. "He said to prepare yourself for him."

All the blood rushed from my face, and a fierce chill hit my spine. I jerked my gaze back to the storefronts and the pastels on the bakery's sign blurred and turned ugly in my vision.

*Prepare yourself.*

I shivered as Jonathan's voice reverberated so clearly in my mind, it was like he was right there.

"That means something," Cole said. His voice was a deep rumble, but I barely heard him. All the years.

All the moments those words were spoken to me when only nastiness came after.

"I can't go back to him," I whispered, and my tangled hands fisted in my lap until pain cut into my palms. "I can't go back to him. Swear it, Cole. Swear I won't ever have to go back."

"Never."

It was a fiercely spoken word like a shot in the tight space in the cab of his truck.

I sniffed and blinked back tears before facing him. "I can't do it again."

He leaned closer, and while one of his arms rested on the armrest the other was on the steering wheel. As he turned to me, there was nothing relaxed or calm about his posture or his expression. "What did that mean? When he said that to you? It means something to you."

I shook my head. "I can't go back there."

"You won't, Trina. I swear it on my life. Tell me what that means."

I peered up at him. With tears running down my cheeks and my chin wobbling, I forced the truth out of me. The ugly, disgusting parts. "That was what he said to me before he planned to hurt me, and I don't mean the times he hit me."

A fiery blast of fury slammed and bounced all over the cab. Cole cursed, and then he moved so quickly I yelped, right as his palm slipped to the back of my head.

"Listen to me," he growled, and that deep, thick voice was so angry I had no choice *but* to listen to him. "Listen to me, Trina and listen closely, okay?"

"Okay."

"Over my dead body will that man *ever* touch you again."

He was so close his breath skated across the tip of my nose as he spoke, but I couldn't pull myself away from the anger swirling in Cole's gaze. None of this was on him, none of this had anything to do with him, and yet he was furious. For *me*. And it wasn't because I owed him.

It was because he spoke the truth.

He loved me.

I only wished I was worthy and good enough for it, but I was still too afraid. That ship had long since sailed.

"Cole."

He blinked, and it was then I realized I was touching him. My fingers brushed over his stubble, and his eyes closed. Leaning into my barely-there touch, a fluttery breath left his lips.

"He will never touch you. Never hurt you again. I don't care if I have to shoot him myself."

"I trust you," I whispered.

I wasn't sure if I believed him, but I trusted Cole, and for me, that was saying a lot.

But this was Cole. The boy who'd loved me before we ever really understood what love was, or at least before I did.

Because love wasn't anger and manipulation and it wasn't coercion and proving yourself right.

Love was this, right there.

Being willing to sacrifice yourself to keep someone else safe.

Loving was giving everything you had.

"Thank you for that."

I dropped my hand back to my lap and pulled away from him. His hand slipped from behind my head as I moved.

"We should go get your girls."

"We can wait. I can spend time with them later—"

"Cole," I interrupted. I appreciated the care and the concern, but we could deal with the rest of this all later.

"What?"

"Let's go get your girls. They need their dad."

And weirdly enough, I was starting to believe I did, too.

———

INSTEAD OF MARIE bringing the girls to Cole's house, we met her at hers. I would have preferred to not see the house he'd lived in with his wife and kids and my already frazzled nerves took another beating when we pulled up the driveway.

"I know Marie wants to meet you," Cole said, "but I think for now it's probably best you stay in the car."

"I understand." I could go the rest of my days without setting eyes on the woman Cole loved enough to marry, the woman he loved enough to have daughters with. I'd stared at the picture of him and his girls far too many times over the last few weeks. He might have hidden it in the nightstand, but that didn't mean I didn't pull it out and memorize every one of their features, cataloging the ones that were so familiar to me and marking the ones that I couldn't place. Far as I could see, Cole was equally present in both girls' physical appearances, but in opposite ways.

Where June was lighter-haired like Cole, Ella was brunette. But it was Ella who had Cole's amber, almond-shaped eyes. June's were a vibrant blue that I had no doubt were brighter in the beach picture due to the sandy shore and cloudless, bright blue sky.

Either way, I was rethinking the decision to meet them at all when the door to the front door opened, stealing my chance to change my mind.

A tiny bundle, tucked beneath a hot pink hat and bright blue puffer coat, charged out of the front door. Her mouth was wide open, and while I couldn't hear her shriek, the joy on her face was clear.

"That's June," Cole said. He was laughing as he opened his door and climbed out of his truck. Like they rehearsed their greeting in their sleep, June slammed her little body into Cole's at the exact moment he crouched to catch her.

"Daddy!" she screamed. Her legs locked around Cole's hips and his face got buried in the collar of her coat, making her pink-booted feet kick with pleasure.

I tore my eyes off him, to see an exact matching outfit on the front steps. Ella's hair was longer than June's, and much darker, but as my gaze lifted, there was no doubt where that came from.

Marie Paxton was beautiful. Dressed in skinny jeans tucked into furry winter boots, her legs were long and slim, and the rest of her was equally elegant. Her soft smile grew as Ella tugged on her hand, and she bent to kiss her daughter's cheek.

More cautiously, but no less excited based on the soft little smile on Ella's cheek, she made her way to her dad with slower steps, but with more purpose than June's wild screech and run. I caught Ella take a glimpse of me, and her already pink cheeks darkened as she gave me a timid smile.

It was then I felt something and turned to the woman on the front steps to the home she'd once lived with everyone now standing in the driveway.

Her eyes were on me this time, and she lifted a hand in a barely-there wave of acknowledgment. Sadness flickered across her face as she dipped her chin toward me.

I had no doubt there was a mix of pity in there if she was as good of a woman as Cole claimed, but there wasn't the animosity I deserved.

The truck door opened in the back, and the cab erupted

with the sweet chatter and squeals of girls eager to see their father.

"My turn to sit there!"

"No! Scoot over!"

"Dad!"

"Please with Mellie's Cakes cherries on top?"

"That's not fair you know those are my favorite!"

Cole shot me a grin from the opened door behind him, a grin and a look that said a million things. Part exasperation, part *aren't they the cutest monsters in existence?* Which meant when he climbed into the truck and closed his own door, I was matching his grin.

It was hard to be scared and sad and all the things I was so used to feeling with such unabashed happiness flooding the cab.

"Girls," Cole said. "You keep chattering about cakes and you'll never get to say hi to Miss Trina."

"Oh! You're daddy's new friend!" June shouted.

"Junie bug, this is Miss Trina."

"Hello!"

"Hi." The second greeting came quieter with a hint of uncertainty in it, and as I turned to face Ella, she was looking out the front windshield.

A quick peek told me her mom was still standing there, and she wasn't sure how to treat me.

"Hi, Ella. Your dad has told me how lovely you are." I looked to June so she didn't feel left out. "You too, Sunshine."

"Sunshine! I love the sun!" the girl shouted.

Ella sank back into her booster seat and buckled up. "Thank you," she said. It was quiet and quickly drowned out by June starting on a story about the beach when Cole grabbed my attention.

"I need to give Marie a quick update about what happened today and grab their bags. You good in here with them?"

"Sure, she's good!" June shouted. "She wants to hear all about my stories, Daddy!"

"Go," I whispered, to him, but I doubt he heard me.

June was off and running, stories to be told, and a captivated listener trapped in front of her.

---

THE AFTERNOON WAS A WHIRLWIND. If the morning started off terrible and worrisome, there was no room left to think of any of it with June and Ella around. June seemed intent on using every word in the English vocabulary at least a dozen times, and Ella, while seemingly content to listen to her sister prattle on and on with little annoyance or frustration, was sweet in her own way.

By the time we were sitting down to dinner, where Cole had whipped up tacos, Ella took the lead in setting the table, and June filled everyone's glasses with water from the fridge, after grumbling that it wasn't her turn.

Somehow, I was starting to think June thought nothing was her turn to do unless it was something she wanted to do. The girl was the Energizer Bunny on steroids, and we were all along for her unending, boundless energy path she carved....but she was adorable. So stinking adorable.

Ella, on the other hand, was the calm to June's storm. I caught her glancing at me through the day, like she was trying to figure me out, so I stayed back and let Cole take the lead, perfectly content to be a visitor.

Which was exactly what I was.

This wasn't my house.

This wasn't anything except a brief stop in time, and I knew, soon, I'd have to start figuring out those next steps myself. Fortunately, it wasn't anything I could think of with June at the kitchen table.

"Who's ready for school tomorrow?" Cole asked.

Ella grinned. "I get to be star of the week tomorrow. Mommy spent all day helping me make a poster of all my favorite things. You're on it, too, Daddy."

Cole chuckled and pointed his fork at his little girl sitting to his right. "I better be one of your favorite things."

A sweet, soft smile bloomed on her cheeks and tears sparked my eyes that I quickly pushed away. He was a *dad*. I could have been the one who worked on a star of the week poster with him, our children...so many eons ago, but it was moments like this, with such precious kids around me, the reality of the decision I made all those years hit hard and wasn't so quickly brushed aside.

I sniffed and looked down at my plate, while June said something about her school.

I sat back, finished my tacos and when I was done and glanced up, I caught Cole's gaze on me.

One arched brow asked the questions I couldn't answer.

*Are you okay?*

No... I didn't really think I was.

But maybe someday, I'd get there.

# THIRTY-ONE

## TRINA

"I'll clean up," I told Cole when dinner and dessert were winding down. The girls were getting restless, and I was still reeling from the regret of what I'd done to our child.

I needed space, my own room to get my head back on straight before I lost it in front of June and Ella. Great first impression for them to take back to their mom.

I took Cole's plate from him. "Go have time with the girls."

His brows furrowed, creating a deep line in between his brows. "What's going on?"

"Nothing." I plastered on a fake smile he could probably read from a mountaintop away.

Scurrying around him, I began rinsing off plates and loading them in the dishwasher. Cole might have known I was faking my smile, but he certainly wasn't going to talk about it then, because he told his girls, "All right you two. Take your plates to Miss Trina, and then we'll get you ready for baths."

"Ugh," June groaned. "I *hate* baths."

"Can I pick the books, Daddy?" Ella asked.

Cole ruffled the top of her head. "Only two tonight though, but yes, you can choose."

"She *always* gets to choose," June pouted.

I turned away to hide my smile from them. June was a handful, and she loved things her way, but her scrunched-up pouty face was too cute for words. Probably why she got her way a lot, too.

"Go on," Cole said. "We'll discuss books and baths for the week. Maybe write out a calendar of nights you girls get to choose to make it fair. How's that sound?"

"I like calendars," Ella declared, and that didn't surprise me either.

I'd been around these girls for a day and their differing personalities were clear as glass.

Their socked feet thundered down the hallway, and after a door clicked closed, Cole was there, behind my back, arms out to my side on the counter.

He caged me in at the sink, and I couldn't move. The warmth from his body held me captive, and I glanced at his hands. There was strength in them, but they were tender too. They were the hands of a man who worked hard, but I could see those same hands cradling the girls when they were small, tucking their little bottoms close to his chest when they cried.

I *really* needed to get out of there.

"Want to tell me what's going on?"

"Nothing." I shook my head and grabbed a plate on the counter. His closeness prevented me from moving much, and the rinsing was awkward, but if avoidance was all I had, avoidance was what I'd do.

"Is it Wolf? Is that why you went silent at dinner and turned into a robot?"

"No." For once, my fear of him had been overridden by something else. *Someone* else, really. "I just wanted to help."

"Trina."

"What?" I reached for a bowl that held cheese.

Cole slapped the water off on his faucet and turned me to face him. I hugged the bowl to my chest, putting the space between us.

"What's gotten into you?" His brows were furrowed, his tone bordering on annoyed. "If you're scared of—"

"I'm not. Or, well, I *am*, but really, Cole. I've been around the girls all day. I thought it'd be good to give you time alone with them."

He reached out, his thumb brushing along my chin, and he tilted my face up so I was forced to look him in the eyes. "You're lying, but I'll let you, because I know you'll tell me when you're ready. But think about this while you're worrying about everything going on in your head that you've probably twisted up over the years."

"I don't—"

"You do." He quieted me with his words, and his thumb switched to his whole palm cupping my cheek. My lips parted in surprise at the way he touched me.

So tender and gentle. So *loving*.

"Tonight, I sat across the table from you, a woman I've always loved, with the girls who have the rest of my entire heart, and I loved every single minute of it. I know you feel guilty for what you've done, and I was angry at you for a long time, but I have June and Ella, and I wouldn't trade them for the world. In a way, you gave me that gift, too. So thank you."

"Cole..." I trailed off, because not only could I think of anything wise to say, or an apology that made it all right, but also because he was leaning closer, closing his eyes.

And then his lips were gently brushing over my forehead, freezing me to the floor beneath my feet. He *kissed me*, with a softness and care I hadn't experienced possibly since I walked away from him. A warm shiver cascaded down my spine, making my body tremble, and then his lips were gone, his fingers brushing my cheek.

"Think about that tonight, too, while you're worrying, okay?"

Like I had a chance of thinking of anything *but* that, now.

---

"ARE YOU OKAY?" Valerie whispered through the phone. "Cole called Kip earlier. Kip's freaking out with Jonathan there."

At least I didn't have to tell her about the morning. As soon as I heard her voice, the strength I'd tried to hold on to all day started to crumble.

"I don't know how I feel about this. He's *here*, Val."

"I'm sorry we didn't know. Kip didn't even know he was out of town, but we're not all that surprised."

"What? Why? I mean, outside his anger, anyway."

There was a pause and then, "We're working on some things here. I don't want to get your hopes up, and I'm not going to tell you what's going on, but there are plans in the works to get Jonathan fired."

"Val, you can't tell me that and not tell me what's going on."

"I can't, honey. But I swear it's for your benefit and protection. Trust me."

I shook my head, even though she couldn't see it. *Knowing* helped me know how to prepare.

"Just, listen," she said, and her voice was barely above a whisper which only scared me more. "There's been information given to Kip, from reliable sources, and things have been snowballing this week. I don't even know if he told Cole earlier but trust me. What we're working on has the potential to send Jonathan away for a very long time."

My head was spinning. "Val..."

"Honestly, if I could tell you more now, I would. But trust me that I'm truly thinking of you right now, and I've never steered you wrong before. You'll learn everything when you can but until then, we can't risk Jonathan finding out. It just might take some more time, but if he's suspicious of anything, it doesn't surprise me he's there to get you. Stay strong though, and trust Cole and Kip and I."

That I could do. I was at least learning how to trust Cole. "Promise you'll tell me when you can."

"Absolutely, honey. I swear it."

It went against every instinct I had to let it go, but Valerie had been the only person I could trust for years.

"Okay, I'll try."

"Good. Now, Kip talked to some of the men who handle his private security. He's used them before... remember when we had that stalker?"

"*You* had the stalker," I grumbled, because it was the truth. Some man started sending her pictures, inappropriate ones where you couldn't see his face, just his unclothed hip area wearing nothing but his birthday suit.

"Regardless, Kip wants to send Jim and some of his men up there to keep an eye on you. They can do things that a man of the law can't. If you get what I'm saying."

"You're not exactly speaking in code." I picked at the duvet covering my lap, and Valerie chuckled. "I'm scared.

The bruises everyone can see are finally gone, but I'm broken inside, Val, and I can't... I had dinner tonight with Cole and his girls, and all I kept thinking about was that he should have another."

"Don't," Valerie said. She snapped the word quietly but firmly. "Don't go down that road. He's *over* it, Trina. He's over it, and the only way you'll truly be able to move on is to forgive yourself. You were young, and you had plans. You made choices, and there's nothing you can do now. You can't *right* the wrong, but you can start living with some happiness."

Man, she was really getting good at this advice stuff.

"It feels so overwhelming to try."

My parents. Ashley and Robbie. The girls. Even Cole and his parents. Maybe it'd all been too much too soon. Maybe I was rushing things, because now everything seemed to be running full speed ahead and I was on the train platform, racing to catch up.

"That man would jump in front of a bullet for you, Trina. All you have to do is reach out and take hold of him."

"That's only one of the things that scares me."

"Then buckle up and tell him to throw on a vest. With Jonathan in town, who knows what's about to happen."

What a lovely thought.

"Maybe he'll slip on snow and fall down the mountain and get buried in an avalanche."

Valerie laughed. "A girl can only dream."

Tell me about it.

A KNOCK on my door tugged me out of the final dredges of sleep. It hadn't come easily last night, and I spent most of the night tossing and turning. Twice I jerked awake, fear rattling my chest and the need to slink through the house to make sure Cole and his girls were okay.

I didn't, but I'd wanted to, so while it had to be early since there was only darkness peeking through the blinds, I'd been half-awake for quite a while.

Relief slipped over me as Cole opened the door. I scooted up on the bed, bringing the duvet and blankets with me.

"Hey," I muttered, wiping sleep away from my eyes and my face. "What's up?"

"You have something to tell me?"

He leaned against the doorframe, arms crossed over his chest. Dressed in green-and-navy flannel plaid pajama pants and a navy long-sleeve T-shirt, he was casual, not angry. Relaxed, but definitely curious.

Handsome as always.

"What?"

"You forget to tell me something last night when you were hiding away in here?"

"I wasn't hiding."

His brows arched, and a smirk curled his lips, barely visible beneath his unshaven scruff.

"I don't know what you're talking about."

"There's a man at my front door. Three of them, actually. Say they're here for you."

"What?" I blinked. Men? Oh... "I called Val last night. She said Kip wanted to send men up here."

"Yeah. Got that." He jerked his chin toward the playroom and stairs. "Would have been nice to know that though so I could prepare the girls."

Damn. "I'm sorry. I wasn't thinking that when she said

he was thinking of sending some men that he was going to overnight them."

Of course Val would. They were probably on the way before we talked.

Cole chuckled and stepped back. "Get dressed and don't take too long. They want to meet you, so you know who they are. They said they'll be mostly invisible, but close to you at all times."

"Great."

Cole turned to leave, but I called his name, and he stopped. "I'm sorry. About not warning you."

"I'm not mad, Trina. Just wished you'd trust me enough to let me in a little bit is all."

He left, leaving a lead weight sinking into my gut.

He was right.

I hadn't given him much of anything, but how did I tell the man who'd always meant everything to me how dirty and worthless I'd become?

I didn't waste time pondering it. There was no point. He knew enough, and he didn't look at me with the same look of disgust I gave myself. Cole was better than me. Always had been.

Quickly scrambling out of bed, I hurried to the closet and pulled on a pair of fleece-lined leggings and a red sweatshirt with batwing sleeves, all clothes Valerie had sent with Cole when they brought me here. They weren't our normal designer brands and styles, much more casual, and as I tugged the sweatshirt over my head, realization struck.

Cole had been at the hospital *hours* after I'd gotten there. I know I saw him. I remembered that in the haze of drugs and pain. And a day later, I'd woken up *here*, with nothing but a suitcase of clothes, packed by Valerie, and every single one of the things she sent with him were casual. Warm and wintery. They were cozy and stylish, but they weren't flashy, and they weren't name brands that were so common in our circles in Georgia.

I trailed my hand over the closet full of sweatshirts and sweaters and Levi jeans and fleece-lined leggings, warm wool socks.

She *planned* this. How long was the question, but there was no way she was able to gather this amount of clothes in the time she had, all of them washed without tags, all of them sent for warm, winter living. And somehow, when disaster struck, not only was she there, Cole dropped everything to be there for me in the middle of the night.

And he'd been there every day since.

"Shoot," I whispered, as I realized how long Valerie had been waiting for this moment for me. How she planned everything. How she worked to get me somewhere safe. Somewhere where someone could help keep me safe.

How long had she planned to send me home?

Tears sprung and I quickly fought them back while I washed my face, brushed my teeth, and ran a brush through my hair so I looked halfway decent for whoever was waiting for me upstairs. Not only the men, but I couldn't scare Cole's girls this early in the morning, either.

I'd call Valerie later and get some answers, but man...I was really lucky to have such great friends looking out for me when I'd been incapable of doing it myself.

Deep, rumbling, and gravelly voices filtered from downstairs, so I headed up, figuring if there were men who showed up to help me, Cole had undoubtedly invited them in for coffee or something.

It was just the kind of guy he was.

Good. Honorable.

He was the kind of man I could trust with everything, and he wouldn't use it against me, he wouldn't berate me for it.

He'd love me through it.

# THIRTY-TWO

## COLE

She was different as she appeared at the top of the stairs. I'd seen Trina with a variety of looks over the last few weeks and in all the years I knew her before. This was something striking, beautiful, even as she appeared without makeup and barely having time to brush her hair.

She was gorgeous like she'd always been, and she still carried herself like she was one step away from stepping on a model's runway, but this morning, there was a shimmer in her eyes. Something lighter. Something more peaceful surrounded her presence as she came straight to where I was in the kitchen, coffee carafe in front of me and five empty mugs.

"Hey," she said, and leaned against me.

Me. She put her weight against *me*. It felt like I had won a gold medal.

What made it even more beautiful was the lack of tension in her body. She was relaxed, pressing her shoulder against my bicep.

"Hello," she said, and it took effort, lots of it, but I tore my eyes off Trina's soft profile to where she was facing the men across the counter from us. "I'm Trina."

"Know who you are," Jim Bower said, the same guy who'd driven the van to take us to the airport. "You're looking good. Well healed."

Trina's frame tightened, and I settled my hand at her lower back. "Jim helped get you out of the hospital."

"Oh," she whispered. "Thank you, for that."

"My pleasure." He dipped his chin. "Would also be my pleasure if he showed up in front of me so I can show him exactly what I think of a man who does that to a woman."

So much for Trina's relaxed stance next to me. She was now so tight it was like she'd stitched her body together, and one tiny move would split all her seams.

"Bower," I growled his name. "Maybe back off a bit?"

He shrugged and then grabbed one of the coffee mugs I'd filled. "I'm an honest guy."

"Thank you," Trina whispered. "As scary as the thought is, thank you for that."

"The other two men are Brock and Rocco." I gestured to each of them. Twins, with shorn close dark hair, eyes even darker, and bodies that could tear some of these mountain pines out of the ground with their bare hands.

"Brock," one said, and lifted his hand. "Nice to meet you, Trina. Rocco and I will be close to you at all times, but don't worry if you can't tell us apart."

"Our mom still has a hard time doing the same." The other one grinned and had a gap in his mouth on the side.

I glanced at Brock, whose expression remained stony.

Hard to believe any woman carried these huge men, and at the same time. Seemed like they could have been created in a test lab for the scariest men on the planet.

At least they'd found their calling in security.

"Not to be rude," Trina said, "but I was told you two would be mostly invisible, and that doesn't really seem possible."

Brock broke his stony expression and winked at her. "We're good at our job. Don't worry."

"Easy for you to say," she muttered and then glanced at me. "The girls okay?"

"Yeah. They're still sleeping."

She turned back to the men. "Um, is there anything besides coffee I can get for you? And well...where are you staying? Here?"

"Outside," Bower said, I snorted. It was dropping into the teens, but I wouldn't be surprised if these men could sleep beneath the stars even in freezing temperatures.

"Really?" Trina sounded much more shocked at the idea than I was.

"No," Brock said, back to being stone cold. "We got a place nearby, but you don't need to know where it is."

"Because it's where you'll keep the bodies?" Trina asked. Her tone was full of lighthearted sass I wouldn't have expected considering why these men were here and what was going on.

Brock's expression remained tight. Rocco chuckled before he hid it behind a cough. Bower said nothing.

"It was a joke," she muttered.

"There won't be any bodies to bury," I told her, and then made sure I met each of their gazes.

*If* something happened to Jonathan, it wouldn't be buried and hidden on a frozen mountain.

"Right," Rocco said, but it sounded more grumbled. Like he wasn't quite on my side.

I bumped my hip lightly into Trina. "Let's get you some breakfast. Need anything else besides coffee?"

"This is good for now, but thanks."

We all settled at the table. Bower went over the plan while they were in town. While Brock and Rocco stuck close to Trina, they'd also be switching off to make sure the girls and Marie were safe at their homes, schools, and work. Bower would mostly be on Jonathan, even if he hadn't been able to find him yet.

He was close, though. He had to be considering yesterday's threats.

Eventually, the girls' bedroom door squeaked open, and the patter of one of my daughter's feet headed toward us.

All the men turned to watch, which meant as June, and her mop of bedhead hair and *Frozen* nightgown reached the mouth of the hallway, all eyes were on her.

I'd meant to go in and wake them up to let them know we had company so they weren't scared, given the size and burliness of the men at my dining table, but it hadn't really been June I'd been worried about.

June proved my assumption right when she smiled at Trina, moved her sleepy eyes over the rest of the men, and settled on Brock.

Rocco's earlier statement that their mom couldn't tell them apart was an utter lie. They might have been identical, but Rocco wore a softer expression. He looked like he heeded his job and got it done efficiently but took no joy in any of the dark sides of it. Brock looked like he ate, slept, and breathed his work, and not only *liked* the darker sides of it, he enjoyed every slow, bloody, agonizing second of it.

"You look like the monster from the Frosty the Snowman movie," June declared, her gaze stuck on Brock. "But with less hair."

If it was possible, Brock's expression hardened further, but Rocco slapped his brother on the shoulder. "You mean that furry snow-monster?" Rocco asked.

June nodded, serious about her decision. "His name is Bumble."

"My name is Brock."

June shrugged, glanced at me, and then back at him. "I like Bumble better."

Jim didn't bother to hide his laugh but let it boom through the kitchen. I flinched at the noise and excused myself from the table.

"Gotta get Ella," I muttered to Trina.

When I reached June, I squatted down in front of her, gave her a kiss on her cheek and hugged her. "As you can see, I've got some more friends visiting. I wanted you and your sister to meet them, so they don't surprise you or scare you, okay?"

"More friends? *Now* are we having a sleepover?"

"No, Junie bug. No sleepovers yet."

"Bummer." Her eyes went wide and round with mischief. "Can I have ice cream for breakfast since I still don't get sleepovers?"

Another round of laughter echoed from the table. I wasn't the least bit surprised. "How about we get you a healthy breakfast before school this week, and then on Saturday we can have it for breakfast."

"My idea sounds better," she muttered.

I'm sure it did. If someone would have told me half of parenting would be bartering with a pint-size pipsqueak, I wouldn't have believed it, but June knew how to get her way and was creative in going about it.

"Let me get your sister up and then I'll make you some oatmeal with brown sugar. That work for you?"

"Sugar sounds great."

I chuckled, kissed the top of her head and went to get Ella.

The day had already started with more excitement than I bargained for, who knew what the rest of it would bring.

———

"WHAT DO you mean he's gone?"

Eddy slapped a stack of files to his desk and followed it with his iPad. "Gone," he repeated. "We can't find him anywhere. Soon as that man left the lot yesterday, he was a ghost."

"There's cameras all over town and on the lights."

He couldn't have vanished. He didn't fly in on the private airstrip. Scranton confirmed it with his own private cameras of the runway.

"I know," Eddy said, "and we got his vehicle turning right out of the parking lot and then left on Littlecastle Highway, but after that, there's nothing."

"That would have taken him to Crystal Mountain. So, what, he ditched the SUV and got in something else?"

"Could have. Still doesn't explain the fact we're scouring every single rental reservation made in the last three weeks for last night and not a single one of them checks out."

I pinched my nose between my fisted hand and thumb, tugging down. This wasn't right.

He had to be here.

"So, he changed his SUV, he's staying farther out in Boone or something, or hell, I don't know... he took off in a helicopter?"

I hadn't heard a word from Kip yet that morning, but he'd been my first call on my way into work.

Hell, for all we knew, Jonathan was full of it and had driven back to Georgia. Maybe he'd lied about staying close to scare Trina. Who knew what went on in that man's mind.

"I don't have time for this crap," I muttered and reached for my iPad. "Not this week. Not when Trina's finally starting to open up again."

She was shutting down just as fast, but she was trying. And this morning, she came straight to me, rested her body against me like she actually felt comfortable with me. I could still feel the weight of her body against mine.

"Those men that guy sent are something else," Eddy said, and he glanced outside. Brock and Rocco and Jim had followed me into the station to meet our chief. Lannister wasn't exactly thrilled they were here, but since they were technically just visitors, he couldn't do much about it, even if I'd gotten an earful after they left to go do their protection thing.

*"They bring trouble, it's going to be hard to cover that up."*

*"I think they'll cover up their own trouble," I'd told him which had earned me a scowl. "What do you want me to do? Leave Trina unprotected?"*

At that, he'd sighed and then relented. The only trouble they'd bring was finishing whatever trouble Jonathan started, and I figured they'd be gone before anyone could pin anything on them anyway. They were the size of mountains and moved like ghosts. Even as a cop, I'd never seen anything like it.

"I'll keep them in check."

Chief nodded and then rolled his eyes. "Make sure you

call the first hint you need backup. We're your family, too, Cole. Family protects family."

I got it. Promised I would and then headed out of his office and back to work. Things were going to erupt soon, and I needed to make sure everyone in the department was ready.

# THIRTY-THREE

## TRINA

"Please, feel free to call or schedule an appointment whenever you need, okay? I know this is hard, but I'm here for you."

My voice trembled, but it'd been doing that for the last hour. "Thank you. I will."

"Seeking help is the first step, Trina. You should be really proud of yourself."

I felt more like I'd been run over and then beaten all over again, but I suppose therapy did that to a person who'd held on to as much as I had, for as long as I had. We'd barely begun to scratch the surface of the last twelve years, and my emotions were shredded. "Thank you, Zoe. I appreciate that."

I wasn't sure I was proud of myself, but beneath all the pain we'd just delved right into, there was a comfort in it, too. As long as I could hold onto the comfort, I was starting to think I could truly do this.

We ended the Zoom call, which had been awkward at the beginning, but then somehow, the therapist Dr. McElroy recommended made me feel like we'd been best friends. As she started asking questions, I found myself opening up before I realized I was doing it.

I closed Cole's laptop he'd told me I could use and pushed away from his office desk. He'd be back with the girls soon and I wanted to have dinner made for them. A quick trip to the bathroom and I scared myself when I saw my reflection. Starting therapy might have been a good thing, but it was going to wreak havoc on my face. I ran downstairs, gave my face a quick wash, reapplied my makeup, and then headed back to the kitchen.

It was now Friday. The week with him and the girls wasn't only exhausting, but exhilarating. I was equally ready for him to take them to Marie on Sunday as I was mourning not have their constant excitement in the house. I'd stopped hiding away in my room after dinner after that first night, and now I stayed in the living room. We played various board games and Jenga after dinner and watched cartoons. When Cole put them to bed, I was close enough to hear him read stories, the giggles as they said their bedtime prayers, and then found myself crying, once again, as Cole sang to them. He was *such* a good dad, and while it hurt, it was a beautiful thing to witness, even if it was from a distance.

Since I wouldn't be seeing them for another week, I'd convinced Cole to run to the grocery store for me so I could cook them all a meal. I wasn't necessarily trying to *win* the girls' approval, and it didn't seem like I needed it because they seemed to be pretty at ease around me, but I figured it couldn't hurt anything, either.

*When I look at you, I see everything.*

Cole's words from last week came to me in a gentle whisper as I grabbed steak from the fridge. And then that kiss.

In all that had gone on in the last few weeks, I hadn't truly considered what he was telling me. I'd been so focused on myself, I hadn't considered he wanted something from *us* or for us. Or me.

He hadn't helped get me out of Jonathan's grip only for me to heal and get better. He wanted me back here.

With him.

The realization slammed into me, stealing my breath even while I reached for the mushrooms to make stroganoff.

He wanted me. He wanted me with him. He wanted me at the kitchen table with his girls.

How? How could he look at me and still see the girl he loved when I wasn't sure she existed anymore?

And what did I want?

I'd loved him once and broken his heart. I'd loved a monster and broken my own.

I wasn't sure I had any idea what love was anymore, or how I could give that to someone else.

My phone rang, startling me and I set down a pot of water I was filling and made my way to the counter.

The screen flashed with Ashley's name and I answered it. "Hello?"

"It's half-priced bottles of wine at Max's tonight. You're coming with me to go see Heather."

I glanced at the clock, the food all over the counter, and the half-filled pot of water I'd just started boiling. "I'm cooking dinner," I said, and through the phone Ashley laughed at me.

"I didn't mean right this very second, although with the day I've had I could use it. Heather's heard you're in town and mad she wasn't invited over last week. You're coming with me so she stops hounding me every five minutes to see you again."

"Oh... I don't... I'm not sure that's smart right now."

I wasn't sure Cole would let me out of his sight. Not with Jonathan still threatening to make an appearance. And with the threat he'd told him about me, I wasn't sure I wanted to go into town.

"Maybe you guys can come here? Tomorrow or something? Or next weekend?"

"No way. You need this. You've been hiding up there for weeks and Max's is the safest place you can be. My parents will watch the kids so Robbie and Cole can come. Or his parents can watch mine there. But you're doing this."

"Ashely... I'm just not sure it's smart." We hadn't heard from Jonathan all week and there'd been no sign of him. I wasn't sure that was a good thing considering the only text I'd gotten from Valerie all week had said: *Sit tight. Trust me.* Cole hadn't gotten much more information out of Kip, either.

As for me, Brock had driven me to a lawyer's office in Boone so I could talk about filing for divorce. Since I wasn't a resident of North Carolina, though, and the state's divorce process was longer and more complicated than Georgia's, I had it on my to-do list to find a Georgia attorney first thing Monday.

I wanted to make it clear to Jonathan I wasn't returning home, ever, and I wanted that done as soon as possible so I could keep moving forward. Regardless, I knew that would upset him even more when he learned.

"What's going to happen? It's not like he can waltz into Max's and take you out. Please. The entire bar would tackle him and then tear him apart piece by piece if he so much as laid a hand on you."

"Lovely visual," I muttered, and then turned on the

water to finish filling the pot. "I don't know. I'll have to talk to Cole."

"Perfect. We'll see you at eight. I'll let Robbie and him figure out the kid situation."

The call went blank, and I gaped at my screen. That hadn't been a yes at all, and I was sure Cole would see the problem with it, too. Shaking my head, I set down the phone and got back to work on dinner.

Heather had always been the wildest one, and Ashley had been the sweet one.

She'd grown bolder over the years. Feistier.

All around me people had changed, but all of them for the good, at least the ones I'd seen so far.

Maybe it was time I started doing the same.

---

"YOU WANT TO GO?"

That was Cole's response to me telling him about Ashley's phone call.

"I assumed you'd say it wasn't safe," I replied.

He glanced at his girls, sitting on opposite sides of the dining table from each other. They were *devouring* my stroganoff. It wasn't that it surprised me, because I'd perfected this meal years ago and it was one of the few comfort, simple foods Jonathan allowed me to make instead of the fancier dishes he'd required me to.

"It'd be fine. If you want to go, we'll go. If you don't want to go, we don't."

"I don't...are you sure?"

He rested his forearms on the table, and while his gaze was stormy, it was also warm. Patient. I imagine being looked at like that every day for the rest of my life, and my body heated. "It will never be my job or my place to tell you what you can and can't do. It's my job to keep you safe while you do it. You want to go, we'll make that happen. We've got Kip's mountain men with us and an entire town who knows us. Is it the *smartest* thing to go and do? Probably not. Absolutely not, really, if you want my honest advice. But I can guarantee you'll be safe while you do it. So if you want to go see Heather tonight, we'll go see her."

"I like Miss Heather," June chimed in. "She makes the bestest Shirley Temple drinks in the whole world."

"And she's super nice," Ella added. "If she's your friend, why wouldn't you want to see her?"

"Well," I started, and then stopped. Because there wasn't a great answer to give a five-year-old. "It's been a long time, Ella. And besides, you only get so much time with your daddy, I wouldn't want to take him from you."

"You can't do that," Ella said. "He's our dad, and he's never going anywhere. He's promised."

A deep, amused chuckle came from the head of the table.

That wasn't exactly what I meant, but I got her point.

Ella glanced at Cole and smiled. June grinned at me. "We love Grammy B too and Papa. We have lots of people who love us and friends. I *always* want to see my friends. And maybe Miss Heather will be so excited to see you, she'll make you a special Shirley Temple drink, too."

It was impossible to be worried and riddled with fear with Cole's girls being so encouraging. "A Shirley Temple does sound good," I admitted to June.

She shrugged and took another bite of her noodles like *duh*.

"Okay then." I shrugged and looked to Cole. "It would be nice to see her."

She hadn't hated me. She hadn't understood but she hadn't hated me. And maybe getting into town would be... nice? Scary, definitely, but nice for sure. I had to face everyone in town sometime.

What better time to do it than with, as Cole called them, Kip's mountain men at my back.

"Then we'll go," Cole said. "And by the way, I know I've already said it, but this dinner is delicious. You're a great cook."

Satisfaction bloomed in me, even if I knew the meal was already good. But sitting around the table with people easily enjoying it instead of judging and critiquing was an entirely new experience for me.

"Thanks, Cole. That's sweet."

---

"WE'LL BE OUT FRONT, out back, and in the bar," Jim said as he pulled into the gravel parking lot behind Max's. "One of us will have eyes on you at all times, so don't worry about anything."

Right. Don't worry. Easier said than done, for sure.

"And I won't leave your side," Cole said, climbing out of the SUV and then holding out his hand for me to slide out after him. "I'm sure you'll recognize eighty percent of everyone in there, but that doesn't mean you go anywhere alone. You got it?"

I got that as soon as I told Cole I wanted to go and he went into ultra-protective planning and slightly-bossy mode. But this wasn't a bad kind of bossy. He was bossy to protect me, not control me, and it made a *wild* difference in how that felt.

"I'll be smart," I promised him, and felt that familiar

zing of warmth hit my fingers and then my chest as his hand wrapped around mine. Would that ever go away?

I hoped not.

*I see everything.*

The words came to mind again, and as we walked into the bar, I wasn't worried about Jonathan. I wasn't worried about Heather. I wasn't worried about seeing anyone else in town I might know.

I was only worried that despite everything I was *trying* to do, I was still going to end up falling short.

I tried to brush it off as Rocco led the way into Max's. He walked in first, holding the door for Cole to grab, but didn't give us any attention, like he was there on his own, and headed straight to the far end of the bar.

It ran along the left side, with three booths in front of it. The center of the small tavern had two, narrow, bar-height tables that could seat twelve. They were meant for people to hang out, greet new people, and have some drinks, but there wasn't exactly room to have full plates of food. On the right side, were two more rows of regular height tables. Some square, some round, Max's Tavern had never been a *bar* bar, with live music or pool tables or darts or all the bar things. It was a restaurant with good, simple food meant to warm your bones after a day of skiing, and drinks meant to cool you off after summer days of hiking. It was the first restaurant and bar ever built in Deer Creek. It wasn't only a staple to the locals, but it was a hotspot to visitors and tourists.

Given the fact we weren't yet fully into the ski and holiday season, the place was full and busy, but there wasn't a wait outside and there were a few open tables.

I scanned it all, recalled dozens of memories I had of being in this place for lunches with friends and dinners with my family and Cole's, and it took me about two point five seconds to take it all in. Almost done scanning the place, I caught sight of the blond behind the bar, who had frozen in the middle of pouring a drink and whose gaze had stalled on me.

I flexed my fingers for Cole to let go. His hand went to my lower back. "She looks more surprised than I thought she would," he whispered to me.

"No kidding," I muttered right back. I took that first step forward, and out of nowhere, Ashley popped into my line of sight.

Her hands were out, and she looked frazzled. "Okay, okay, so I fibbed a bit."

"What in the ever-loving slice of weird voodoo is going on?" Heather shrieked.

Fortunately, we were close enough she didn't have to shriek too loud, and as Cole guided me toward the bar, where Heather's appearance turned more surprised by the second, and then happy, he barked to Ashley, "Explain. Now."

"Well, okay, so she didn't know Trina was in town, but I knew she'd want to see her, and I thought if I tried to convince Trina to come and Heather didn't know, it'd be easier for her to say no, so I fibbed... but just a little...because see?"

She flung out her arm toward Heather, who had handed off the half-mixed drink, and had somehow disappeared from behind the bar, and was running straight toward me.

"Not cool," Cole growled.

I didn't have time to think about any of it because Heather was barreling down on me, her mouth opened into a wide, cheek-aching smile, and her arms were extended. "I don't know what's going on or why you're here, because this feels like an incredible fever dream, but holy *freaking* cow, Trina!"

She threw her arms around me and yanked me to her. She'd trapped my arm beneath hers in her rush to get to me, and I grunted as pain flared in my ribs as she swung me back and forth. "Holy cow," she repeated. "Holy freaking cow. You're here, you're actually here, and it's so incredibly amazing and surprising to see you."

I could barely breathe, much less respond, so I stayed still and took Heather's fierce hug while she kept rambling.

But man... that felt good. It felt good to be held by her and have her so overwhelmingly excited to see me.

"I can't breathe," I finally rasped.

Heather laughed and let me go, only to hold on to my hands. "You're beautiful. So beautiful. I'm sorry, I just...I can't believe you're *here* here. And with Cole." She blinked and her gaze swung to him and then Ashley and Robbie, who'd joined us at some point. "And...like you all *knew* this."

"I know," Ashley said and lifted her hand. "I know. And well, I didn't tell you because I wanted to respect Trina's privacy, and everything, but I felt bad." She turned to me. "And I'm sorry I lied to get you here, but I couldn't hold it in anymore, and I didn't want to keep hiding it from Heather, so I'm sorry. But I *told* you she'd be excited to see you. Didn't I?"

"You did," I replied, and tugged on my hands that were still connected to Heather's. "And it *is* good to see you. You look incredible."

"You're as beautiful as always," she said, peering at me as her eyes narrowed. "But sad. And hurt." Her gaze stalled on the scar at my temple. The stitches had been removed a week ago, and most of my bruising was either gone or yellowed so I could easily hide it, but if felt like Heather saw it all. "I'm guessing there's a story there."

"There is," I confirmed, but this wasn't the time or the place to share it.

She frowned. "Okay then. Come, come sit at the bar. I'll kick people out if I have to. I'm obviously working, but man..." She threw her arms around me and hugged me tight. "It's *so* great to see you. Injuries and stories, aside, I've missed you."

This time, I was able to hug her back. "You too, Heather. It's good to see you too."

She dragged us to the bar, and like she'd promised, she kicked out a group of men and pointed them to the closest booth. "Sorry guys. This is my best friend who I haven't seen in far too long. She gets center stage tonight."

I didn't quite like the idea of being the center of anything, especially not the attention she was putting on me, but the men left with barely a grumble, and then Cole was planting onto a stool while Heather scooted around back behind the bar, beneath an opened area, and then popping up on the other side.

"Let me guess," she said, grinning at Ashley and me. "Half off double bottles?"

"You got it," Ashley replied for me.

# THIRTY-FOUR

## COLE

It was a strange feeling, to feel like I knew someone so well, and then realize there was so much more to learn about that same person. Beyond Trina's fears and obvious insecurities, I'd learned she changed in other ways, better ways over the years, too. After the surprise of a lifetime when we walked in, something I wasn't as quick to forgive Ashley about even if it worked out okay, Trina settled in at the bar.

She wasn't a drinker. Not that that alone was a surprise, I'd noticed it the other nights there'd been alcohol around. She had a glass, maybe two, but they took her so long to drink, that there was no way she was even close to tipsy. Definitely not drunk. Her years of modeling had changed the way she carried herself. There was a grace in which she carried herself, like she was floating above the ground when she walked, and even when she sat, the way she tilted her head or moved her fingers was done with a smooth, yet precise manner. Every move of her body was more of a smooth glide that was mesmerizing to watch. It made everything she did, even sipping from a glass of wine or shifting on her stool, elegant and refined.

A far cry from the girl who used to trip over her snow skis on her way down the bunny slope.

Her laughter was soft as she caught up with Heather and her smile was more timid. I wasn't sure if that was from age and growth and the world she lived in, or the fact someone had silenced and terrified her all those years. But even quieter and less frequent, it was no less beautiful.

I had taken the seat next to her, and Robbie was on my other side, while Heather got caught up with Trina, breaking only when she needed to take care of another customer at the bar or mix drinks for the servers.

"Feels like no time has passed and a lifetime all at the same time," Robbie said next to me, swirling his water glass in his hands.

We were both sticking to water. Robbie because he and Ashley had met us here and he had to drive, me in case something happened.

"It's weird, isn't it? And yet, not."

Heather was as vibrant as she'd always been. Engaged once, she'd ended it when the guy she was with kept pushing back the wedding and then started bringing up moving to Raleigh to be closer to his family. She took that to mean he didn't want to live the quiet life in Deer Creek, and since Heather never intended to leave, her man did. She stood on the other side of the bar from Trina, over her surprise and acting like she'd seen Trina every single day of her life for the last twelve years.

Being back together with all the people I'd grown up with that hadn't left our town for bigger cities or different states was oddly comforting, despite all the changes and growing we'd done along the way.

Heather stepped away to pour drinks for a few men at

the end of the bar, and Ashley turned to face the rest of us. "So, I have another confession."

"I'm still not over the first one," I told her.

"Well, then you'll have to get over two of them."

"What is it?" Trina asked.

Ashley worried her bottom lip. "You know I teach with your sister. I mean, not *with* her because she does AP Calculus, not English, but the school is small."

"Spit it out, Ash."

"I kinda forgot to mention that the high school teachers usually come here, the women at least, for a quick drink on Fridays."

It wasn't that I hadn't known that. There were lots of nights when I didn't have the girls that I went and hung out at Robbie's while she came here. But...I closed my eyes and shook my head. "You're kidding me."

"Kari is coming?" Trina squeaked. She glanced at me, face already paling, and then back to Ashley. "Why would you do this to me?"

For the first time, Trina looked truly panicked. Not fearful, not worried, but panicked like her worst nightmare was coming true.

I couldn't blame her, fully. She and her sister had never really gotten along, but that was because they were different. Too far separated in ages to be friends or enemies, Kari was always soft spoken and an ardent rule follower. She never understood Trina, much like the rest of us, really, but it wasn't that Kari didn't understand her sister, it sometimes felt like she thought Trina's excitement over life and more laid-back personality was *wrong* somehow.

"Yeah." Ashley cringed. "And it's not that she's coming here, it's that she just walked in."

"What?" Trina's head whipped toward the front door.

How I missed it, when I'd been trying to clock everyone who entered was beyond me, but there she was.

Kari Knapp was near the front door, wearing a knee-length puffy coat and the saddest, most worried expression I'd ever seen on her.

She glanced at a table to the right, and then back to us. One step turned to two, then another, and Trina was sliding off her stool. She stayed close, one hand on the stool's back like she needed the support as her sister made a much slower, almost painful walk to her little sister.

"Mom and Dad said you went to see them," she said, and while her voice had always been soft, it was difficult to hear over the sounds of the bar and conversations around us. "They said you didn't want to see me."

"I wasn't sure I was ready to see anyone yet." Trina attempted a smile, but it wobbled before it fell completely.

"I wasn't always nice to you," Kari said and glanced around. All of us were watching, and if she read it right that we'd jump in at the first hostile word spoken, she was right. "But Mom told me some things, about what you told them, and I'm really sorry. About, well... everything. You don't deserve that."

"Thank you," Trina said, her voice now shaking.

The woman had to have cried enough tears over the last few weeks to create a new lake.

"I'm glad you're here," Kari said. "And that you're safe. When you're ready, I'd like for you to meet your nieces. Missy looks just like you, and she'd love you."

"I'd love that." Trina lifted her arm and then went to her sister. Kari hesitated for a second, but then returned the move and soon, the sisters were hugging.

It was short, and awkward, and then Kari was pulling back, wiping a tear beneath her eye. "We'll talk soon?"

"Yes. Definitely."

"Good." She glanced at all of us again. "See you all soon." She squeezed Ashley's shoulder as she walked by, and Trina slumped back onto her barstool. Even her slump was graceful.

"That was short and not as painful as I expected it to be."

"We've all grown and changed, sweetie," Heather said. "Kari, right along with the rest of us heathens."

Trina chuckled, and then glanced at Ashley. "Any more surprises for us?"

"Not from me," she quipped, and then leaned in and rested her hand on Trina's forearm. "I should have told you, but I guess...Kari and I have talked over the years. She's grown a lot, and she's kinder now. I knew that'd be hard, but you were worried about meeting me, and you didn't need to be. I just wanted to show you how much you're loved, how much you've always been loved."

It was a hell of a way to orchestrate it, but I couldn't blame Ashley for wanting to give that goodness to Trina when all I wanted to do was the same.

"I need a minute," she whispered, and slid off the stool. "I'll be back, but I need a minute alone."

"Trina—" I warned. We *talked* about this.

"Rocco's watching," she said, "Jim's out back. I get what you're saying, but I just need a minute to get my head on straight. Okay?"

The last thing I wanted to do was let her out of my sight, but I relented. We were safe in Max's, and she had eyes on her everywhere. "Okay. Take the time you need."

She curled her hand around my shoulder and squeezed it tight. A strange look crossed her face as she scanned mine and then her tongue appeared before she ran her lips together.

I knew that look. I'd seen it on her a thousand times, and *damn*...it wasn't only shocking, but turned my blood to a simmering heat.

She was staring at me like she wanted to kiss me. Or climb onto my lap and hold on to me. All things I'd allow. If I wasn't trying to be so cautious with her, I'd stand and give her exactly what that look suggested. Instead, I curled my hand over hers, brought it to my lips, and kissed the back of her hand.

And then I watched every step she took to the back of Max's, until she disappeared down the hall and swung my gaze toward Rocco who was doing the exact same thing.

Confirmation she'd be safe, for however long she needed, I finally turned back to the bar.

From the other side, Heather stated, "You're still in love with her."

I shrugged and grabbed my water. "It's Trina."

# THIRTY-FIVE

## TRINA

I couldn't wait to get to the moment where life stopped throwing me curveball after curveball. Where it settled and I stopped being thrown for a loop every time someone from my past approached. Where I quit feeling regret bubble to the surface and when I was able to stop living in fear.

It'd take time, I knew that. I just wanted to be able to go about my day without waiting for the proverbial monster to jump out from around the corner.

I used the restroom, washed my hands, and then turned the faucet to ice cold. Shoving my hands and wrists under the water, I scrubbed them together until the icy chill distracted me from my spinning thoughts.

Done, I rested my back against the wall and closed my eyes. This would stop.

It would all stop soon.

I was doing the work to leave the past where it belonged. I was strong enough to leave Jonathan for good. I was healing. I was working on all of it, and maybe Ashley and Cole were right. The sooner I realized people loved me and didn't hold the past against me, the sooner I'd start feeling the same. Maybe.

Time.

I just needed more time.

I opened my eyes. I might need more time, but tonight I had friends. I had people who were good to me. I had Cole, who kissed me like he truly *did* still love me, and not the girl I used to be. He kissed me like he saw the woman in front of him even if I wasn't so sure who that woman was anymore, or who she was becoming.

*What if...?*

What if she could become whatever she wanted, craft a new dream, create a new life? One that wasn't held back by all my regrets and fears, but focused on something different?

A soft smile curved my lips. I started at the reflection, at the face reflected. The smile, that maybe, for the first time since I left this town, contained hope, held true, real-life hope. "I can do this, and eventually, it will be okay."

For the first time, the night didn't feel so dark and the days ahead not so difficult.

I turned and opened the door. Stepping outside into the hall, I turned, intent on heading straight back to Cole when a hand wrapped around my arm.

I froze as the cloying, familiar scent I'd hoped to never smell again, hit me so hard my stomach churned. I opened my mouth to scream, and a hand wrapped over my mouth.

"You didn't think you could actually hide in plain sight and get away with it, did you?"

*Jonathan.*

All that bubbling hope popped like a thousand bubbles. I kicked my legs, tried to break away but he only dragged me harder and soon, there was the metal bang of the door and the frigid cold air of the night air sending goose bumps peppering down my arms beneath my sweater.

"Those men Kip sent, might have been large, but they're idiots. And Kip should have known better than to think he had a chance in hell at keeping me from what I want."

I screamed against his hand, fear flashing straight in front of my eyes. Jonathan spun me around, making me lose my footing. The world spun, and my vision went hazy. It took me a moment to grasp what I was seeing, what Jonathan had spun me around to see. Jim Bower. Lying splayed out on the ground, face down, a dark pool of what had to be blood, but I refused to believe it was, pooled on the ground beneath him.

"No!" I screamed against the hand still pressed to my mouth, and then felt the burning blast of pain and heat against my cheekbone.

"Shut up. You're only making it worse for you. Should I tell you the things I'll do to you once I get you back home? Should I tell you how much it's going to hurt?"

"I think you should take your hands off the woman and let her go."

Relief swelled inside of me at the new voice. Brock. Someone was here. Thank *God*. My shoulders fell as Jonathan jerked me around again, this time with something hard pressing into my back. He adjusted so quickly his other arm wrapped around the front of my throat, and he held me against him as Rocco came crashing through the back door a second before Cole followed. Rocco had his own gun drawn, pointed directly at me and Jonathan, Cole's was loose at his side.

Adrenaline rushed through me, making me warm and

possibly psychotic because I burst out in a laugh and looked directly at Cole. "Probably shouldn't have gone alone, huh?"

"Shut up!" Jonathan snapped and jerked me backward.

I cried out in surprise more than pain.

Cole showed no hint of humor and scowled instead. "You don't think you're getting out of here with her, do you?"

Jonathan chuckled, and the cold tone in his voice turned mocking. "You don't think I'm leaving here without her, do you? It's not like you've been that difficult to take down."

With Jim still on the ground, unmoving, his point was clear.

"Takes a special kind of coward to shoot a man in the back," Rocco retorted. "Good news for you, when I shoot you, it'll be straight to your chest, so you see it coming and I get to watch the life bleed out of you."

"Nonsense," Jonathan clipped and stepped backward, away from the door to the tavern, away from the three men, all with their guns ready.

They wouldn't shoot, though, and Jonathan knew it. Not with me as his shield. He could do whatever he wanted to me, and they wouldn't do a thing to stop him.

His slow backward steps were mirrored by theirs. With very step he made away from them they made a small stride toward us.

"My wife and I will be headed home and trust me when I tell you I have plans to correct her behavior, so this doesn't happen again. You won't mind, will you, Mr. Paxton?"

"I think you'll be the one who minds considering as soon as you cross state lines you'll be arrested."

"Lies. All lies," Jonathan snapped, but he stopped moving. With his arm around my throat, his other swung out from behind me and his gun was now pointed directly at Cole.

"Cole!" I shouted and got jerked back against him with his hand tightening on my throat. I choked as he squeezed.

"Shut up." His hand loosened enough so I could suck in a breath.

Cole acted like he wasn't watching Jonathan choke me.

"Yeah, see, I got a text a minute ago. Apparently, an APB in Georgia has gone out on you. How many women have you assaulted in the last several years? I mean, other than your wife?"

"What?" I rasped, and my jaw fell open. I blinked at Cole, trying to make sense of his words, but it was Brock who filled in the gap.

"Eight women so far have come forward, thanks to the help of some of our team." He turned to me. "Board meeting was called this afternoon, and all the evidence was laid in front of Mr. Wolf here. He's been asked to resign immediately. Seems Kip and Valerie have been working hard on your behalf, Miss Mills."

My head spun with the news. The reminder of my conversation with Valerie. I knew they'd been working on something, but this?

"Mrs. Wolf," Jonathan clipped and yanked me even closer to him until my entire body was pressed against his. "And they're lies. Aren't they, Katrina. You know I wouldn't do that."

I couldn't speak. Couldn't breathe. We'd been married for almost nine years in all those years there'd been *women*? He'd cheated on me. The entire time. It was a punch I hadn't seen coming. I'd truly meant *nothing* to him. And how messed up was it that that hurt? After all the other things he'd done...he still had the power to hurt me.

"I hate you," I seethed, unable to stop the bile rising in my throat. Assaulting women... the fact he could say he'd never do that...

What was wrong with him? He was so much worse than I already believed him to be.

"I hate you with every fiber of my being." I twisted, because screw him. Screw being trapped by him again. It would *never* happen. Not again. I was done living in fear.

Cole's voice rang out as I struggled, and I froze as something round and cold pressed to my temple.

"Keep moving and you'll end with your brains splattered on the pavement."

"Doubtful," I snapped back. "You need me to portray your perfect little image, don't you? You're sick."

"And you were the broken and used and desperate little girl that fell for me, weren't you?"

His words hurt, but the impact was dulled as he grabbed me tighter around the throat with his gun to my head.

"Now, if none of you want to see her brains on the ground, I suggest you all stop moving." He swung out his gun and then brought it back to my temple.

None of the men stopped, but their movements slowed.

We were almost to the end of the parking lot. At some point, he'd have to let me go. I'd move then. Or the men would. I just had to stay calm.

There was no way he was going to get away with this.

I shoved what Brock said out of my mind. I'd have time to deal with it later.

"Freeze! Police! Hands up!"

A cacophony of voices erupted, and lights exploded behind us.

Jonathan froze and then swung us around. Our backs

were now to Cole and Brock and Rocco and I wasn't thinking that was such a great thing, but I wasn't sure that mattered anymore either, because in front of us, was what had to be the entire Deer Creek police department. Fully decked out in gear, guns drawn. How they'd arrived without anyone hearing them was a miracle.

But they were here.

Jonathan swung again, and this time didn't get far.

"I wouldn't move," Rocco said. Based on his tone, there had to be a smile on his face even though I couldn't see him, but he was sounding like he was enjoying this.

Somehow, the lightness in his tone helped me relax.

He did something, and Jonathan jerked as he barked out a cuss word, and then his arm from my throat was gone. The gun at my temple gone with him.

I collapsed onto the pavement and gasped for breath, and then two strong arms I'd recognize anywhere were wrapping around me.

"It's okay," Cole said. "It's okay. We'll get you out of here, and I'll explain everything, okay?"

"He hurt other women," I rasped. My throat burned, and the bile that had seared my throat earlier returned except this time there wasn't any forcing it down.

I threw up all over gravel and pavement, on my hands and knees, and while I was certain there was still shouting, still noise and mayhem and madness all around me, all I heard was the ringing in my ears and the softly spoken words from Cole while he gathered my hair.

"It's okay, Trina. Get it all out." One of his hands rubbed up and down on my back. "It's okay. You're safe now, Trina. And that monster is going to go to jail for a very long time."

"I wish you would have shot him," I admitted.

He huffed and ran his hand up and down my back again in large, swooping gestures. "Me too, honey. Me too. But you're safe, and that's all that matters in the end."

I gathered myself, spit, and then pushed off my hands so I was still on my knees. "He was arrested."

Jonathan was currently in the back of a police car, smirking at me. He'd been evil and an idiot, and now he'd get what was coming to him. Whatever happened to those women, whatever he'd done to anyone other than me, I'd be joining their fight to ensure what Cole said was correct. That Jonathan went away for a very, very long time and could never hurt anyone ever again.

For the first time since he'd revealed his true colors to me, I met Jonathan's smile and gave him one of my own. Hopefully, he read into it what I intended. A smile of vengeance, a smile prepared to fight tooth and nail, and a smile that said he would get what was coming to him.

He caught my smile and looked away.

I grinned up at Cole and held out my hand.

Like I knew he would, he took it and guided me to my feet. I was barely on both before his arms were around me, holding me tightly to him. "I love you, Trina. I love you so much."

This time, I hugged him back. It came as naturally as breathing. Which was probably why I opened my mouth and found myself saying, "For the first time in a long time, I love myself too."

He pulled back and grinned down at me. I reached up and cupped his cheek, which meant I was close to see the ways his eyes softened as I smiled back. "And I'm pretty sure I love you, too."

# EPILOGUE

## TRINA

**Three Months Later**

ONCE I DECIDED to stop living in fear and start reaching for freedom, the changes I went through were wild. The night Jonathan was arrested changed everything.

First, and most importantly, Jim Bower recovered from the gunshot wound. He'd bled out a lot, and that had been the most dangerous, but after being stabilized, I learned that Jonathan hadn't hit anything vital. It was the fall to the ground that knocked him out, leaving him with a nasty concussion that took six weeks to heal from. Fortunately for Jim, he was in the hospital healing from surgery and the gunshot for half of it. Unfortunately, considering the number of times I talked to Kip and Valerie during that period, I learned he was not the kind of man who enjoyed sitting around and doing nothing. He'd become a friend of sorts, and he reached out, guilty and horrified he hadn't caught Jonathan sneaking up on him and that I'd been in any sort of danger at all.

We talked, and I forgave him because there was nothing to forgive, and in the end, that act of forgiveness toward him led me to start forgiving myself too. Well, that along with therapy.

A lot of therapy. So much therapy I could have put a bed in my therapist's office and moved in.

Jonathan wasn't only arrested for attempted murder, but it turned out that during our marriage, he'd not only assaulted and manipulated his assistant, but many other women she had the job of scheduling time for with Jonathan. This all came out when I was finally able to call Valerie.

She admitted she'd been keeping it from me, but it was Jonathan's assistant who went to Kip and told him what had been going on after I was hospitalized the last time. It was Lexi's bravery that sent Kip and Valerie on a mission, and while there were now ten women who had come forward, all being abused or manipulated or assaulted by Jonathan, we assumed there was still more.

As soon as the sun rose the following Monday, I called a lawyer Kip trusted and filed for divorce. By then, Jonathan was back in an Atlanta jail and was being held without bail until his trials could start. He was fighting all the charges and since he was wealthy and his attorney was well-connected, they kept getting pushed back, which sucked for all of us involved. He'd also fought the divorce tooth and nail and while I'd signed a prenuptial agreement, given the proof of his infidelity and assault—caveats I couldn't believe he'd even put in the prenuptial agreement in the first place—I was set to soon become a very wealthy woman.

And all of it, every single penny was either earmarked to be donated to multiple domestic violence women's shelters in the southeast region or put into creating my new dream.

Deer Creek's Pregnancy Center would be open in the summer and would serve not only the woman in our county, but anyone who found themselves in situations where they were uncertain how to navigate. I was currently working on hiring doctors, nurses, and counselors and we'd rely heavily on volunteers as well. Our jobs were not to judge or convince or push women in any specific direction. We were there to instruct and care for every woman who walked through our doors needing assistance. We would also offer classes, whether that be pregnancy or birthing or the first year of a child's life afterward, and if their choices veered toward the one I made, we provided appointments and transportation. Looking back, I made the choice I did not purely out of naivety and stubbornness, but an alarming amount of fear. And while I was healing from my guilt, I also recognized not every woman would, so I wanted to ensure our center was accepting of all choices, whether they'd be mine if I had to make them again or not.

I stepped back, squinting at the bright and freezing February afternoon sky, and the building in front of me that was now a shell of a closed down dentist's office. It would soon be all mine, and I squeezed the hand of the man standing next to me.

The man who hadn't left my side. The man who'd been there for me every step of the way in the last three months. The man who held me while I cried after therapy, the man who was silent while I screamed and raged, and the man who joined me in now frequent laughter.

"It's happening." I grinned up at Cole.

"You're doing great." He grinned back at me. "But we didn't finish our argument this morning."

I rolled my eyes. It was a stupid argument, one that he was being stubborn about. "I need to get an apartment and do this on my own."

I was still living in his downstairs bedroom. Some nights, Cole came down and joined me and held me. Other nights, I went up to his, but most of the nights, we slept alone. We hadn't taken that step yet, and I still wasn't ready.

My body hadn't truly been *mine* in a healthy way in a very long time, and the thought of taking those next steps still made me tense with fear.

Cole continued to assure me it didn't matter.

"And you're not alone. You never have to do anything on your own again."

I knew that, too. Not only had I grown in friendships with all the friends I used to have, but Marie and I reached a quick and cordial friendship. Cole had been right about the kind of woman she'd been because the night everything went down and Cole called her, she'd rushed to *me* and hugged me and told me she was thankful I was okay. She'd come over so Cole could tell her what happened, and then she'd stayed the night in Ella's bed with her daughters. But the next morning, she'd acted like we'd known each other for years.

My parents and I were close, and I went over to their house every Sunday for potluck after church like I'd done every weekend of my life since I was born, even if I wasn't ready to step back through the church doors. Kari brought her husband, Dan, and her daughters Missy and Elsie, and while she was right, Missy did look a lot like me, it was Elsie's sweetness that stole my heart.

So yeah, I wasn't alone. But I still couldn't see why Cole got mad every time I talked to him about moving out or looking at apartments. "I just feel like where we're headed, it's best to wait. I don't want to be *living* with you, with the girls, if we're not married. It feels like so much change for them, too fast."

The girls, for the most part, were perfect little angels, even with June's rambunctiousness. She was the one that brought the joy to everyday living, but there were still moments where she wanted her dad and her mom together. Not her dad and her mom *friends* with me. I didn't blame her. She was still so young, and I tried not to take it personally.

But it was her I was most worried about, who thought it would help the most if I left.

"Then we should do that," Cole said.

I flinched back at him and laughed. "What?"

He didn't laugh back. He sank to one knee in the middle of the parking lot, in front of my soon-to-be pregnancy center, and held out his hand. And in that hand was a box. "I've waited since I was fifteen years old to ask you this question, Trina, but will you marry me? Will you let me love you for all the days we have yet to live?"

Tears burned my eyes, and they came so fast I couldn't blink them back. "What?" I shrieked, and my knees wobbled. "You're crazy. Get up. We're not doing this."

Cole, steady and happy as always, shrugged. "What better way than to start our Valentine's night out with an engagement ring on your finger and something to celebrate?"

"You're insane!" I cried and was still laughing. This was...this was *mind-boggling*.

It'd only been a few months. And sure, yeah, a lot had happened, but...

This was Cole.

"Marry me, Trina. Make me the happiest man in the world. Let me love you forever. Give me that honor."

This was *Cole*, I thought again. He was it. He was everything.

"Yes." I finally nodded, still crying. Not so much laughing anymore, either. "Yes, I'll marry you!"

He slipped the ring, a gorgeous, round diamond onto my finger and stood. He brought his hands to my cheeks, making me shriek from the iciness of them, but that coldness quickly turned to warmth, and then a slow-burning heat as he bought his lips to mine and kissed me.

Almost thirteen years ago, I'd left town certain I'd never return and while life had thrown a lot of darkness my way, it was always being with Cole when I shined the brightest, and I had no doubt, from this day forward, he'd do everything in his power to ensure our lives kept getting brighter and better.

---

THANK you for taking the time to read Love Me Gently. I hope you love Trina and Cole's story as much as I do. Reviews are gold to authors. I'd be forever grateful if you could leave a review at the retailer where you purchased this book.

Want to pre-order Love Me Boldly? There are twists and turns you never see coming. Pre-order today: https://amzn.to/4go9yyX

Stay up to date on all my new release and sales! **Join my newsletter today!** https://bit.ly/42MPeEo

# THANK YOU

2025 will mark my twelve-year anniversary in the writing and publishing world from when I published my first book, Just One Song. I truly had no idea that publishing one book as a "bucket list" challenge to myself, would lead to this amazing, decade-plus career. From the friends I've made along the way, to meeting other authors and book signings and meeting readers, my world is so drastically more amazing than anything I could have ever imagined. I'm so unbelievably thankful to every person who takes a chance on one of books. Thank you for being a part of this wild journey with me!

HUGE thank you to Nina and all the incredible women at Valentine PR for throwing your full enthusiasm and support behind me and these books. I love with working with you.

Thank you so much to my editing team for all your amazing hard work and refining the hot mess drafts I send you.

Shannon, you're the best. Always. Forever. Your talent is astounding and I'm thankful I can call you a friend.

Ratula, I couldn't do this without you. Thank you so much for being so incredible!

To my Sweeties: I love you ladies and your excitement for my books!

To all the bloggers who devote their time and passion into reading books, book tours, release events, leaving reviews, promoting and pimping – you are all rockstars! Thank you for all the love over the years.

My family— I love you all to the moon and back. I don't know what I would do without you in my corner, cheering me on every step of the way. Your support is everything to me and I love you all with all of my heart.

To my friends who have encouraged me for the last several years and always been there to support me. Tamara, Cassy, Niccole, Bree, and Lauren. Thank you so much for loving me!

And last but definitely not least – to you, the reader. I'm blown away with every release how much you adore my books. You have made my dream a reality and I hope I can cheer you on with yours. Please don't forget to leave reviews on Goodreads or whichever retailer you've purchased this copy from. It helps us so much!

# ABOUT THE AUTHOR

A long-time dreamer, Stacey Lynn has always loved the emotional journey of two different and complex individuals finding their way to a happily-ever-after.

The author of over fifty romance novels, many of which have been best-selling titles on Amazon, AppleBooks, and Barnes & Noble, she loves being able to turn her vivid imagination into a career that brings entertainment and joy to her readers. Focused on emotional, small-town romance, she happily admits her books might require keeping tissues nearby.

Born in Texas and raised in the Midwest, she now makes her home in North Carolina and loves all things Southern. Blessed with her ultimate tall, dark, and handsome hero, and four children, she loves every minute of her wild and wonderful life.

Subscribe to her newsletter so you can stay up to date on all her new releases. www.staceylynnbooks.com

OTHER BOOKS BY STACEY LYNN

**A Deer Creek Novel ~ small town romance**

Love Me Gently

Love Me Boldly – May 2025

**The Kelley Family ~ small town romance**

Undeniable Love Novella (free on all retailers)

Unending Love

Unstoppable Love

Unbreakable Love

**Nashville Steel ~ football romance**

Sneak Attack

Time Out

Tight Spot

Risky Game

**Las Vegas Vipers ~hockey romance**

Final Shot (free on all retailers)

Game Changer

Dream Maker

Rule Breaker

Shot Taker

Goal Chaser

Secret Keeper

## Ice Kings Series ~hockey romance

Playing With Fire (free on all retailers)

Playing To Win

Scoring Off The Ice

Hooked One Her

Hard Checked

Fighting Dirty

## The Rough Riders Series ~football romance

Dirty Player

Filthy Player

Wicked Player

Cocky Player

## Love and Lies Duet ~angsty slow burn, romance

All the Ugly Things

All the Beautiful Things

## Love and Honor Duet ~angsty, romantic suspense

Twisted Hearts

Unraveled Love

## Love In The Heartland ~small town romance

Captivated By You

This Time Around

Long Road Home

Before We Fell

## Crazy Love Series ~small town romance

Fake Wife

Knocked Up

28 Dates

Weekend Fling

## The Fireside Series ~small town romance

His to Love

His to Protect

His to Cherish

His to Seduce

## Just One Series ~rockstar romance

Just One Song

Just One Week

Just One Regret

Just One Moment

## Standalones

Remembering Us

www.ingramcontent.com/pod-product-compliance
Lightning Source LLC
Chambersburg PA
CBHW031202020726
47499CB00002B/455